Ready For You

USA TODAY BESTSELLING AUTHOR

J.L. BERG

ALSO BY J.L. BERG

THE READY SERIES

When You're Ready

Never Been Ready

Ready to Wed

Ready for You

Ready or Not

The Ready Series Box Set

When You're Ready - 10th Anniversary Edition

THE WALLS SERIES

Within These Walls

Beyond These Walls

Behind Closed Doors

The Cavenaugh Brothers - A Box Set

THE LOST & FOUND SERIES

Forgetting August

Remembering Everly

BY THE BAY SERIES

The Choices I've Made

The Scars I Bare

The Lies I've Told

The Mistakes I've Made

The Secrets We Keep

By The Bay Series: A Box Set (Books 1-4)

STANDALONES

Fraud

The Tattered Gloves

The Affair

GARRETT

All I could see was blue and white. It stretched out beyond my field of vision, encompassing the grassy terrain completely, as if the entire football field had exploded into a sea of satin.

I was a high school graduate—finally.

Proud parents hugged their sons or daughters, congratulating their success with wishes for bright, happy futures. My fellow graduates had banded together, standing united on that vast green grass, feeling proud and utterly relieved. We had finally made it. Twelve years were behind us, and we had nothing but endless possibilities in our future. I smiled at the thought. There was only one person I wanted in my future, both imminently and permanently.

As my parents took what was probably the hundredth picture, I saw her. Chocolate-brown hair tumbled down her back, contrasting against the stark white robe she wore. When her gaze turned upward, our eyes locked briefly from across the field, and she smiled.

Mia Emerson. *My Mia.*

She'd been the first girl I noticed freshman year and the only girl I'd paid attention to since. She was my world, and I couldn't wait to spend the rest of my life with her. It wasn't exactly the life our parents had imagined for us, and I knew they would disagree with the plans we'd made, but everything would work out. With Mia by my side, everything would always work out.

Tomorrow was the beginning of us.

With slight hesitation, she shyly walked up to my large group of family members laughing and talking loudly. She was always a bit timid around my parents even though she had no reason to be. My mother and father adored her, and nothing would change that, not even the bomb we were about to drop tomorrow morning.

"Mia!" my mom said, greeting her enthusiastically, while pulling her into a tight hug. "Congratulations, my dear!"

"Thank you, Mrs. Finnegan."

"How many times do I have to tell you, sweetheart? There's no Mrs. Finnegan around here. You can call me Mom or Laura."

Mia gave her a sweet smile and nodded.

Mia hadn't known how to react to my family the first time she met them. Her family was vastly different. They loved her in their own way, but hugs and feelings were never easy to come by in the Emerson household. Mia came from wealth, and her family did things a certain way. My touchy-feely, middle-income family looked like *The Beverly Hillbillies* compared to hers, especially her mother.

"Garrett, put your arm around Mia. I need a quick picture!" Mom said, holding her digital camera up once again.

My father chuckled, giving my mom a squeeze, as she held the camera and waited for us to pose. My mouth curled into a grin, and I wrapped my arm around Mia's waist. I knew when my mom had said *picture*, she really meant we would be here for an eternity. Laura Finnegan was unable to take just one picture. I didn't mind. Mom clicked away as we smiled and laughed. I'd gladly hold Mia in my arms forever.

"Okay, okay, Mom! I think that's enough! He's going to break the camera!" my older sister, Clare, joked from behind us.

I turned around and gave her a stern look, and she laughed. Her giant basketball stomach bounced up and down as she turned her head to shield her laughter. If she got any bigger, I swore she was going to deliver an entire litter of babies and not just the one she'd kept telling me was in there. Her husband, Ethan, bent down to place a tender kiss on her round stomach. My big sister was going to be a mother. That freaked me out a little. I spent a moment too long staring at her stomach, wondering—

"Hey, I've got to meet my parents for dinner. Pick me up later?" Mia said suddenly, bringing me out of my wayward thoughts.

Her brilliant teal-blue eyes found mine, and I nodded, pulling her closer.

"I'll be there," I promised before bending down to kiss her softly.

Our kiss lingered a bit before she got embarrassed, giggling and pushing away. My parents already knew we were head over heels in love. *Did she really think I was going to keep my hands off just because my mom was around?*

Mia shot me a sly grin, promising retribution that I was sure to enjoy later, and then I watched her walk away, disappearing into the crowd of blue and white satin.

Had I known this would be the last time I saw her, I would have never let her go.

I would have fought for her. I would have done something, anything.

I would have done anything, except stand there and watch her disappear…forever.

Chapter One

I gasped, desperately seeking air, as I tried clawing my way back to reality. Oxygen filled my airways too quickly and burned a fiery path to my overworked lungs. I felt myself gripping, holding on… trying not to let go.

Don't let her go. Not again. Come back, Mia. Come back!

My eyes flew open, and I found myself back in my cramped, lifeless bedroom, back in the present.

Back to hell.

I couldn't count the number of times I'd relived that day. I would relive what had started out as a perfect day in my past, and I'd wake back up to the hell that had become my life. It was like some sick, twisted curse I'd been given to remind me just how fucked-up fate could be.

The sheets felt cold against my sweat-slicked body, and my heart rate was still racing a marathon. A marathon I never won. Night after night, I'd awake from the same nightmare, my heart racing as I tried, over and over, to change history through my dreams.

Good luck, buddy.

I'd given up on that hope years ago. Sitting up, I ran my hands over my face and tried to calm my nerves. Out of the corner of my eye, I caught the glint of a mostly empty bottle of tequila sitting on my nightstand. Looking through my hands, which were still covering my face, I saw the bra first, then the dress, and finally the heels. They were all scattered among my own clothes on the floor.

My head began to pound like a drum as I slowly pieced together the night before, remembering the copious amounts of alcohol I'd consumed. I'd wandered into a bar after another long day at work, and there was a woman.

Sarah or Sierra? It didn't matter.

I'd told her she was beautiful and offered to buy her a drink. She'd laughed at my lame jokes, throwing her head back with enthusiasm, while resting her hand on my thigh. Her laugh had been all wrong—high-pitched and too bubbly. But nothing ever was right. I'd bought her another drink, and finally, I'd followed it up by asking if she would like to have a third one—back at my place.

Shit.

Running my hands through my disheveled dark hair, I slowly turned to my right, and there she was—the owner of the dress.

Siena or Samantha?

Sadie?

I had no clue.

I was not a player. I wasn't one of those guys who would bring a different woman home every night and brag about it to his coworkers the next day. I didn't have notches on my bedpost, and I actually really hated the one-night stand routine. But I wasn't a saint, and sometimes, the solitude and quiet of being alone would get to be too much, overwhelming me to the point where I would become so weighed down by it that I thought I might drown. That was when I would end up here—with a nameless woman and a fucking mess to clean up.

She really was beautiful though.

I'm a giant asshole.

"Hey—" I started but stopped short, remembering I had no idea what to call her.

She stirred a bit, stretching like a cat, which made the sheet draped over her fall away to expose her naked body. I turned away.

"Oh." She giggled a bit. "Good morning, Adam," she nearly purred.

Adam, huh? I never gave my real name, but I hadn't ever used that one before.

She reached out, searching with her fingers, but I jumped off the bed before she could touch me. I was sober. There would be no touching now. I threw on my clothes and began running around to pick up hers. Once that was done, I risked turning around.

Sitting up now but using the sheet to cover herself, she had that look. It was the same look they would all give me when I did this one-eighty routine. Her eyes darted around the room, and the confidence from her good-morning purr was now replaced with insecurity and awkwardness.

"Am I missing something? I thought we had a good time last night," she said quietly.

I huffed out a breath. "We did," I said even though I didn't remember any of it. "But you need to go. I'm sorry."

She nodded silently, and I tried to ignore the sight of her lip quivering as I put her clothes on the bed before walking out.

My apartment was small, bordering on claustrophobic, and it took exactly five steps to reach my kitchen from my bedroom. If I were to give someone a tour, it would last about ten seconds. I had one solitary bedroom, and it was barely big enough to fit my bed, nightstand, and dresser. There was one bathroom, and the kitchen and living room bled into each other so much that they were really considered one entity. To complete the bachelor pad, I had a small kitchen table that most people would probably consider more of a card table.

My sister, Clare, hated this apartment. She would refuse to use the bathroom because it was too close to the couch, and she felt like people could hear her pee. She'd said the word *pee* in a hushed tone, like it was a bad word. I'd tried not to laugh, but she was kind of ridiculous. Also, she was right. We could hear her pee, but I wasn't about to tell her that. She would make me move.

After visiting for probably the tenth time and still refusing to use my bathroom, she had finally asked, *Why do you live in such a shithole, Garrett?*

It was a good question. I had a good job—one that would pay for a place that could eat my current apartment for breakfast. But why bother? It was just me. It would only ever be just me.

Just as I started to pour myself a cup of freshly brewed coffee, the smell beginning to do its job as my droopy eyes were prying themselves apart, my mystery date appeared in the kitchen. She looked awkward, tugging at her wrinkled black dress, as she stared at the floor. I got the feeling that she wasn't the type of girl who did this often.

"I'm going to take off," she said softly, her timid brown eyes peeking out from tousled blonde bangs.

"Okay," I answered, feeling like the worst kind of asshole on the planet.

She waited for a second, obviously stalling to see if I would follow up with anything. When I didn't, she reached for the door and took a step forward, but I stopped her.

"Hey, I'm sorry. I just…I'm…" I didn't know what to say. *I'm fucked-up? Permanently?*

She looked up at me with those sad brown eyes that were now rimmed with tears—tears that I'd put there.

"Just answer one question. Is your name even Adam?"

"No," I answered honestly. I didn't volunteer my real name. What was the point?

Her watery eyes peered up at me as if searching for something. "You're hurting…over a woman?" she asked, surprising me.

My silence was enough of an answer for her, and she seemed to recover a bit from her revelation. Seeing me as a victim suddenly made her feel better. Well, at least there was that.

"The tattoo on your arm…is it for her?"

Inquisitive little thing, wasn't she? I really needed to stop getting drunk.

Her eyes wandered down to the tattoo in question, stopping at the black tip of script peeking out of my T-shirt sleeve.

"No," I bit out. "That's for someone else."

Date night was definitely over.

MIA

It had been eight years since I was in my home state of Virginia. Eight years since I'd left the boy who stole my heart on a hot summer night under the stars. Eight years since I'd given him nothing more than a tear-stained note, destroying everything we'd planned. Eight years since I'd driven over that state line and never looked back, ruining my life from that moment on.

Now, fate had brought me home again. Why? I didn't know, but like a magnet, I'd felt drawn back here, and I only hoped it wouldn't be a mistake.

Virginia was beautiful and picturesque as I made my way down the tree-lined back roads dotted with small farms and forgotten towns. My roots were here, buried in the sweet Southern air and the historic countryside. Crossing the city limits into Richmond felt like coming home for the first time in almost a decade. No matter where I had gone, where I'd settled down, I never felt more at home than I did here. This is where I truly belonged and it was about time I came to accept that.

A few miles deeper into the city, I was pulling up to the curb of my longtime friend Olivia Prescott, or Liv, as I liked to call her. It had been years since we last spoke. That had been my fault, not hers. I'd cut ties with everyone from my former life when I quietly left town the night of our high school graduation. After what I'd done, I'd felt too ashamed to face anyone, even those I was closest to.

The house was drastically different than what I'd ever envisioned for Liv. Her family, like mine, came from money. Initially, it had been why we became friends. Our parents had attended the same country club, and we would end up attending many of the same functions together. We quickly realized that we had a lot in common, and we had become fast friends.

Liv had hated the country-club life almost as much as I had. It was so stuffy and stifling in there. I would feel like my lungs were tightening every time I'd walked inside those pretentious gilded walls. Our mutual hatred for the place had created a close bond, and we had always sought each other out when we were forced to attend parties or formal events. Our parents hadn't approved of our friendship. We had been expected to act a certain way, and neither Liv nor I had fit the mold of the perfect daughter. Being together had only exacerbated the situation in our parents' eyes.

I'd finally taken a stand against my parents, but by the time I had, it had been too late, and it had ended up costing me everything. I could only imagine what Liv had gone through alone. As I stepped out of my car, I took my first good look at Liv's house, and I knew she must have done the impossible. She'd done what I should have that night so long ago. She'd broken free.

Her house was small, too small for a trust-fund baby, which we both were—or at least, we used to be. Her trust fund was substantially larger than mine since she came from a family that had a name everyone knew. My family was well-off, more so than most, but my parents always strived to appear greater than they were. My father was a lawyer, a very successful one. I never understood why he'd felt the need to kiss ass with the rich elitists of the city. But maintaining their image had been everything to my parents—or rather my mother. My father loved me, but he had been my mother's puppet. She'd always come first. When I'd finally walked away, I'd told my mother to screw herself, and I'd left my inheritance behind. I hadn't heard from either of them since.

Liv lived in a part of town known for being eclectic. The neighborhood was full of artists and college students. Within walking distance, there was access to great restaurants, shops, and bars. The houses were small, historic, and full of Victorian charm. Most were divided into duplexes or townhouses to accommodate the amount of students attending the nearby university. But Liv's home looked to be all hers with only one address painted in hot pink stenciling on a wooden sign hanging by the side of the mossy green front door.

I pressed the buzzer and waited. I admired the bright colors she'd chosen for her trim and porch, and I hated the fact that she could keep her plants alive. I had the exact opposite of a green thumb. *What would that be? A black thumb?* Well, whatever it was, I had it. If they could, plants would scream and run away from my presence, knowing I would be their ultimate demise. I also couldn't cook worth a damn. I was the antithesis of Martha Stewart.

The door was suddenly thrown open, and I was engulfed in a sea of ebony hair as Liv dove forward and threw her arms around me.

"Mia!" Liv squealed, pulling back from her hug attack to give me her signature megawatt grin.

I always loved Liv's smile. It could light up an entire room. Her smile was genuine and encompassed her entire face. Her brown eyes twinkled and warmed, her right cheek dimpled, and her entire personality shined through. *God, I had missed her.*

"Amelia Emerson! You haven't changed a bit! You're just as skinny and gorgeous as ever. But wait, hold on," she said, stepping back to assess me for a moment. "Turn for me."

I rolled my eyes and did as she'd said, making a complete turn on her front stoop. I hoped her neighbors couldn't see this little spectacle. I would be staying here for a bit, and I didn't want them to think I was Liv's crazy relative coming to visit.

"Your boobs got bigger!" she practically announced to the entire block.

"Oh my God, they did not!" I said, folding my arms over my chest.

"They did so," she fired back, pulling my arms away to expose the area in question.

Suddenly, I felt underdressed next to my long-lost friend. She was very put together—in a strange way. It was much different than the Liv I remembered. She had on a gorgeous maxi dress that hugged her curves and highlighted her own rack nicely. Her jewelry all looked handmade, nothing like the pricey designer pieces our parents use to buy. The bold silver necklace and matching earrings she wore accentuated her long neck and shiny black hair. Her appearance was very eclectic and artsy but in a hip and sophisticated manner.

I looked like a bum standing next to her. Since I had been traveling all day, I wasn't wearing anything fancy. I had on a faded Old Navy tank top and a pair of jeans I'd probably owned since college. Besides the pendant around my neck that I never took off, I didn't have any other jewelry on. To complete my fashion train wreck, I was wearing flip-flops that didn't even match.

Yay, me.

"Well, whatever you say, but I still think they are bigger. Is that a thing? Are they supposed to get bigger in our twenties? Because mine sure haven't. I heard they sometimes grow with pregnancy, but that shit definitely isn't ever happening to me, so I'm stuck with my mediums. I've never had any complaints though. What do they say? A handful is all you need."

I just stared for a moment, thrown off guard by what she'd said, but I laughed it off. Shaking my head, I said, "You haven't changed a bit."

"Oh, but I have. Can't you tell?" She tossed her hands up as if to acknowledge her surroundings as validation of her epic change.

"Yes, you need to tell me all about this," I said, waving my pointer finger in a circle to incorporate her entire look.

"Oh, I plan to. Let's get you inside and make some tea."

Of course she drank tea.

As we made our way through her home, I took notice of the hand-carved wood artwork on the walls and the unusual paintings scattered everywhere. I couldn't help but wonder how my privileged friend had gone from being a senator's daughter to wearing moonstones and making tea.

I settled into a chair at her worn kitchen table and drew my knees up to my chin.

"Still folding yourself into a ball, Mia?"

It was the second time I'd heard her say my former name. I'd given that name up when I left my old life behind. When I'd walked away from Virginia, I'd stopped being Mia, and I'd started using my proper name, Amelia.

Mia was the name *he* had given me, and I couldn't bear to hear it. I didn't deserve it anymore.

"I go by Amelia now," I simply said.

"Okay," she said, sending me a strange look. "Still folding yourself into a ball, *Amelia?*"

"Yes, I guess some things never change."

She gave me a long stare as she filled up the teakettle. "No, they don't."

We moved from awkward conversation to silence for a while as she moved about the kitchen, pulling out snacks and tea from some weird tin. She was so different, yet I could still see parts of my old friend there. Some of her mannerisms were the same, like how she bit her bottom lip as she became impatient while waiting for the water to boil and how she rocked her hips when she was standing. I used to call her a valley girl for that silly movement after seeing the girls on *Clueless* do it. She would just laugh it off and keep doing it.

Liv finished pouring our tea—some weird herbal blend and set the mugs on a tray along with a plate of cookies. She brought everything over and set it on the table and joined me. I added a bit of cream to my tea and grabbed a spiced cookie to nibble on.

"So, are we going to talk about why you ran out of here like a demon on graduation night and then never came back? Or are we going to continue to ignore it?"

I knew she would ask, yet I still hadn't prepared an answer.

"I…had to leave. I just…I'm sorry, Liv. I'm not ready to talk about this yet."

I looked up, expecting to see hurt or anger, but she was radiating understanding.

"Okay, I can deal with that—as long as you'll be ready to talk someday."

"Okay," I agreed, not knowing if that day would ever come.

As we continued to eat our cookies and sip our teas, something was tugging at me, something I needed to know. It was more than what Liv had been doing since high school, more than whether that ice cream store was still down the street from my old house. I needed to know about him.

"Liv, I need to know. Does Garrett still live here?"

Saying his name out loud hurt. I didn't think I'd actually said those precious syllables in years. Hearing it spring free from my lips felt like I was cutting deep into my own flesh. It felt raw and ragged, like gravel against my vocal cords, and I was ashamed for even saying it.

She gave me a sympathetic gaze. "I don't know. After you…after that night, he hounded me for days that turned into weeks, trying to get a clue as to where you went. When I finally convinced him I was in the dark like he was, I didn't hear from him again. He went off to college, and that was it."

We were supposed to go to college together—the beginning to our *crazy life*, as he'd called it. We'd picked out all of our classes together. He was going to be my brainy architect, and I was going to be his sexy teacher. But I'd left, and he had gone alone.

Now, I was here. I wondered where life had taken him.

I only hoped he was happy.

Chapter Two

MIA

It had been a week since I came home, back to the place I'd sworn I would never return. When I'd fled down that dark, deserted road on that night so long ago, I'd promised myself I would do him the favor of never returning. After I'd caused so much pain, he deserved that at least.

So, why now? After all this time, why had I come back?

Once again, I was running.

It seemed to be something I was highly skilled in. When the walls of my carefully built life in Atlanta had started to cave in on me, I'd needed out, and I had bailed. I'd packed up everything I owned, and I'd found myself on the interstate, headed for home. It always felt safe and secure here, and I liked the person I had been here—before the end.

In the week since I'd returned, I temporarily moved in with Liv. Living with Liv was great. After so much time and how different we had both become, I had been afraid that things would be awkward and that the friendship we had once shared would be gone. But it wasn't, and we naturally fell into that sweet spot—somewhere between best friends and sisters. I hadn't realized how much I missed her until I had her back, and I didn't think I would ever forgive myself for pushing her away for so long. The fact that she'd opened up her home and life to me after eight long years and one email just showed the type of person she was. I didn't deserve such compassion.

She wanted me to move in permanently, but I'd spent years living with others, and for once, I wanted to live on my own. I needed to live on my own. I was twenty-five years old, and I didn't think I even knew myself. Who was I without someone else? I'd come here in search of something. *That had to be it, right?* I needed to find out.

I picked out a great house not too far from Liv. It was old and needed work, and it was pricey because of the neighborhood, but I took it on the spot. With my pre-approved loan and sizable down payment—thanks to years of saving money—it would be mine in a week.

After throwing together breakfast this morning from the last of the groceries, we decided a trip to the farmers' market might be fun. Liv said she would go every week to get local produce, rather than buying from the grocery store. According to Liv, big-business grocery stores that choked out small farmers were going to be the death of our society.

"Who the hell are you?" I asked as we roamed around the streets filled with vendors selling everything from kale to nuts to strawberries.

"I'm the same girl. I'm just an upgraded, more worldly version," she said.

Her sassy smirk reminded me of a younger Liv.

"But how did this upgrade happen? I mean you didn't just wake up one day and decide that trust funds sucked and hemp bracelets were way cooler."

She gave me a pointed looked and snickered. Then, she continued her search for the perfect tomato, squeezing one and then another, as I watched.

"It was college actually." She picked up a juicy red tomato and turned it over in her hand before placing it on the scale with the others she'd picked out.

The man on the other side of the stand told her the amount she owed. They finished their business, and we moved on.

"I was sitting in a sociology class. It wasn't my major at the time. It was just something I was taking to fill a general ed requirement. The professor was lecturing about the African society and how they had been basically crippled by the AIDS epidemic. I remember sitting there, staring at these pictures in my textbook. I was bored out of my mind. I looked down at my nails to see a chip in my Very Berry nail polish, and I was just beside myself. I was so annoyed because I'd had a manicure only three days earlier. My professor was in front of the class, speaking about people dying, and I was pissed because my nail was chipped. I mean, how bitchy is that? I don't know. I guess I just had a light bulb moment."

"You were not a bitch," I said, trying to defend the friend I once knew.

"No, I know that now, I guess. I've done alright, despite my parents trying to turn me into the most pretentious being on the planet. But I still came from wealth, and I knew it. I always had someone to take care of me. My father was there to pay my tuition and rent, and a huge trust fund was waiting for me when I turned twenty-one. I was set for life."

"So, you became a hippie?"

"No, bitch!" She laughed. "I told my parents that I didn't want my trust fund anymore and that I didn't see the point of going to college to prepare for a career if I wouldn't need to work. I wanted to make my own way. So, I switched majors. I dropped business for sociology."

"Oh, man. Your dad must have been so pissed."

"Yeah, he didn't take it too well," she said.

"And then, you became a hippie?"

"Oh my God! I am not a hippie!" She giggled.

"I know. I just like giving you shit."

"Well, at least that hasn't changed," she said, giving me a shoulder nudge.

We continued shopping, and I helped by picking up carrots and freshly baked bread that smelled like heaven. Liv hadn't been kidding when she said she visited the farmers' market a lot. Almost every vendor knew her by name and would give her a special price or throw in a few more veggies or goodies into her bag with a wink and a grin. She'd give them a hug and ask how their families were doing. They really loved her down here, and it wasn't surprising.

After college, Liv had gone to graduate school and gotten her master's degree. She now earned her living as a family counselor. She worked with families who were going through hard times, like divorce, death, or other difficult transitions. From what she'd shared, I could tell it wasn't easy work, but the love she had for others radiated through everything she did.

With our bags loaded, we started to make our way back to the car, weaving through the crowd and enjoying the sounds of people talking and soft music playing. I smiled when I heard a child laughing. I turned to see a child being thrown over his father's shoulder.

"Garrett! Stop it! I'm too old to be carried!" The child laughed.

"You're never too old to be tackled, Connor! We've got to get you ready for football!"

That voice—even after eight years, I would recognize it anywhere. My stomach fell to the concrete, and my feet cemented to the ground. I was frozen, completely frozen. Everything slowed. The street noise melted away, and each and every shopper disappeared until I saw him. He had the boy slung over his shoulder. They were both laughing and breathless from their horseplay. He looked older, but it was still him. He still had the same jet-black hair, emerald eyes, and dazzling smile. A beautiful blonde woman was smiling at the two of them as they joked around.

My heart finally caught up to my brain, and it felt like a jackhammer was beating hard and fast in my chest. My hands shook, and my knees suddenly felt weak and wobbly. I had no idea how much time had passed since I saw him.

Minutes? Hours?

I didn't know, but it couldn't have been long since Liv was just now noticing my crazy behavior.

"Amelia, are you okay? You look like you just saw a ghost," she said.

When I didn't respond, she must have glanced up because I heard her gasp. She'd seen him, too.

"I-I need to get out of here—now," I gritted through my teeth.

"Are you sure?"

I just nodded and started to turn. I couldn't face him. He probably hated me.

He had a kid. That hurt. My hand went to my chest, trying to rub out the pain settling there. He had a child. That meant the blonde standing next to him was probably his wife. *Garrett was married.* It had been eight years. Of course he would be married. I didn't know why I was surprised, but he wasn't supposed to be here. He had moved away. He was supposed to stay away. I couldn't be here if he was still here. I couldn't breathe if he was still here.

"Come on, sweetheart, let's get to the car," Liv said gently, grabbing my arm and guiding me toward the car.

I just gave a brief nod as I let her lead me.

We hadn't made it three steps before I heard the words that made my heart come to a screeching halt.

"Mia? Mia, is that you?"

GARRETT

Since the night she'd left with nothing more than a hastily scribbled note that reduced my heart to ashes, I'd been haunted by Mia's face everywhere I went. I'd seen her the very first day of my freshman psychology class, sitting in the front row, as I remembered how much she had wanted to earn her degree in child psychology, and eventually teach.

Maybe it will give me a leg up on our own hellions, she'd always said.

I would see her in the airport every time I flew. If I caught a glimpse of a brunette beauty with brilliant blue eyes, I'd wonder where she was going and who she was going to see.

And now, with Connor on my shoulders and Leah next to me, holding her daughter, Lily, I saw her again across the farmers' market. Out of the corner of my eye, a wisp of brown hair caught my attention, like it always did. But this one was different. This brunette had just the right amount of natural auburn mixed in, and the way the shimmery strands reflected the sun reminded me of summers gone by. I pivoted around just in time to see her face before she turned away into the crowd. My heart recognized her before my mind did, and my heartbeat galloped to full speed the second my eyes saw her.

I'd spent so many years imagining this moment—the day when I saw her again. I didn't know how many hours I'd wasted, wondering what it would be like to have Mia walk back into my life. Would she come running back, apologizing for everything and begging for forgiveness? Would she look the same? Would she still want me like I wanted her? Or would she have moved on in the way I couldn't?

Before I could even register the fear and trepidation of the unknown that would have me running in the opposite direction, straight for the sanctuary of the ignorant and unaware, I called out to her.

She turned, and I saw her, all of her, for the first time in eight years.

She looked shell-shocked, frozen, and scared. She had a death grip on the woman beside her.

On a closer look, I recognized Olivia Prescott. We'd gone to high school together. I hadn't seen her in years, but I remembered her because of Mia. They had been best friends, so we'd spent a lot of time together. The last time I'd seen Olivia, I hadn't been the sanest of men. I probably owed her an apology.

"Hi, Garrett," Mia said softly.

She didn't seem surprised to see me. That paired with the death grip and panic on her face led me to believe she'd spotted me first...and she must have been fleeing when I called out to her.

She had chosen to run, rather than face me—again.

Fuck, that hurt.

"You look well," she said politely.

"You, too," I answered awkwardly.

Now that I knew she didn't want to see me, I wasn't really in a talkative mood. Any scenario I had envisioned of our long-awaited reunion didn't include her trying to dodge me in the middle of a crowd. I thought I at least deserved a, *Hey, how are you, Garrett? Sorry I bailed on you right after you asked me to marry you. Yeah, that was a shitty thing to do.*

Whatever.

"Garrett, are you going to introduce us?" Leah asked, turning to me with an expectant look.

She had Lily balanced on her hip, which was getting harder to do. Lily had just passed her first birthday, and she was a fidgety little thing.

"Gah!" Lily screamed her version of my name, clapping her hands. Then, she held them out to me, using the universal signal for, *Take me!*

I took Lily into my arms and turned back to Mia. She quietly watched, her eyes darting between Leah and me as, she bit her lip. I remembered she would always bite it when she was nervous. It used to drive me wild. Unfortunately, it still did.

"Leah, this is Mia and Olivia—two friends from my high school days. Mia and Olivia, this is Leah," I said simply. "This dude right here is Connor, and the princess in my arms is his little sister, Lily."

Mia was silent for a second longer than what would probably be considered socially correct, but she finally smiled. "They're lovely, Garrett. Really, you have a beautiful family."

Tears rimmed her eyes, and for one split second, I really wanted to just thank her and turn around to leave. I wanted to make her feel the pain I'd felt when I went to her house and found that letter along with that same pain I'd felt every fucking day because I couldn't find a way to move on.

For one brief moment, I wanted her to think it had been easy for me to live without her. I wanted to let her believe that these children were mine and that the beautiful woman by my side was my wife. In this one second of hesitation, I believed it would all be so easy if I could just walk away, leaving her with the impression of the great success Garrett Finnegan had become.

I didn't though. I wasn't a jackass. But right then, I really wanted to be.

"Oh, I'm sorry. You misunderstood," I said. "Leah is my sister, Clare's, best friend. You remember Clare, right?"

She nodded, and I saw her squeeze Olivia's hand.

"Leah is like a sister to me. We hang out quite a bit, but she is definitely not my wife. I'd consider taking this one though," I said with a wink. I gave Lily a tickle in the ribs, which caused her to squeal.

"So, you're not..."

"No, I'm not," I answered.

More awkward silence filled the space between our two small groups. Connor started kicking a rock on the ground in front of me, and he gave me the look that kids would give when they wanted to leave. It was the look that basically said they were going to spontaneously combust if they didn't vacate the premises immediately. *I knew the feeling.*

"So, Mia…what have you been up to since graduation?" Leah, the oh-so-nosy one, asked.

She knew who Mia was and knew I hadn't seen her since high school. We'd had a few heart to heart conversations over the years. I hadn't spilled all the gory details to Leah, but she was smart enough to put two and two together. Until she had some answers, she wasn't going to let this woman leave.

"I went to college in Portland and ended up settling in Atlanta, but I just moved back to Richmond last week. Olivia is letting me stay with her until I finalize everything with my house loan."

"You went to school in Oregon?" I said out loud before I had a chance to filter.

"Yes," she answered.

I grumbled as I continued my fascination with Connor's rock-kicking. I'd looked for her everywhere. We were supposed to go to a state school together. We had even gone apartment hunting, envisioning what our life would be like as we toured each place.

"What brought you back? Family? Work?" Leah asked.

"Um…I'm not really sure. I don't have a job yet…and I don't have any family anymore."

My head jerked up in surprise at that last statement. Were her parents dead? They had moved shortly after she left. Her father had taken a prestigious position in New York City, and at that time, I'd started to wonder if she would ever come back.

"So, you're looking for a job then? What do you do?" Leah asked.

"I majored in accounting, but I don't think I want to go back to an accounting firm. I'm looking for something else…anything else."

This was not the girl I had known. She looked similar. Her hair was the same color, her eyes were just as mesmerizing, and her body…shit. I thought she'd looked beautiful before, but when she'd left, she'd still had the body of a girl. Now, she was all woman, and I was honest enough to admit I wanted every inch of her.

Still.

Although her appearance was nearly the same, every word coming out of her mouth reminded me that the woman standing in front of me was not the girl who'd left me eight years ago.

"Well, there's a job opening where I work at the hospital. Do you think you'd be interested?" Leah asked.

I shot Leah a look, and she glanced back at me sweetly, like she had no idea that she was meddling.

"Um, I guess that depends. What kind of job is it?" Mia asked with a hint of a smile.

It was the first time I'd seen her smile in eight long years and I was glad to know at least that hadn't changed.

"Working the nurses' station. Do you have any medical experience?"

"I used to work at the student clinic in college," she answered.

"That could work. Why don't you stop by on Monday? I'll get you on the interview list and put in a good word."

Mia nodded and thanked Leah, and we started to say our good-byes.

Just as Mia was turning to walk away, she turned back. "Leah, what department do you work in?"

"Oh, duh! Labor and delivery on the third floor."

Mia looked stunned for a moment, but she quickly recovered and thanked Leah again before leaving.

Leah, the kids, and I walked back to the car.

"Well, you handled that one like a pro, Goober. Were you even going to talk to her? You could have at least asked her out to coffee? Asked for her phone number? You should have done something to make sure she wouldn't walk out of your life again," Leah said as she strapped Lily into the backseat.

"I think you just took care of that for me, didn't you, Miss Meddler?"

She grinned. "That's Mrs. Meddler, thank you very much, and you'll thank me later."

I wasn't too sure about that. Having Mia back in my life sounded like a bad idea. The last time had left me in ruins. I wasn't sure I could survive a second round.

Chapter Three

MIA

"So, that happened," Liv said.

It was later in the afternoon, and we were sitting around her living room, sipping tea. She really had a thing for it. She had an entire cabinet devoted to the beverage. She probably kept some exotic tea company in business. The girl was kind of psycho when it came to the stuff.

No tea bags for hippie Liv.

She hated it when I called her that, so I had decided to make it my mission to do so as much as possible.

She considered herself *evolved.*

Whatever. When you had canisters of tea leaves, didn't eat meat, and bought organic everything, the word *hippie* might fly out of my mouth on occasion.

"Yep. Sure did," I answered from my seat on the couch.

I hadn't moved in hours. I was just sitting there, like a pathetic wounded deer. I was drinking the mugs of tea

Liv had brought in, eating the cookies she'd stuffed in my hand, and staring into space, like a zombie.

"You got anything stronger than tea?" I finally asked, having had my fill of tea for the next millennium.

"You mean, like, coffee?"

I looked up at my friend with pure shock and horror written all over my face. She was grinning from ear to ear and had her arms wrapped around her front, looking smug.

"You better be kidding," I threatened.

"It got your attention at least. Of course I've got booze. Even *hippies* drink," she said, emphasizing the word she so loathed.

"Why don't I go make us some drinks, and you go order us a pizza? We'll meet back here in five."

I nodded and started looking up the phone number to the locally owned pizza shop down the street where we'd ordered from a few days ago. I ordered a large veggie pizza and cheesy bread, and then I waited. After a minute or so, I was bored. *What did people do before smartphones? Stare at walls?* I'd been doing that all day, and I was over it.

I picked back up my iPhone and did the one thing I'd sworn I would never do. I stalked Garrett on Facebook. In all the time I'd been gone, I had never looked him up—not on the Internet, Twitter, Instagram…nothing. I hadn't wanted to know if he had a girlfriend or a wife. I hadn't wanted to take the chance of possibly seeing wedding pictures or vacation photos with his kids. Not knowing had been the key to my survival.

But now, I knew, and like a dam bursting, I wanted to know everything. *Did he go to college, like we'd planned? What does he do? How is his family? Is he happy?*

My search turned out to be a bust when I found his

profile was locked down tighter than Fort Knox. The only thing I could see was his profile picture, and that was enough to set my heart into double-time. I hadn't thought it was possible, but he'd grown even more handsome since the last time I saw him. All those boyish features I remembered had been replaced with hard, lean muscle, broad shoulders, and a gaze that could set my panties on fire.

"I wondered how long it would take you," Liv said, reentering the living room with two large drinks.

She handed me one, and I instantly took a sip, not caring in the least about what it was. As long as it was alcohol, it was my kind of drink tonight.

"Are you sure?" I said through tear-stained eyes. "We can wait. We don't have to do this now. You know what everyone will say."

He looked into my eyes, finding a path into my very soul with a single glance.

"I don't want to wait, Mia. I'm ready now, and I don't care what everyone will say. I know you're the one, so why wait? We've already started our lives together. Now, we just have to make it official."

"He was perfect," I blurted out, staring at the picture of him still lighting up my screen. "He asked me to marry him."

"What? When?"

"The day before graduation."

"And you said...no?" she asked hesitantly.

I put down my phone, shutting off the screen and severing my view of Garrett and his many lickable features. "I said yes."

"Oh. So, why did you—"

"Leave?"

She just nodded. It was one of those things I wasn't ready to share yet.

"Mia—I mean, Amelia…fuck. I'm calling you Mia, okay? I can't look at you and call you anything else. You're just going to have to deal."

"Okay."

"Okay? That's it? I figured you'd put up more of a fight than that, but okay. You know, if you'd changed your mind, you could have just told him. You were eighteen. Getting married is a huge deal at that age. Hell, it still is at our age. The idea scares the shit out of me. That's why I'm planning on never going down that road. I'll never let a guy get that close."

I remembered the night Garrett had asked me.

We'd parked at the edge of the river, and we were lying on an old blanket that he always stored in his trunk. For hours, we'd been staring at the stars while talking about our new life. We were scared and excited. Everything was changing, but we were together, and we knew we could do anything if we had each other. We were so young and innocent, yet we were full of grown-up emotions we hadn't been prepared for.

Right in the middle of our conversation about apartments, he said, "Stand up."

"Why?" I asked.

"Just do it!" He grinned.

He bent down on one knee, and I giggled, thinking that was something men only did in movies. I knelt with him on the blanket. The frogs croaked, and the water rushed by as I held his hands. We both laughed and cried as he proposed.

He curled his fingers into my hair and kissed me softly until I said, "Yes."

Then, he completely surprised me by pulling out a ring. I had thought the entire thing was spur-of-the-moment, but he had planned it, every single minute. He placed the ring on my finger. It was a delicate white gold band with a small diamond placed in the center.

"It's not much, but you already own my heart, so this is just a placeholder for that."

"It's perfect."

And it had been.

I briefly touched the spot on my left hand, now ring-less and empty. "I didn't change my mind about him."

"Then, what made you run?"

"I didn't deserve him."

I still didn't.

GARRETT

Dropping Leah and the kids off, I briefly stopped inside to say hi to Leah's husband, Declan.

Then, I headed into the office. I didn't have to since it was Saturday, but this was what workaholics did. It was what anyone with an addiction did. I had to feed it constantly. Otherwise, the pain would start to surface again, and I'd be forced to deal with it. So, when everyone else was as far away from the office as possible, hanging out with friends or playing with their kids, I was scanning my corporate key card and taking the elevator up to the floor holding the Richmond office of the pharmaceutical company I'd been working for since college.

There were two types of workaholics in my opinion. There could be more. I hadn't done an official study. Psychology was always Mia's thing—or at least, it used to be until she'd apparently decided to become an accountant instead. But as far as I could see, people either worked themselves ragged to get to the top or they did so to avoid their own pathetic lives. I was the latter pretending to be the former. I played the part well. As the young team leader, I was known as a rise-to-the-top, do-anything-to-succeed corporate star. Honestly though, I couldn't give a rat's ass about this place.

I hated my job—like, really fucking hated it.

No one would ever know it by the way I acted. I would take on every project and account I could get my hands on. *Someone couldn't work late? I'd take it. Michelle needed to cancel her trip to Dallas because her kid was sick? Sure, I'd go for her.* To my coworkers, I was their saving grace and a team player to the end, and all my hard work had paid off. I had been promoted faster than any other sales executive my age. I'd made more deals and earned more bonuses, raking in more cash than anyone else in the company. Within a few years, I would be running the entire Richmond office, if not somewhere larger.

Did I want to? Hell no.

So, why was I still here? It kept my mind occupied.

It was the workaholic logic. As long as I was working, as long as I was immersed in something, I could keep my mind off her, and I would be fine.

When I'd been about to graduate from college, I had hoped to get a position at an architecture firm, but everywhere I had looked, I had been turned down. It had been my major and my dream in college. Unfortunately, the country had been in an economic shithole, and building and construction had hit an all-time low.

I had been forced to look outside my field. I'd taken the first job I could find—pharmaceutical sales. I had the face for it, doctors loved me, and it paid well. I had become addicted—addicted to the hours, addicted to the mind-numbing nothingness it gave me. So, my design work had become nothing more than a pastime, and I'd become Garrett Finnegan, pharmaceutical salesman extraordinaire.

The elevator dinged, and I exited on the fifth floor. I took a right toward my office, and I walked past the sea of cubicles, now dark and full of lengthy gray shadows. Offices were always a bit creepy in the off-hours. During business hours, there would be so much noise that the air was thick with it—phones rang, keyboards clicked, people chatted and shuffled around. But in the late hours, when it was just me, it would be dead silent and eerie, like the building recognized an intruder and silently watched me as I swiftly made my way through.

I unlocked the door to my office and immediately went to the coffeemaker in the corner. Coffee was an overworked man's best friend. I was selfish, and I had bought my own coffeemaker a few years ago. It was one of those single-cup fancy things that could make tea, cappuccino, probably hot-wax my car, and build a spaceship. All I knew was that it was easy, and it made the shit fast. The girls in the office were always telling me I should get the fancy shit, like some caramel-and-hazelnut-drizzled-coconut crap. Did I look like I wanted coconut in my coffee? If I could put an IV into my vein and pump this stuff directly to my heart, I'd go for it—as long as it was black.

While I waited for my wake-up juice to brew, I booted up my computer, and I looked out the window into the city, tapping my foot. This view always used to calm me. I loved this city. I'd gone to college about two hours away, but I'd immediately moved back after I graduated. My parents lived just outside the city limits in a quiet, beautiful neighborhood with aged trees and white fences.

When I had moved back, I'd wanted to be in the midst of everything, so I'd picked an apartment within walking distance of tons of great restaurants, bars, and anything else I might need. I could take the bus to work if I wanted, and I could walk or ride my bike to practically anywhere. The city that usually relaxed me was now setting me on edge. Suddenly, my favorite place to be was making me feel uneasy and nervous.

She was out there somewhere.

I never expected her to come back.

I never expected her to come back and not want to find me.

The gurgling sound of the coffeemaker caught my attention, and I turned to find my computer was ready as well. With my freshly brewed cup in hand, I sat down and got to work, pulling up my email, reports, and various other things.

Five minutes later, I was staring at the same report, and I hadn't made any progress.

Mia was back. My mind couldn't get past that, and I was having a hard time processing what I would do now that she was back in my life.

Was she back in my life?

Did I want her to be?

I looked at the clock. Thirty minutes had passed.

Fuck.

Leah had seemed to think it was simple. Mia was back, and I was here. We were both single—although Mia had never confirmed that fact—and we had history.

Leah had said, *See? Easy, Goober!*

No, not easy.

Mia wasn't some teenage crush. She was the one, and I'd spent my entire adult life trying to convince my heart otherwise—without any luck. Losing her once had left me a shell of what I had once been. Losing her again would utterly destroy me.

Would I be willing to take the risk if I were offered it? If Mia could be mine again, would I take it?

"What do you mean, she's gone?" I asked, my voice sounding hoarse from the shock.

"She's gone, Mr. Finnegan," Mia's mother said coldly.

"Where did she go? I need to find her. I'll go after her."

"I'm sorry. She made her intentions clear when she left. She does not want you to know her whereabouts, and she said to give you this."

She handed me a folded note. I opened it to see Mia's handwriting, and I read through it quickly.

My eyes flew up to Mrs. Emerson. "She can't mean this. She would never do this."

"I don't think you know our daughter very well, Mr. Finnegan. Good night."

No, I couldn't do it. She'd betrayed me, betrayed us. No matter how much my heart and body still wanted her, I could never forget that.

A knock pulled me out of my thoughts, and I saw Kara, another sales executive, standing in my door. She was dressed down today since it was a Saturday, but she still looked put together in a flowery summer dress and sandals.

"I see you're burning the figurative midnight oil as well?" she said.

"Funny thing, when you start working sixty-plus hours a week, they start regularly giving you that much more work."

"I know, right? I'm fairly certain I didn't have this much to start with, and I was working fifty hours then."

Kara had been stopping by my office, casually flirting, for a couple of months now. She'd just gotten out of a serious relationship, and I bet she was thinking I'd be the perfect follow-up.

I'm not.

But then, I remembered seeing Mia and how she had moved back into town and had purposely tried to avoid me. As I remembered the night when I'd sat on that street corner in the rain, clutching that god-awful letter, while screaming in agony with no one to cling to for support as my entire world was crumbling down, I decided I needed a clean break.

Maybe Kara could be my break—or maybe not, but I wouldn't know if I didn't try.

Looking up at her as she was talking to me about her upcoming trip to Charlotte, I noticed she was incredibly pretty. It wasn't something I'd ever bothered taking note of before. I didn't know why, but everyone who worked here was good-looking. It wasn't written in our job requirements, but pharmaceutical reps tended to be on the hot side. It certainly never hurt our sales. With golden brown hair and chocolate eyes, she had a sweet and trusting look to her.

"Hey, Kara, do you want to go out to dinner with me tonight?" I asked suddenly, interrupting her mid-sentence.

Her stunned look gave way to a dazzling smile. "I'd love to, Garrett."

"Great. Let's get out of here."

Chapter Four

MIA

I was not a fan of hospitals, specifically the department I was headed toward, but I needed a job. I couldn't sit around anymore, and I didn't like depleting my hard-earned savings account like a bum.

Somehow, in the last two weeks, I'd managed to interview for the position in the hospital, get the job, and move into my new house. Between learning everything that went into my new job and trying not to panic that I was now a first-time homeowner, I was exhausted.

"Hey, Mia," Leah said, greeting me as I took my spot at the nurses' station.

We didn't always have shifts together since she was only part-time, but I did enjoy seeing her. We had become fast friends, especially now that I knew she wasn't Garrett's wife. It definitely helped that I didn't want to rip off her head.

"Hi Leah. How are you? Did Lily get over her cold?" I asked.

During her last shift a few days ago, she'd mentioned that her daughter had come down with a cold, and she had hated having to leave her at home.

"Oh, yes, she's doing much better. Daddy, however, is miserable."

"Your husband got it?"

"Oh, yes, and let me tell you, men are giant pains in the asses when they are sick."

I laughed while listening to her plunge into all the craziness she'd been through during her husband's "horrific illness".

"And I told him, 'If Lily, *the baby*, can get over the cold, I'm sure you can suffer through.'"

"What did he say?" I asked, trying to imagine Leah's super-hot husband sick and cuddled up on the couch.

I'd recently found out that she was married to Declan James, the ex-actor turned movie director. I'd forgotten he had moved to Richmond. Hearing her talk about a guy I'd seen in several of my favorite films was weird.

"He told me that it was much worse for him because he's bigger. He then tried his best to convince me he needed to be taken care of by his sexy wife. Sponge baths and thigh-highs were encouraged."

I snorted out a laugh, and Leah left to make her rounds.

Working closely with a member of Garrett's family, even if she wasn't related, was turning out better than I had expected. I had worried that she would try to set us up or delve into my personal life right away, asking if I was seeing anyone or wanting to rekindle my relationship with Garrett. But since starting here, she hadn't said a word. I felt like she was actually getting to know me for me, rather than acknowledging me only because of the ties that bound us. It would be nice to have another friend.

"Hi," a quiet voice said, pulling me from the list I was working on.

A young woman, probably in her early twenties, was standing before me, leaning against the counter. Her belly protruded in front of her, and she was rocking from side to side, breathing in and out. Dark blonde hair was thrown up into a haphazard bun on the top of her head, and sweat was trickling down her forehead.

"Hi. Do you need something? Can I get your nurse?"

I'd seen this particular woman walking the halls when I came in earlier. I'd learned it was common practice for women to do that during labor. As long as they hadn't had an epidural, which made it impossible for them to leave the bed, they were free to move about the cabin. Several of the nurses had told me that walking could help alleviate some of the pain.

"No, no, I'm fine. It would just be nice to have someone to talk to, if you aren't too busy?" she asked, looking down at my printed spreadsheet.

I put it aside and gave her a reassuring smile. "No, I'm not too busy. How are you feeling?" I asked, knowing she probably felt like crap.

"Oh, well, I've been better, but it's not as bad as I thought it would be—at least not yet. I'm Tessa," she said.

"Amelia, but you can call me Mia," I answered back, surprising myself. After hearing it so often now, I guessed it wasn't so hard to acknowledge anymore. "Do you have anyone here with you?"

She shook her head as a single tear ran down her cheek. "Nope, it's just me."

"Well, now, you have me."

Over the next fifteen minutes, Tessa told me about her pregnancy—the joys, the sorrows, and the hard decisions. "I never thought I'd be having a child alone, but I knew I didn't want to give her up."

"It's a girl?" I asked, my voice quivering a bit.

"Yeah, that's what they tell me. The first time I saw her on the ultrasound, I knew I'd never be able to look away again, you know?"

"Yeah, I know."

Three hours later, Tessa gave birth to a beautiful baby girl named Beth. I was able to visit before they took Beth up to the nursery. The baby was beautiful, and her mother was beaming.

"Nothing quite like it, is there?" Leah said as I returned to the nurses' station.

"No," I answered.

"I still can't believe that little thing went natural. I was sure she would cave at the last minute and claw me to death, asking for an epidural. God knows I did."

"Maybe she had something to prove. To herself, to the world? Being all alone, she didn't have anyone with her to hold her hand," I said.

"You're right. Those mothers are usually the strongest of us all. She's going to do just fine, I think."

"I sure hope so."

"Holy shit! What happened to your leg?" she asked, leaning halfway over the desk for a closer inspection of my leg which was peeking out from the desk.

"Oh, it's nothing," I answered, trying to tuck my legs back under the work space. I attempted to pull my pant leg back down to cover the angry-looking bruise.

"That doesn't look like nothing."

"I'm installing new floors in my house. I was

ripping up the old wood, and I lost my balance and control of the crowbar. I kind of whacked my leg with it. It hurts by the way, if you were thinking of trying it."

"Looks like it. That's a mother of a bruise. You're redoing the floors of your house…by yourself? Why?"

"Well, my house is a fixer-upper, and I'm trying to do it on the cheap."

"Is it worth your limbs?" She arched a brow in question.

"I still have all my limbs!" I protested.

"Yeah, for now, but come next week, you're going to be coming in here, spouting blood everywhere. I won't know how to fix you because I only deal with vajayjays. You need some help."

Famous last words.

GARRETT

There was this song by The Offspring called "Bad Habit." In middle school, my friends and I would listen to it because it had about half a million curse words in it. We'd sneak the CD into my room, play it on my stereo, and pretend like we knew how to headbang. We would mouth the lyrics instead of singing the words out loud because we were too afraid of facing the wrath of my mother. Soap would have been involved in my punishment for sure.

As I pulled up to the curb of Mia's newly purchased house in a neighborhood that was blocks away from my own, the profanity in my internal monologue was putting that song to shame. I noticed right away that the front of her house looked like a construction zone with piles of wood near the alley dumpster and boxes of new wood on the porch.

"Fuck," I cursed out loud just to make sure I was hearing what my brain was screaming.

Why was I here?

Because I was the nice guy.

I was the guy who had heard his ex-girlfriend had bashed in her shins while trying to take out her hardwood floors and came to help.

Had she asked? Nope.

Did she know I was coming? No.

I was here because I was a glutton for punishment.

Intent on moving on, I'd taken Kara out that Saturday after I ran into Mia at the farmers' market. I was done. I'd wasted eight years of my life waiting for—what? For her to come back? For closure? I didn't know what the hell I had been waiting for, but by the time I figured it out, I could be the ninety-year-old crazy cat man who no one wanted to visit.

So, Kara and I had gone to one of my favorite local spots, and we'd had a good time. We'd talked and commiserated over work and our summer plans, and then…nothing. I had walked her to her car, and I could see that expectant look on her face. She'd wanted more, and God, I'd wanted to give it to her, but I just couldn't. I had looked into her eyes, and they were all wrong. Mia had intensely blue eyes, almost bordering on aquamarine, and the deep brown of Kara's eyes had just mocked me, reminding me of what I'd lost. I'd realized I wasn't ready to move on. I'd told her that I had a great time and that I would see her on Monday. That had left her in a stunned and bewildered state as she stood by her car in the middle of the parking lot.

I'd made excuses every time Kara asked me to lunch or out for drinks. I'd been trying to dodge any more awkward exchanges. There was a reason I would give a different name to the few scattered women I'd taken home from bars over the years. I couldn't stand the thought of hearing another woman whisper my name before our lips touched or call out my name as I made love to her. I'd only made love to one woman, only heard one woman say my name as I came inside her, and even though I needed to, I never wanted to change that fact.

Out of the corner of my eye, I saw her. Wearing cutoff shorts that barely covered her ass and a tank top that exposed her tanned skin, she bent over to drop a pile of lumber in the already accumulating pile in her front yard. I was moving before my brain could even register it. She looked up and caught my gaze just before I closed the car door. We both stood there, frozen in place, unable to look away.

It was me who took the first step forward. I walked across the street until I was in front of her, closer than I'd been in eight years. If I reached out, I could touch her, tuck that stray hair behind her ear, or show her exactly what was racing through my mind as I watched her nervously bite her lip.

"Hi," she said hesitantly.

"Hey." *Yep, that was a good start. I was the master of small talk.*

She looked at me expectantly, and I realized I should probably explain why I was there.

"Leah said that you banged up your leg pretty bad while ripping out your floors the other day. I thought you might need a hand." I shifted awkwardly and ran my fingers through my hair, unsure of what to do with my hands. I wanted to touch her, yet I didn't. I'd never had a conversation without touching her, and now, I felt twitchy and unnatural.

"You talk about me?" she asked.

"Oh, uh…I mean, Leah mentioned you the other day when I went over to her house for dinner. But I didn't ask about you," I said. Ouch, that hadn't come out the way I meant it to.

Judging from the way her eyes widened and dodged mine for a moment, I gathered she had taken it exactly how it had come out.

This was going fan-fucking-tastic.

"Look, do you want help or not?" I asked in frustration.

"No, I'm fine. Thank you." Her arms were crossed, and she looked pissed.

Well, that made two of us.

The never-ending stream of curse words started up in my head again, and I was seriously ready to just say, *Fuck it*, and leave. But then, she turned slightly, and I saw the bruise on her leg along with the Band-Aids on her hands and arms. Mia was never one for grace. She could trip over her own two feet.

"I'm not leaving. Get your ass back inside."

She opened her mouth to protest, but I stopped her, placing my finger on her lips. It was the first contact we'd had since she walked away from me all those years ago. The heat from her soft lips seared my skin, and I heard her gasp from the contact.

Our eyes locked as I said, punctuating each word, "I'm. Not. Leaving. Understand?"

She nodded her head in agreement, and we both turned to make our way inside. I rubbed my hands together, trying to savor the warmth I'd felt from her mouth, but it quickly disappeared—just like her.

There wasn't much in the way of furniture. A red couch was tucked in the corner, still covered in plastic. It was obviously new. A table that looked like it had seen quite a number of years and a couple of chairs sat in the kitchen.

"There isn't much yet. I'm waiting to get more furniture until the floors down here are done," she said before turning around.

"Why did you get such a big house in the first place?" I asked, giving an appraising glare.

This was supposed to be our thing—buying an old house and fixing it up. We had planned to do this together. While on the phone or cuddled up together on the hood of my car as we looked up to the stars, we used to talk for hours about what kind of house we wanted and what we'd do to it.

This was our dream, not hers.

"Uh…I don't know. It was all I could afford."

Bullshit.

"So, where do you want me?"

"What?" she asked, suddenly flustered.

"Put me to work, Mia. That's why I'm here." I tried not to laugh at her reaction to my words. It was good to know I could still ruffle those stuck-up little feathers of hers. God knows I'd spent a good part of my teenage years doing so.

"Hey," I whispered, leaning forward in my desk chair.

Nothing.

"Hey," I muttered softly. This time, I took a piece of binder paper, wadded it up, and tossed it at her head.

That had gotten her attention as she let out an audible gasp and turned around in her seat to face me.

"What do you want?" she asked coldly.

Brr...

"Your name. I want your name."

"Why?"

"So, I know what to call you on our date," I answered with a sly grin.

I'd been watching this girl in my homeroom class ever since the first day of school two weeks ago. She'd come from a different middle school, so I had no idea who she was, but the second I'd seen her, I'd wanted to know her.

"We are not going on a date!" she scoffed.

"Of course we are, and I can't ask you out on a second one if we don't go on a first. See where I'm going with this?" I replied back.

"And why would I go on a date with you?"

"Because you're already falling madly in love with me. It's hopeless."

I was honestly waiting for her to smack me. When I saw just a hint of a smile appear at the corner of her mouth, I knew I'd gotten to her.

"Amelia," she said.

"Huh?"

"Amelia—that's my name, stupid." She giggled.

"That's kind of a stuck-up name, Amelia. I'm picking something else."

"You're renaming me?" She laughed.

She was now completely caught in my trap.

"Yep. From now on, you will be known as...Mia."

"Oh, um...are you good with a crowbar?" she asked, pointing to the large tool propped up against the far wall.

"Better than you, I'd wager." I pointed to her leg.

She gave me a sour look before showing me what still needed to be ripped up.

"You know these are original floors that you are tearing out, right? They're probably over a hundred years old," I said as I started pulling up the oak in the dining room.

"Yes, I know that, but they can't be rescued. Apparently, the owners before me didn't care so much about the historical value of them because they were trashed. They looked like someone had taken a sledgehammer to them and then left an entire litter of cats to urinate on every board for a month."

"Is that what smells in here?"

"Did you think it was me?"

"Well, I mean—"

"Garrett!" she shrieked, leaning over to playfully hit my arm.

She realized what she had done a second after she did it, and she stepped back. It was scary how easily we had just fallen back into our normal banter. It made me wonder just how little effort it would take to tumble back into everything else.

Rather than suffer through the impending awkwardness, I started my job of taking up the wood floors. She busied herself by sweeping the four-thousand nails that were being thrown all over the place from each board being pried out of place. We worked through the afternoon.

In the evening, Mia asked, "Hey, do you want to order a pizza or something?"

"Uh…actually, I have to go to my sister's for dinner tonight." I didn't really, but I'd reached my threshold for the day. The silence was getting to me, and if I had to spend one more hour in here watching Mia bend down in those shorts, trying not to see her ass cheeks peek out from the bottom, I would go crazy.

"Oh, okay. Well, you better get going then." Dodging my gaze, she became very interested in a spot on the wall that needed to be patched.

"Yeah, I guess I should."

I walked to the door and stopped. I swung around on my heels, finding a surprised Mia behind me.

"What time tomorrow?"

"Excuse me?" she asked in surprise.

"What time do you want me to come back over tomorrow?" I repeated.

"You're coming back?"

Our eyes met, and I nodded. "Yes, I like to follow through with things until the very end."

The double meaning was not lost on her.

MIA

Like clockwork, he showed up at my doorstep the very next day.

Then, the day after, he returned when I was done with my shift at the hospital.

He even came back the following night, holding a bag of takeout in one hand and a change of clothes in the other. This was the second day he'd arrived in a suit. It was further proof that the boy I'd left on the football field after graduation day had disappeared, replaced by a man I barely recognized.

This new Garrett was not the lighthearted boy I remembered. He was a little rough around the edges and a bit bossy, and he had a hardness to him that I didn't recognize. It wasn't what I was used to, but if I had to admit it to myself, it was sexy as hell. I had adored playful, carefree Garrett. He was always loving and gentle, and he'd dedicated himself to me completely. But grown-up

Garrett was full of mystery and angst. I didn't know what he would do from one minute to the next, and I hated myself for liking it.

He wasn't for me, and I didn't need to add complication to his life again. He was just doing me a favor with the floors, and I needed to keep my distance. If the past had proven anything, it was that he deserved someone a hell of a lot better than me.

"You brought food?" I asked as he breezed past me toward the kitchen.

"Well, you have absolutely nothing in your refrigerator, and I nearly starved to death last night, so I decided to take matters into my own hands. You know you're a grown-up now, right? Food doesn't grow on trees. You have to actually go to the store, pick it up, and prepare it."

He was also incredibly sarcastic. That, unfortunately, wasn't new.

"I know I am a grown-up, Garrett," I huffed, crossing my arms over my chest.

His eyes immediately dropped, hungrily watching the way my breasts strained against my tank top from the pressure of my arms. His emerald gaze traveled back up to meet my eyes, and I blushed like a teenager. I looked away to find plates for the Chinese food he'd brought over, but I could see him smirking out of the corner of my eye. He knew he'd gotten to me.

"You still wear that necklace."

It was a statement, not a question. I'd wondered if he would say anything about it. I'd caught him staring at it on the first day he'd shown up to help. We had been hours into destroying my floors. Leaning against the wall, I'd tried to catch my breath, and I'd quenched my thirst with a glass of ice-cold water. When I had looked up, I'd seen the crowbar on the floor, and his eyes had been locked on my chest. I'd instantly heated, thinking he was blatantly checking me out, but then I'd realized the heat in his eyes was from anger, not passion. He'd seen the sterling silver key pendant with his birthstone in the center hanging from my neck. He'd given it to me for my sixteenth birthday, and I'd never taken it off since he'd placed it there.

"I've never taken it off."

He just grunted and continued pulling out cartons of takeout. His eyes drifted up to mine briefly, and he held our stare as if he wanted to say something, but then he let it go. We loaded up our plates, sat down at my kitchen table, and silently ate our moo shu pork and fried rice.

"Why?" he asked, breaking the silence.

I stilled, unable to look up and meet his penetrating gaze. "I…I needed to keep a part of you with me."

I looked up and our eyes held for a moment before he pushed away from the table, startling me.

"I'm not hungry anymore."

I finished my dinner alone with my knees pulled into my chest, and then I pushed my plate away. I listened to him in the living room, tearing up the floor like a madman. I could hear boards flying and nails hitting the walls. The tears rimming my eyes threatened to spill over as he took his anger and hurt out on the floor. I finally rose from the table to clean up our plates and glasses.

What had I done to this man? Had I really thought this would be better? No answers, no closure had turned into just anger and lost hopes. I'd done this.

It was just another reason he deserved so much more.

After another few minutes, I heard his movements

slow and return to a normal pace until he stopped altogether, and I heard him empty a bottle of water in a few chugs. The broom then began making slow, methodical sweeps across the room, and I figured it might be a safe time to enter.

All that double-time pace must have caused him to work up quite a sweat. When I came into my living room, I was faced with Garrett the God. *Holy shit, that man should warn people before he takes his shirt off.* There were a lot of new additions to the twenty-five-year-old Garrett, starting with a set of eight-pack abs and a chiseled chest that made me think dirty, dirty things. Garrett 2.0 also came with a few tattoos, which I usually wasn't attracted to. But on him? *Yum.*

I realized about a half a second too late that I'd been caught in my ogle-fest, and I immediately turned away, trying to hide the blush spreading across my horrified face.

"Um…I can do the sweeping if you want to take a break," I offered, still unable to turn toward him.

If I looked at him, I would be looking at all of him, and then we'd be back to where we were a few minutes earlier —me swimming in my own drool, thinking of all the various ways I could get him up to my bedroom and the many, many things I could do with him once we were there.

"All right," he said, holding out the broom just inches from his glistening body.

The pads of my fingers grazed his stomach as I took the broom, and I was pretty sure I'd whimpered as that tiny part of my body came into contact with his. Up until that moment, I'd thought eight-packs were a myth, a legend told by magazine editors and sorority girls, but no, they were real. That eight-pack was no joke.

I felt his eyes on me as I finished sweeping up the mess he'd made, and then he quietly watched me as I bent down and picked up each and every nail that had been strewn around the room.

Sick of feeling like an animal in the zoo, I decided to end the silence. "I thought you worked, like, a billion hours a week? How have you managed to get so much time away from the office?"

He seemed a bit taken aback by my question, but he gave a hint of a smile. His eyes always crinkled in the corners when he smiled. It made him appear younger, more like the boy I remembered.

"Been talking to Leah about me?"

"I mean, she was talking about you. I didn't ask," I answered, basically repeating the words he'd said to me days earlier.

"Hmm…well, to answer your question, I don't have to work a billion hours a week. I just choose to."

"Why? Why would anyone want to work that much?" I asked.

His eyes flew to mine in a heated glare. "Some people enjoy what they do. Maybe I'm just driven."

"What do you do?" I asked.

"I'm in pharmaceutical sales."

"Oh, please!" I said, laughing, "That's total bullshit! You? In sales? You have to hate it. The Garrett I knew would have cut off his left arm before taking a job like that."

I could see by his expression that I'd hit home. His eyes lost focus, and he wouldn't meet mine.

"Yeah, well…I guess we all change, don't we? The girl I

knew would have never become a tight-ass accountant, so I guess we didn't know each other as well as we thought we did."

"No, I guess not."

The rest of the evening was spent in stifling silence as I tried to remember the boy I once knew. I wondered if I would ever understand the man who was standing before me.

Do I deserve to?

GARRETT

"You look lovely, sweetie," my mother said over my shoulder.

I gazed into the floor-length mirror wedged in the corner of my parents' bedroom. I'd snuck in here a few minutes earlier to try and adjust the monstrosity of a bow tie that was currently choking the life out of my windpipes.

"I feel like a penguin," I muttered. I readjusted the bow tie for the hundredth time.

"A very handsome penguin," she amended.

She spun me around, which was not an easy task. I was only sixteen, but I was a football player, and I practiced every waking moment. I was a walking, talking muscle machine, not that I was bragging.

"Are you ready for tonight?" she asked.

"Mom, it's just a dinner." A dinner I had to wear a freaking tuxedo for.

"Garrett, Mia's family is different from ours."

"I know, Mom. They're loaded," I scoffed.

"It's more than that. They think very highly of themselves and the people they associate with. I don't want you to get hurt."

"Mia would never hurt me," I said adamantly.

"You really like this girl, don't you?"

"I love her, Mom."

Vibrations on the nightstand next to my bed tore me from my dream, bringing me back to reality. My eyes blinked open, and I groggily searched around in the dark for the source of what had awoken me. Palming my phone, I hit a button, hoping it would end the incessant buzzing.

Without bothering to see who the hell was calling me at this unholy hour, I said, "Hello?"

"Garrett? I'm sorry. I didn't know who else to call."

"Mia?" All remnants of sleep fell away at the sound of her panicked voice.

"I think someone just tried to break into my house," she said.

"Did you call the police?" I was already standing, pulling on a pair of jeans over my boxers.

"No, I think they're gone. A car drove by, and it might have scared them off, but I'm frightened they might come back. I didn't want to call the cops. What if it was a cat? Or a drunk frat boy? I'm sorry. I'm being stupid…and I woke you up…" she trailed off.

"Look, I'm already dressed." I paused, throwing a shirt over my head. "I'll drive over now and check things out for you. Then, you'll at least be able to go back to sleep."

"Okay."

"I'll be there in ten."

I ended the call, grabbed my keys, and threw on a pair of shoes. I ran toward my front door, and the small mosaic mirror next to it caught my eye. Clare had bought the mirror for me while on her honeymoon a few years ago. I took a quick look at my refection as I undid the lock.

It was two in the morning. My ex-girlfriend—ex-fiancée, if I wanted to get technical—had just called. And what had I done? I had jumped out of bed to be her knight in shining armor.

"What the fuck are you doing, Garrett?"

My reflection had no answers, so I just turned toward the door, opened it, and walked out—toward Mia, which is where I always seemed to go. The irony wasn't lost on me that in an entire city filled with thousands of people, Mia and I lived less than a few minutes, a few city blocks really, from each other. The one person I needed to be the farthest away from was basically my neighbor.

In the time it took the radio DJ to run a few commercials, I was knocking on Mia's door, impatiently waiting for her to answer. My eyes scanned the area, looking around for anything out of the ordinary. I was planning on walking around her house, but first, I needed to make sure she was safe.

The door creaked open, and there was Mia, standing in pink boy shorts and a tank top. My eyes quickly swept down her body, remembering how she'd felt under me, over me—

Fuck.

She'd just been scared out of her mind by an attempted robbery, and here I was, practically drooling at her door like some pervert, trying to figure out if I could see her nipples through her top.

And I could.

My hungry gaze obviously gave away my thoughts because she hastily covered her exposed body with the matching robe that had been hanging open.

Mentally shaking my head to clear away the pornographic thoughts, I asked, "Are you okay?"

She nodded. "Yeah, I haven't heard anything else. I'm

sure it was nothing." She looked embarrassed and flustered.

"You don't know whether it was nothing, Mia. Why don't you go make yourself some coffee or something? I'm going to go check everything out. I'll be back in a few minutes."

She agreed, and I turned to make my way around her house. I checked her window locks and gate. I found footprints near the entrance of the locked gate at the side of her house. They weren't mine or hers. Of course, I couldn't tell if the owner of the footprints had sinister intent, but it was enough to piss me off.

I walked back through her front door and turned to lock it behind me.

"We're replacing all your locks tomorrow. You've got twenty-year-old locks out there, Mia. And you're getting a dog."

She was just sitting down with two cups of coffee at the kitchen table as I made my announcement. She turned and gave me a dumbfounded look. "I'm getting a what?"

"Locks. You need new locks."

"No, the other part," she said.

"Oh, you're getting a dog."

"Says who?" She crossed her arms over her chest.

I'd noticed it was a common trait of hers. The thin robe she was wearing did nothing to cover up her round breasts. Her pouty stance only pushed them higher, making them strain against the thin pink fabric.

"Says me. You are a single woman in the middle of the city, Mia. You need protection."

"So, rather than being rational and getting something like—oh, I don't know—a security system, you decide I need a dog?"

"Yes. Security systems are expensive and can be dismantled. Dogs can be trained, and they are good companions."

Her eyes narrowed, and she threw her hands up in exasperation. "You are exhausting. I am not yours to boss around, Garrett."

"Oh, I know that, Mia. You made sure of that a long time ago," I practically spit, venom lacing my words.

I regretted the words the second they had left my mouth. I saw the hurt on her face as she looked ashen and gutted.

"I'll look into the dog. Thank you for coming over," she whispered.

Pinching the bridge of my nose, I turned away. The coffee she'd made was still sitting on the kitchen table. It was probably now lukewarm from my icy words.

"Hey, why don't you head upstairs? I'll make sure everything is locked and secure," I offered.

She didn't even argue. She just retreated upstairs. As I listened to the soft sobs echoing down the hall, I took a deep breath and tried to center myself. I didn't understand her. I couldn't comprehend why a girl who had left me looked so destroyed.

She left me, damn it.

I should be the one with the right to bleed, not her. *What puzzle piece was I missing here?*

After cleaning up the coffee and quickly checking the locks again, I quietly jogged my way up the stairs, and found her bedroom. The stark white walls and dark wood furniture decorating the room looked washed out against the soft light emanating from the small lamp at her bedside.

Curled up with a sheet pulled all the way to her chin, she was staring out the window at the crescent moon.

"Why did you come here, Garrett?" she asked softly, her attention still focused on the window.

Against my better judgment, I walked over to her bed and sat down next to her. I resisted the urge to touch her, to caress her cheek, to bend down and taste her quivering lip, and to tell her everything would be fine.

"I had to be sure you were safe," I answered honestly.

She didn't respond. She just continued to stare out the window, like she was searching for an answer from the man on the moon.

"Do you remember that dinner you had me go to?" I asked, remembering my dream from earlier tonight.

"The one at the country club?" she asked.

"Yeah."

"I had strappy black heels on. You kept staring at them all night," she said wistfully.

"They were the fanciest and sexiest damn things I'd ever seen. They made your legs look endless."

I caught her gaze with mine, but she quickly looked away.

"You weren't the only one who noticed. My mom caught you staring at my legs several times that night, if I remember correctly."

I turned away, giving a hint of a laugh. "Your mom never was much of a fan of mine, especially that night. I showed up in my rented tuxedo, which was definitely not designer, and your mom's nose curled up so fast that I thought she was allergic to me."

Her eyes finally disengaged from the window, meeting mine, and she gave a small ghost of a laugh. "The only

thing my mother was allergic to was being kind, generous, or understanding."

"You say that like she's not around anymore."

"I wouldn't know."

Her answer was final, so I didn't push it.

"You were always willing to do anything for me."

"I would have gone into hell for you," I said adamantly.
"For both of you."

Chapter Six

MIA

"So, then what happened?" Liv asked as we settled in on the couch.

It was Saturday night, and we were slumming it in our yoga pants and hoodies at my house, getting ready to order Thai food and watch a movie on Netflix. I'd managed to push around the couch and old secondhand chair I'd picked up in a way that mimicked an actual living room despite the lack of flooring. It looked pretty depressing now, but I had a vision in my head of something much better, and someday soon, it would be beautiful. Until then, Liv and I would have to settle for sitting on crappy furniture.

On my half-completed floor.

On a Saturday night, no less.

In our pajamas.

I thought we were miserably failing our age bracket.

"He just left. He locked the door and walked out," I finally answered.

I omitted that part when I recapped Garrett's late-night visit.

There hadn't been much to say after that. He'd left. Lying awake in my bed, I'd listened to my echoing breaths moving in and out of my lungs, the sounds quietly filling my empty bedroom, as I'd wallowed in regret. I'd thought about my parents and the choke-hold control they'd had over my life back then.

Those heels I'd worn the night Garrett came and picked me up were a complete act of rebellion. Olivia and I had been told to go out and buy suitable ensembles for a formal dinner. Credit cards had been thrown at us, and we'd been sent on our way.

Olivia's parents could throw money around, charging things every single day without worrying about the consequences. My parents, on the other hand, would rack up the debt and then worry until my dad's next big court case, hoping he would make enough to pay the cards off. The trust fund my mother had liked to brag about wasn't even money my dad had earned himself. It had been money my grandparents had set aside for me. I had no doubt it was gone now. My parents always lived beyond their means, and they thought they hid it well. My mother would sell her clothes on eBay to make extra cash, or she'd wear an outfit once and return it, telling me it hadn't fit right when I knew it had.

While I'd known what they were doing, what I hadn't understood was why. Why try so hard? Why not just live a happy existence, like everyone else?

Garrett came from a well-to-do family. His father had a well-paying job, and they always lived within their means. I'd never seen a happier family. Why couldn't mine be like that?

When I'd returned home with my sexy designer pumps that were not on my mother's acceptable list of clothing, she'd had a full-out panic attack.

"How could you do this, Amelia? Don't you understand who will be there? I should have never let you go to that school. It's a terrible influence," she said, clearly flustered.

"No, Mom, I don't understand," I answered bluntly.

I didn't bother to correct her on the fact that they probably couldn't afford to send me to a private school because of her massive clothing budget. Olivia's parents sent her to public school to fit a certain image for her father's political career, but I was under no illusions that my parents were doing the same.

"My school is perfectly fine," I snapped.

I was angry. She was making a big deal out of nothing. I wanted to look grown-up for once. I was sick of looking like a porcelain doll. Look but don't touch. I wanted my boyfriend to see me in something sexy for a change, rather than the mother-approved garments I was always in.

"You just don't care about anything, do you?" she huffed.

"It's just a pair of shoes, Mom."

I stormed out the door and got ready for the evening.

I didn't talk to my mom for the rest of the evening, even when I showed up with Olivia and Garrett. Just as I'd thought, no one gasped or fainted when I walked in, looking like a traitor in my inappropriate heels. It wasn't like they were covered in rhinestones or glitter. They were designer, and they had cost a fortune. But in my mother's head, she had a vision of what a sixteen-year-old should look like, and it was not this.

I'd spent the evening laughing and dancing with Garrett. It had been the first time I'd ever enjoyed being in that awful country club my parents loved so much. I hadn't paid attention to anyone else other than my best friend and boyfriend. They'd made everything better. I'd thought I had won the battle with my mother that night, and I felt exhilarated. When I woke up the next morning and found my shoes had disappeared, I knew I hadn't.

When I was chaperoned to every other shopping excursion from that moment on, I knew I would never win. I had been pretty sure the only reason she'd allowed me to keep Garrett around was because she'd known I would only rebel further if she tried to take him away, and she had been petrified of a scene.

"So, have you heard from him since?" Liv asked, bringing me out of my head and back to the present.

"Nope," I answered.

He hadn't shown up since then to help with the floors, and he hadn't called to say if he would be returning. I thought it was safe to say he was done with me, and I didn't blame him.

"That man is very different from the boy I once knew," Liv said wistfully.

I didn't say anything. I just nodded in agreement.

The more time I'd spent with him, the more evident this realization had become. This man was Garrett, but he wasn't my Garrett, not anymore, and I couldn't help but feel responsible. When I would look into his eyes, I could see pain, hurt, and anger. Those were emotions I'd never encountered before with the bright-eyed boy I'd left so long ago. When I'd decided to leave and never come back, I'd thought he would be better off because of it. I always pictured him happy with that carefree attitude of his. In my head, he had gotten married, and he was content. It hurt to think of it, but it was what had kept me from rushing back every day. It was the only thing that had allowed me to come back now. I'd thought that after so much time had passed, someone like him couldn't possibly be alone.

Seeing him on that busy street in the middle of the farmers' market, carrying the young boy on his shoulders was exactly how I'd pictured him in my head. But that wasn't his life. After all this time, he was alone. Had I done that?

Before I had time to contemplate that, my doorbell rang. Our food had arrived.

Let our sad Saturday night begin.

I rose from the couch and gathered the money we'd pooled together off the kitchen counter. I headed for the door. Thanks to an overbearing Garrett sending over a locksmith, every door and window lock had been replaced with shiny new locks to keep the bad guys out. After flipping the new lock that had just been installed, I pulled the door open.

"Did someone order in on a Saturday night?" a feminine voice asked.

I found Leah standing on the other side, holding up two bags of food, as she sported a wry grin.

"Did you take up a new side job?" I asked, wondering why she was at my door.

"Nope, but I bet I could make a lot of tips dressed like this, huh?" she said, giving a glance at her attire.

She wasn't kidding about the tips. She was dressed to kill. Mile-high nude heels made her already long legs look endless, and the pink dress she was wearing clung to her like a second skin. I didn't know anyone who could pull off something like that, but she did so flawlessly.

"So, what exactly are you doing, looking like a guy's

wet dream on my doorstep?" I asked, motioning for her to come in.

She breezed past me and strutted toward the kitchen. She put the bags of food in the fridge.

Wait, what? I want to eat that.

"I ran into your delivery guy on your porch. I paid for your food. You're welcome," she said with a grin. "But you won't be eating it tonight."

"Hey, hot stuff," Liv said, greeting Leah like they were old pals, as she came into the kitchen.

"Hey. Olivia, right?"

Liv nodded. "You can call me Liv."

I gave Leah a look that said to get to the point. My food was currently cooling in the fridge, and I was getting cranky.

"So, you guys are seriously sitting around in your pajamas on a Saturday night?" Leah glanced down at our frumpy clothes.

I was pretty sure I could see a stain on my hoodie that had been there since college. *I was so sexy.*

"Yep," we said in unison.

"That's just sad. You are too young for this shit. Come on, let's get you upstairs."

She grabbed both of our hands and began dragging us up the flight of stairs.

"Wait, what are we doing?" I asked.

"We are going out. I have excuses for PJ Saturdays. It's called two kids. You two, however, do not have any excuses. Tonight, Clare and I both have babysitters, and you two will be joining us on our night out."

I thought about arguing, but from her determined face as she started rummaging through my closet, I didn't think I had a choice. She was a woman on a mission.

"How many cardigans does one woman need to own, Mia?" Leah asked, poking her head out of my tiny closet.

It was such a mess. I was surprised she hadn't been swallowed up by it yet.

"I get cold easily, and they're always on sale," I answered defensively.

I heard her muffled laugh somewhere in the depth of my closet.

"Well, in this"—she emerged out of the mess, holding up a black mini skirt and glittery tank top—"you will be so hot that we will all have to put out fires behind you."

My eyes went wide at the sight of those two pieces. I'd bought them on a whim off of a sale rack when I was feeling daring, but I had never actually worn either. Leah and Liv were both looking at me with big Cheshire Cat grins that said I would be wearing that outfit tonight.

Well, here goes nothing.

After a bit more rummaging, we found a red dress for Liv that accented her dark hair and alabaster skin and a pair of matching heels.

Leah, of course, insisted on redoing my makeup. Liv got off easy, applying her own. But I was, in Leah's opinion, too sweet-looking and needed to get a bit dirty.

After thirty minutes, I looked in the mirror and gasped in surprise. My eyes were smoky and sultry, and my cheekbones were sculpted yet subtle. My lips looked luscious and understated in a peachy gloss that brought out the reddish highlights in my hair.

I put on my micro mini skirt and tank, and I slipped into my patent leather heels. I checked myself out in the full-length mirror on the back of my door.

I look hot.

If only my mom could see me now, she'd have a heart

attack. No, she'd have to have a heart for that, and she definitely did own anything that beat or expressed emotion.

All three of us piled into Leah's car, and I tried not to giggle as I sat down next to the infant seat in my sexy ensemble. It seemed sort of ridiculous.

"So, you have a babysitter, and you aren't spending the evening with your husband?" I asked Leah as she merged onto the interstate, headed for downtown.

I'd seen pictures of her husband. Hell, I was a fan of her husband, and if I were her, I didn't think I'd be able to leave the house. He was sex-on-a-stick hot, and from the way Leah had spoken, she mounted that stick as frequently as possible.

Lucky bitch.

"Oh, he'll be there," she said with a sly grin.

"What exactly does that mean? This isn't a girls' night out?" I asked.

"Oh, it is...sort of. The guys are out on their own, and we are out as well. I found out where they are going though, so we'll just happen to be at the same place."

I was so confused. "Why are we doing this?"

"Do you see the way I'm dressed?" she asked.

"Uh...yeah, it's kind of hard to miss."

Liv was already laughing. Apparently, she got it, but I was still lost. Was I that naive?

"She's showing up to drive her husband nuts. That's awesome...and kind of evil."

Leah shrugged. "Hey, when you're married, you've got to do things to keep your husband on his toes. Showing up unexpectedly, looking hotter than sin, will drive him insane."

"And Clare?" I asked, wondering if she was in on the plan.

"Oh, I was at her house before I came and got you. She's all sexed-up, too. Logan will lose his shit. Our good friend, Ella, is coming with her as well to surprise her husband, Colin."

Awesome. So, the entire gang will be there. I suddenly felt awkward and out of place. Hanging out with a bunch of married couples didn't sound like a fun night at all.

"So, why are we going with you? We don't have any husbands to drive nuts," I said.

"No, you don't. But you have the rest of the bar," she said with a mischievous grin.

GARRETT

My brother-in-law was the last person I'd expected to see at a karaoke bar in the middle of downtown on a Saturday night. As I entered the packed hot spot with several of my coworkers, I saw him sitting in the corner with his two best buddies as they were laughing, drinking cold beers, and trying to ignore a drunk sorority girl singing a horrible rendition of No Doubt's "Just a Girl."

I hadn't really wanted to come in the first place. Nothing sounded better than a beer, but I'd rather enjoy it at home by myself—without the noise.

God, I was fucking lame.

I turned to Kara, who was leading the pack of us. "Hey, I see my brother-in-law. I'm going to go over and say hi for a second."

She glanced over at the table I was pointing at, and she immediately zeroed in on Declan, one of Logan's best friends. Her eyes widened in what could only be described as wonderment.

Oh, great. She's a fan. I gave a sigh. "Do you want to come with me?"

She nodded enthusiastically and took my hand. That shocked me a little, but I figured she didn't want to get lost in the crowd. So, I wove us through until we finally made it to the small group. Logan, Declan, and their friend, Colin, instantly rose to greet us.

"Hey, man! I didn't know you were coming down! Take a seat!" Logan said with a hard pat on my back.

"Just coming by to say hi," I said, so he wouldn't feel obligated to find us seats. "I didn't know you were such a fan of karaoke," I followed up with a grin.

He laughed and shook his head. "I'm not—at all. Colin chose the place, and he didn't realize it was karaoke night. When we got here, we talked about going somewhere else, but he thought it would be funny to watch. So, here we are."

"So, I shouldn't expect you to hop up there and bleed out your heart to all these women?"

"The only woman I sing for is your sister," he said sincerely.

Logan and my sister had been married for a few years now, and I honestly couldn't imagine a better man for her. After her first husband, Ethan, had passed away, she had been left alone to raise their infant daughter, and I'd thought she'd given up on ever finding anyone again. Logan had come into their lives and taken care of both of them. When he had been diagnosed with cancer a few years back, Clare had then taken care of him. I'd never seen a stronger couple.

I gave a quick nod to everyone else at the table, and

then I noticed Logan glancing down at my hand still joined with Kara's. I quickly let go, not wanting to give the wrong impression to either of them.

"Logan, this is Kara, my coworker. A bunch of us came down here to unwind after a long day. She, uh…saw Declan and wanted to meet him."

Kara blushed, and Logan grinned. As the son of a billionaire, Logan wasn't invisible to the public eye either, but since marrying and settling down, his popularity had died down significantly. When you were famous for being a rich playboy and suddenly you're not anymore, people lose interest.

Declan, however, was an actor—or he used to be. He'd stopped taking roles over two years ago when he stepped behind the camera and started directing, but that didn't mean people stopped recognizing him. He was gaining some serious credibility as a director. He hadn't shown up in the tabloids as much, but the women could still point him out in a crowd.

"Well, we wouldn't want to disappoint a fan, would we, Declan?" Logan said over his shoulder to his good friend.

Declan just shook his head and chuckled, standing to greet us. "It's a pleasure to meet you, Kara," he said in a voice that oozed sex appeal.

Kara's blush spread even further. "Can I get your autograph?"

"Uh…sure. You got anything for me to sign? I'm afraid I don't really carry anything like that."

She dived into her purse and rummaged around, looking for something, but she only found a pen. Nothing to write on. "I have a pen. You could sign me," she said with a giggle.

I heard Colin choke on his laugh as he had been

sucking down his beer. Declan gave a half-grin, but he handled it like the pro he was.

"That's very sweet, but I gave up signing body parts a long time ago," he said, holding up his wedding ring as an explanation.

"Of course. I was just being silly," she answered, fumbling now and looking highly embarrassed.

Didn't this girl just go on a date with me? Next to Declan James, I was suddenly chopped liver, not that I was jealous. It actually made my life a hell of a lot easier.

Declan reached down and grabbed a napkin off the table. He took the pen from her hand, and he scribbled something on the napkin. When he handed it back to her, she thanked him. They took a picture, which of course caused a domino effect, and he had to take many more pictures with several other women who were suddenly brave enough to come over.

After about fifteen minutes, he politely thanked them and said he was going to join his buddies for a beer. He sat back down, and everyone, thankfully, dispersed. The conversation Logan, Kara, and I had been having started to come to a close. Just as Kara and I were about to say our good-byes to everyone and join our coworkers again, Logan caught someone's eye over my shoulder and cursed.

"Motherfucker!" Declan joined in.

"Is that my wife?" Colin asked.

I turned to see my sister and her two best friends entering the bar. I lost interest immediately when I saw who was walking behind them.

Mia.

She was dressed in a short skirt and fuck-me heels, and I had to brace myself against the wall for a second to recover from the impact. Mia had always been beautiful and sexy in a natural way. She was never overdone but never plain either. Tonight though, she was dripping sex from head to toe, and I wanted to kill every man in the bar who was eyeing her as she walked in.

She wasn't mine though. I had no right. My hands fisted at my sides, and I took a cleansing deep breath that did absolutely nothing to calm my nerves. I tried to turn back and start another conversation with Logan, but he was now entirely focused on Clare. He stood frozen in place, completely mesmerized, as he waited for her to join him. When Clare reached his side, she grinned, and he whispered something in her ear, which caused her to blush.

"Funny meeting you here, handsome," she whispered.

"My night just got much, much better," Logan said.

Yuck, I really didn't want to witness sexy time between my sister and her husband.

Declan and Colin were engaged in similar acts with their wives—eye-fucking the shit out of them and whispering God-only-knows-what in their ears. I looked over, and Mia and Liv were casually leaning over the bar, waiting to buy a drink. She glanced over at Leah with a grin. It died immediately when her eyes found mine, and her face fell even more when she saw me standing with Kara.

Shit, she thinks I'm on a date. I needed to get out of here. Nothing good could come from this.

"Goober!" Leah said, finally realizing my presence.

"Hey, Leah," I said.

"I didn't know you were going to be here! I thought we were just crashing our husbands' night out. To what do we owe the pleasure?" she asked, settling herself on her husband's lap.

Declan looked mighty happy with his new arrangements for the evening. His hand was caressing up and down Leah's bare thigh. I shuddered and looked away. It was like being at a family get-together, but instead of playing Parcheesi, everyone had decided to make out instead.

Gross.

"I showed up with a few of my coworkers. This is Kara," I said. "We should probably head back. You guys have a nice evening."

"Hold up!" Leah said.

I paused. Damn, I knew I wouldn't get off that easy.

Leah could smell bullshit like a shark could smell blood.

"Why don't you and Kara join us?" Leah asked.

Now that the offer had been extended, I knew it wouldn't be refused. One glance at Declan's number one fan, and I knew we were staying. Two additional chairs were added, and then we were settling in and ordering drinks as Mia and Liv joined us.

"Mia! Look who's here!" Leah said with an evil gleam in her eye.

I hated Leah right now. Family or not, I wanted to strangle her.

"Hi, Garrett," Mia said meekly.

I reciprocated. "Evening, Mia."

Clare's eyes flew up to mine, and I could see the apology written all over her face. I had no doubt that she remembered who Mia was and how much she had once meant to me and in her Logan-frazzled mind, she'd forgotten that we were both now sitting at the same small table. Together. Clare knew how uncomfortable this situation was for the both of us.

The table was silent. Had it not been for the loud noise of the bar and the wailing voices from the karaoke going on behind us, I was fairly certain I could have heard a pin drop.

This isn't awkward. No, not at all.

"So, who's singing first?" Leah asked loudly, clapping her hands together.

We all groaned.

The question was followed by a handful of, "No," and "Hell no."

"Oh, come on! It's karaoke night and no one is going to sing? Come on! Anyone? Clare? Oh, I know! Mia, what about you? You need to do something crazy tonight, especially in that outfit! Get your ass up there and sing."

I glanced over at Mia, and her eyes were wide.

"I don't think so," she answered.

"Oh, come on! Why not?"

"I can't sing," she answered.

I laughed out loud. "Lie," I blurted out.

Mia's eyes heated in anger, and I felt a bit of triumph. *Good, feel anger.* I'd been living waist-deep in the shit for years.

"The girl I once knew would have gotten up there and sang her heart out at the first chance."

"So, Mia...what do you like to do when you aren't being all prim and proper and shit? I asked, fiddling with her hair.

We were sitting on the grass and sharing a crappy slice of pizza.

"Why do you keep calling me Mia? It's not my name, and I don't curse. It's not polite," she said, exasperated.

I knew she wasn't really frustrated though. The curve of a smile on her face said otherwise.

I grinned, ignoring her comment about my language. I pulled a piece of pepperoni off my pizza and tossed it in my mouth. "Neither is Amelia. It's too formal and uptight for a teenager. Mia is more your style. I like it."

"Hmm..." was all she said.

A silence fell between us as she picked at her salad. I'd skipped the salad. She should have, too. Salad from the school cafeteria was scary.

"I sing."

"What?" I said.

"You asked what I liked to do. I like to sing."

The grown-up Mia gave me a hard stare, and then she slowly rose from her chair. Everyone at the table cheered and hollered at the accepted challenge. I just gulped in fear. I was a fucking fool. I didn't want to hear her sing. It would end me.

Maybe she'd lost that talent. Maybe it'd gone away with age, and she now sucked at it. It could be true. I hadn't heard her sing since she returned. She hadn't let out a hum or an absentminded chorus, not one single note, as she'd cleaned the floors.

She walked over to the corner where the stage was set up. She huddled in close with the DJ, who was standing under a banner that proudly boasted he had every song ever known. She bent over the book of songs, and then she finally pointed and nodded, having made her decision. After the person in front of her finished singing Boyz II Men's "I'll Make Love to You," Mia quietly took the stage, and I stopped breathing.

The lights all pointed toward her, and a few males, who would be dead soon, hooted and howled as she wrapped her slender fingers around the microphone. She gave me a pointed look right before the music kicked in, and "The One That Got Away" by The Civil Wars filled the bar. She was seeking her revenge on that stage. I'd pushed her and forced her up there, and this song was her way of throwing it back in my face.

As soon as she sang the first note, the entire bar went quiet.

I heard Clare whisper, "Holy shit."

Mia went into the first verse, her seductive voice owning every note like it was hers. This was not normal drunken karaoke singing where patrons cringed and wished the person up there would pass out. This was a performance, and everyone in the bar was mesmerized.

If anything, her talent for singing had only grown with age. Her voice was fuller, sexier, and she owned the stage as she took full possession of the song. Bewitched, the men were hanging on her every note. Every woman in the place wanted to be her as she took hold of the mic and sang the high notes effortlessly.

My eyes never left hers, and I was up and out of my seat before the last note roared from the speakers. Unfortunately, so were several other men. As soon as she stepped off the stage, a handful of suitors met her at the bar, all trying to get her attention with offers to buy her drinks.

She smiled and laughed and I felt my hands cramped from the hard fists they were making. I shoved them in my pockets and pushed through the crowd of adoring fans.

"Come on, let me buy you a drink, sweetheart?" a jackass in a suit said smoothly.

She blushed and opened her mouth to answer, but

before she could, I grabbed her arm and pulled her from her spot at the bar.

"Garrett!" she yelped in surprise.

"Can I speak to you?"

"What? Um…sure," she replied in guarded hesitation.

I wrapped my hand around her waist, trying hard not to think about how good that felt, as I pushed us through the heavy crowd. My possessiveness of her didn't go unnoticed by many of the other men, and they quickly backed off.

Good.

I guided us toward the hallway which led to the kitchen and back door. It was fairly quiet.

"What the hell is this about?" she yelled.

Touching her had been a bad mistake. My hand was on fire, and I was about to lose any ounce of restraint I had left.

I shoved her against the wall, and she sucked in a breath.

"Do you enjoy driving me crazy?" I asked. My hands tightened around her waist as I pressed my body against hers.

"I don't know what you're talking about," she said.

Her voice was husky, and it gave me memories of that same voice crying out my name while I came deep inside her.

"Don't you? That little show up there wasn't for me?"

"No."

"No?"

My hands slid lower, and a slight moan escaped her lips as her eyes lost focus. My attention shifted, and I found myself transfixed on her mouth. She had the most perfect lips, soft and pouty and made for kissing. She saw me staring, and she stopped breathing in anticipation. I moved in to kiss her. I needed to remember what it felt like to live, to feel my heart beating in my chest.

And then, I remembered everything she had taken away from me.

She can't mean this. She would never do this.

Those words haunted me. I pushed away with an angry growl as she sank against the wall.

"Go home, Mia," I barked over my shoulder as I stalked away in anger.

Anger was my true love and my only soul mate.

Chapter Seven

After a fitful night of sleep, I awoke in a tangled mess of sheets to the sound of thunderous banging coming from my front door. I glanced at my clock with fuzzy eyes and saw that it was barely eight in the morning on Sunday.

Who the hell was bothering me this early? Sunday mornings were sacred and precious. I would sleep in, drink coffee, read for hours, and enjoy doing absolutely nothing.

Why was someone bombarding my solitude?

And why is that person knocking so damn loudly?

I threw on a sweatshirt, which was three sizes too large for me since it technically wasn't mine, and I ran downstairs to see the person I would be yelling at. I pulled the door open and found a very angry Garrett on the other side.

"What took you so damn long?" he asked harshly. His

eyes moved around me and started to roam my living room.

"I was asleep," I answered shortly, folding my arms over my chest.

"Alone?"

"What? Yes—not that it's any of your business."

He barged past me and headed for the kitchen. Moving around the room like he owned it, he opened my dingy white fridge that had seen better days and started pulling out eggs, cheese, and bacon. From the cupboard, he picked out the bag of coffee I'd just bought from the specialty shop down the street, and he started a pot.

"What are you doing?" I asked, stunned by his display.

"Making us breakfast. I'm starving."

"You came over here to make me breakfast?"

"No, I came over here to take you to get a dog. The breakfast is just an added bonus."

I sat down in a chair at the kitchen table, tucking my feet underneath me, as I watched him. He turned on burners, and he began to scramble eggs. I'd never seen him cook before. That was something we'd talked about when we discussed moving in together and getting married—who would do the cooking and who would clean. We'd joked that we would live on macaroni and cheese and ramen for the rest of our lives and eat off of paper plates to keep from having to do dishes.

Obviously, he'd learned to cook more than those two dishes. Someone had taught him how to cook, or he'd learned on his own. I didn't want to think about someone doing all the things I was supposed to do with him.

"I never agreed to a dog," I said with a touch of annoyance in my voice.

"No one ever gave you a choice. You moved into this house by yourself. You need some sort of protection."

"I don't want to adopt Cujo," I huffed.

"I didn't say you had to adopt a snarling, man-eating dog. But you need one that will be attentive and bark if it senses an intruder."

"And a security alarm won't do that?" I challenged.

"I like dogs better," he answered plainly.

"Then, why don't you have one?"

"My place is too small, and I'm a guy." He shrugged.

He'd never really mentioned his place, but considering how quickly he'd gotten over here the other night, I was assuming he lived close. How close, I didn't know. The thought of him being just streets away at night sent my heart into double-time.

Garrett threw some bread in the toaster and continued to mix the eggs. He grabbed a handful of cheese and sprinkled it on top before turning off the burner. He glanced over at me, and his eyes lingered on my legs tucked neatly beneath me. My shorts were mostly covered by my sweatshirt, so it looked like I was bare underneath it. From the way his eyes heated, I didn't think he'd actually taken the time to look at me until now.

"Is that my sweatshirt?"

I looked down and immediately blushed. "No, it's my sweatshirt."

"You mean, it's a sweatshirt you stole and never gave back," he corrected.

It was one of the few things I had taken with me when I left home. I had been leaving the life we planned, but I'd still wanted some pieces of him. So, I'd granted myself pictures, my necklace, and this sweatshirt. I hadn't deserved more than that. I wore it all the time, and I'd completely forgotten I had it on when he came rushing in.

I needed to change the subject. "So, are we going to talk about last night?" I suddenly took a great interest in my fingernails. I couldn't look at him. Instead, I stared at the chip in my purple nail polish while waiting for an answer.

"Nope," was all he said as he dumped the eggs equally on two plates.

After he buttered the toast, he brought everything over to the table and chose the seat across from me. The food he dropped in front of me smelled delicious, and my stomach growled in response.

"Okay."

I didn't really know where to take the conversation from there, so I chose silence—awkward, long silence. It seemed to be the thing we excelled at nowadays. We used to spend hours, days talking, and now, we could barely speak a sentence without digging ourselves into a hole.

"Look," he finally said with a huff, "I got jealous. It was a dick move. It won't happen again. I want to be your friend, Mia, or at least I'm trying to be."

He was being nice. What he really meant to say was, *I'm trying to be your friend despite everything you did to me.*

I finished my eggs and took a final bite of my toast. "Friends?" I asked.

"Friends," he confirmed. "And friends do things like take friends to choose a furry companion. So, go upstairs and get ready. I want to be there when they open."

It was the first time I'd seen him smile. It was a forced smile, but it was still something. I nodded and rose with my plate in hand. I rinsed it off and placed everything in the dishwasher. I could feel his eyes on me as he finished eating. Without saying another word, I finished up in the kitchen and raced up the stairs to my room and shut the door, locking it behind me.

How could I be friends with him? How could I be around him and not want him? I'd just agreed to a terrible idea. *Friends? What the hell was I thinking?*

I can't be just friends with the man who owns the other half of my soul.

I was so screwed.

GARRETT

The ancient pipes rattled, and I heard the shower kick on. I tried my best not to imagine Mia stripping down in the bathroom above me, that old sweatshirt of mine falling to the floor, before she stepped into the warm stream of water with the dewy drops of liquid cascading down every curvy inch of her sun-kissed skin.

Yep, I tried.

It didn't work.

Finished eating, I got up from my seat at the table and began scrubbing the few dishes left out with a bit more vigor than necessary. When I'd just about taken all of my frustrations and probably some of the glaze right off of the plate, I put down the sponge and placed everything in the dishwasher, making sure to delay it an hour. I was pretty sure I was the only one in the house who needed a cold shower.

With nothing to do but wait, I paced. I walked through her living room and down the hall to her empty office. Nothing but unopened boxes filled the room. She'd barely unpacked. She had probably been too involved in remodeling the house.

Why was I here? Why did I wake up at the crack of dawn and drive myself over here, only to torture myself further? This was supposed to be our dream, our future. But it wasn't. She had chosen to end that dream and leave. Did I need a constant reminder of that?

I heard the shower shut off, and I wandered back into the living room, sinking into the sofa. It smelled like her. She smelled exactly as I remembered—like fresh oranges in summer. It was some sort of lotion she used, and it drove me crazy. I had smelled it on her last night as I leaned in to kiss her.

And then, everything had gone to shit.

Memories had come racing back in a flash, firing through my brain like a pistol. I couldn't get out of that bar fast enough. I'd made some lame excuse to Kara and bailed. I'd needed air and space, space from Mia.

Yet, here I was, not even twelve hours later.

It had taken forever for me to fall asleep, and when I had, I'd dreamed of her. This wasn't a new thing for me. When I slept, I always dreamed of Mia. But last night, I hadn't dreamed of eighteen-year-old Mia leaving me in that crowded football field after graduation. I'd dreamed of grown-up Mia—the Mia who had worn a tight black skirt and sang with a seductive huskiness that made me ache with need.

In my dream, I hadn't pulled away. I'd kissed her and taken what was rightfully mine. In my dream, I hadn't stopped, and I sure as shit hadn't told her to go home. No, in my sleep, I'd dreamed of bringing her home where I had spent hours making her remember every touch, taste, and feel my body had to offer.

I'd woken up covered in sweat and sporting the biggest hard-on of my life. Groaning, I'd jumped out of bed and gotten in the shower. Hissing as my hand reached for my cock, I'd pictured her, and I'd fisted myself over and over, remembering how she looked when I sent her over the edge. As I had cried out her name in my release, I had known I would want her until the day I died.

No matter what she'd done in our past, I would always want her. I could turn away and show restraint a thousand times, and it would never lessen the hunger I had for that woman.

Before I'd had another thought, I was dressed and in the car, driving to her house.

It wasn't until I'd driven up to the curb that I'd realized it was barely eight in the morning, and I'd had no excuse for being there.

Then, I'd remembered the dog.

She needed a dog, and I'd take her to get one. *Friends did that, right? We could be friends.*

By the time I'd reached the door, I'd convinced myself that my need could be tamed with friendship. If I needed to be around her, I would be her friend.

Go home, Mia.

I remembered my angry snarl in the bar and her hurt expression. *Did she go home?* I didn't have a right in the world to order her around, but at the moment, I had been livid. I'd been livid at myself for wanting her and angry with her for being so damn desirable. If I couldn't have her, neither could anyone else. So, I had told her to go home.

Childish? Maybe. So, I'm an asshole. Whatever.

As I'd raised my hand to knock on the door this morning, I'd suddenly feared that she hadn't listened. What if she'd lashed out and found the first guy she could and taken him home?

Anger could do strange things to one's mind, and when I had seen her as she opened the door, I had been ready to murder the bastard inside who had been lucky enough to touch her. I hadn't calmed down until about five minutes later when I finished scrambling the eggs and hadn't heard any movements above.

I was going psycho. This woman was making me insane.

The woman in question breezed past me and entered the living room. The smell of oranges followed her, and I tried not to think about how much that scent affected me. She'd changed into a pair of jean shorts and a tank top. The fact that no bra straps were peeking out made me nearly groan out in frustration.

No bra. Awesome.

"You ready?" she asked, cocking an eyebrow in my direction.

There were so many possibilities with that question, but I went with the high road and settled with a nod.

I followed her out, and she paused a moment to lock her front door before we climbed into my SUV. She sat awkwardly next to me and fiddled with the ring on her right hand while I pulled away from the curb.

"That's a beautiful ring. Did someone special buy it for you?" I asked.

I was fishing for information. She'd been back less than a month, and I didn't know anything about her, other than what I'd observed.

"What? Oh, um…no. I bought it in New Orleans a few years ago."

"You've been to NOLA, huh?"

She swallowed and made a noise that must have been a *yes*. "I went for a business trip. It's beautiful."

"I wouldn't know," I said absently.

"You haven't done much traveling?" she asked.

"I travel for work but not much beyond that. I've been all over the Midwest, and up and down the East Coast, but that's about it. We have territories, and mine has changed a bit over the last few years, but it has still stayed relatively boring. Nothing as exciting as New Orleans."

More awkward silence filled the small space, and I played around with the air-conditioner knob, trying to make it cooler. It was summer, and the inside of the car was about a million degrees.

After another minute or two, she commented, "Your date seemed nice. She was very pretty."

"Oh, that was Kara. Yeah, she's nice, but she wasn't my date. She's a coworker."

"Oh," was all she said.

Then, I announced our arrival at the animal shelter.

The employee had just flipped the sign, officially opening for business, when we walked through. With two stories, this very modern-looking animal shelter was large and well-funded. They housed many of Richmond's abandoned cats and dogs.

We were greeted immediately by the sounds of barking, lots of barking. It filled my ears and left them ringing. We checked in at the front desk. Mia filled out some paperwork and answered some questions on what type of animal she was hoping to adopt. We were told to wait for someone who would be with us shortly.

About three minutes later, a man approached us and stuck out his hand in a friendly greeting. "Hi, I'm Leo. I'm one of the managers here. I hear someone is looking to adopt today," he said with a grin that was all for Mia.

Leo was about our age, maybe a few years older. He

was tall and lean and had that save-the-world attitude to him. I would bet he was a vegan and ran fifty miles a day.

"Yes, I live alone, and I wanted a little company," she replied.

Leo looked over at me and back at Mia, obviously making up his mind that she was fair game. Then, he made his move. "Well, let's see what we can do." He glanced down at her paperwork. "Amelia, what a beautiful name," he said.

I wanted to punch him. As he led us around and showed us several dogs, all I could think about was how close his hand was getting to her side or how much I wanted to dropkick him when he made her laugh.

"Oh my gosh, Garrett! Look at him!" she said, kneeling down to pet a golden retriever mix.

The dog instantly wagged his tail and nuzzled up to Mia.

"Sam is new to our facility. He's young, probably only a year or two. It's rare for us to keep retrievers in here for long even if they aren't purebred. They're a popular breed and very loyal," Mr. Know-It-All said.

Mia looked up at me and smiled. The dog gave her a big lick, and she laughed. I couldn't help but chuckle a bit.

"I think he likes you, Mia," I said.

"Mia, that's a lovely nickname," Leo said.

"It's my nickname," I replied coldly.

Mia must have sensed the tension because she shot up from her crouch. "I think Sam is the one! Can you grab the rest of the adoption paperwork, Leo?" she asked as Leo and I continued to have a staring match.

"Sure. Be right back, Mia." He grinned and turned to leave.

My hands fisted, and I fought back a growl.

"What the hell was that?" she asked.

"I don't like him."

"Well, that's obvious. The question is, why?"

"He was flirting with you. He's working, and he's flirting with you. It's very unprofessional."

Her lip quivered as she tried to maintain a straight face. "You're jealous," she said.

It wasn't a question.

"Am not," I answered.

"Are to."

"Am not. So, what if I am?"

Her grin widened, knowing she'd won the argument.

"I'm pretty sure the only male I'll be cozying up to in the near future is the one right here."

It was too bad she was pointing at the dog.

Lucky bastard.

Chapter Eight

MIA

"Do you want to help me unpack some of these boxes?" I asked, looking up from the enormous mess spread out in front of me on the floor.

Sam's dopey brown eyes just stared at me blankly as he lifted an ear and cocked his head to the side. He did this a lot. I figured it was the doggie equivalent of, *huh?*

"You know, if you're going to live here, you need to start pulling your weight."

Sam wagged his tail and licked my fingers. He really was a sweet dog. When I'd asked what had brought him into the shelter, Leo had told me his owner was moving overseas and couldn't take him. So, at least it sounded like he'd come from a good home before we found each other.

"Okay, but if you don't help, there will be no treats later."

I paused. I was carrying on a conversation with a dog. *Had my life really come to this?*

I gave Sam a long stare and eventually shrugged. "Eh. Oh, well." I could do worse.

It was Monday night, and I'd just come home from a long shift at the hospital. Leah and I had shared the same work hours today, so we'd spent some time catching up after the weekend.

"So, did you have a good time on Saturday?" she asked.

"Um...well, it was interesting."

"Interesting?" she repeated, obviously wanting me to delve deeper.

"I, uh...hadn't expected Garrett to be there," I answered honestly.

"Oh. Well, I hadn't either. I hope you don't think I was conspiring behind your back."

"No, I don't think you would do that." She gave me a wry grin.

I amended my answer, "Okay, at least, I didn't think that was your intention on Saturday."

"Better. Never underestimate my evil powers, Mia, especially when it concerns two people I care about," she said.

It made me feel special but also a little uneasy that she cared about me. I'd seen the way she looked at Garrett and me in that bar. She might not have put us together that night, but I had no doubt that she wouldn't try in the near future.

I wished she would give up on that hope. I really liked Leah. She was fun, fearless, and loyal. I could see the devotion she had for her family and friends, and I was honored to be included in that small group, but I wasn't the one for Garrett, not anymore.

I couldn't be, not after everything I'd done.

He deserved so much better.

The default ringtone on my phone startled me out of

my scattered thoughts, and I reached into my pocket to retrieve it. It was a phone number I didn't recognize. Normally, I wouldn't answer, but the area code was from Atlanta. I'd left friends behind with little explanation for my quick exit. I didn't want them to worry, so I took a chance and answered it.

"Hello?" I said.

"Amelia," the male voice said in relief.

I was momentarily stunned. *How did he get this number?* I'd changed my number, and I'd only given it out to a handful of people before I left. A chosen few had known where I was headed, and I purposely hadn't included him.

"Aiden?"

"It's so good to finally hear your voice. I was starting to think I might forget the sound."

"How did you get this number?" I asked.

But I hadn't meant to sound rude. He didn't deserve that.

I immediately reworded my question. "I mean, how did you find me?"

"Maggie gave me your number. It wasn't easy. She was very persistent for a long time, but she finally caved. You have a loyal friend. I'm a wreck, Amelia, an absolute wreck."

"I'm sorry, Aiden. I don't know what to say."

"Say you'll come back."

Visions of our last night together came crashing back —candles, flowers, and tears. That was what I remembered the most, except for the part where I'd run and never looked back.

"I...I'm sorry, Aiden. I've got to go."

I ended the call before he could say another word. He tried calling back once and then twice before he gave up. I couldn't give him what he wanted. He didn't see that now, but he would eventually. He just needed time and space.

Another hour or so passed, and I continued to empty out the boxes that had been gathering dust in my office. I wasn't sure what I was going to use an office for—considering I worked in a hospital, filing patient records and avoiding pregnant women—but it was an extra room, and I didn't know what else to use it for. I took a quick look at the computer stacked up in the corner and thought about setting it up, but I decided to put it off for another day.

My stomach started to grumble right around the time Sam's ears perked up. He jumped up and started barking seconds before the doorbell went off. I guessed Garrett was right about one thing. No one would be able to get past Sam.

I glanced down at my watch and realized dinnertime had long since passed, and it was now eight o'clock. A quick sweep around the room proved I hadn't done nearly enough. There were still several boxes to go through, and the ones I had opened up just made more of a mess. I had hoped to find places for some of this, so when the floors went down, I'd have less to move around. I was starting to think that was a really stupid idea.

I brushed my hands back and forth on my black yoga pants, trying to get rid of some of the dust that had accumulated there, and I went to join Sam at the door. He was jumping up and down and wagging his tail like it was Christmas. Dogs had the best enthusiasm. Humans could learn a thing or two from our four-legged companions. There was very little left on this earth that brought such excitement to our faces.

I opened the door, and I really shouldn't have been

surprised by what I found. Garrett was standing in his work clothes, holding a bag of takeout and a duffel bag.

"Are we having a sleepover?" I asked, pointing to the large bag slung over his shoulder.

His lip twitched. "No, I brought clothes to change into. Can't lay down floors in a suit."

"Who said anything about laying down floors tonight? It's late."

He let himself in, which was quickly becoming a habit of his, and breezed past me. He dropped the bags of food and his duffel on the kitchen counter and turned. "It's late? How old are you?"

I folded my arms over my chest and gave an exasperated sigh. "I have to get up early for work tomorrow," I said.

"So do I. In fact, I bet I have to wake up earlier."

"Do not," I challenged.

"Mmm…do so." He leaned against the counter and mimicked my stance, folding his arms over his broad chest.

On me, it was pouting. On him, it was anything but, and it was super sexy.

"Ugh, you are infuriating! What time do you have to be up, smartass?"

"About four."

"In the morning?" I squeaked.

"Yep." He shrugged.

"Why so damn early? Don't you have an office job?"

He adjusted his stance and shrugged off his jacket. He started loosening his tie, and I watched with fascination.

"Well, smartass, I like to go to the gym in the morning. No one else really does, so it's quiet that early. And yes, I have an office job. I like to get into the office before everyone else, so I usually show up around six."

He pulled off his tie and undid the first two buttons of his shirt.

The whole process, watching him slowly take off his tie had been mesmerizing. I didn't want him to stop. *Why did he stop?*

He looked at me expectantly.

He'd said something, hadn't he?

I realized I'd been staring at those open two buttons longer than socially acceptable, and he'd noticed. His lips curled into a grin, and he'd been waiting to see how long it would take for me to come back from whatever fantasy I'd just inserted myself into.

"You sound kind of like a loner," I finally said. I was very proud of my little rebuttal.

"I'm just picky about who I spend my time with, I guess."

"Sounds like a loner."

"Coming from the girl who's spending her evenings with her dog," he shot back before picking up his duffel and taking off toward the bathroom.

"At least it's someone!" I yelled.

Lame comeback. Good job, Mia.

"Well, *friend*, I guess it's a good thing I have you now, isn't it?" he said with a wicked grin over his shoulder.

He disappeared behind the door, but he didn't lock it. That hadn't gone unnoticed to my very attuned ears.

I stared at the closed bathroom door and shook my head. *Oh, Garrett Finnegan, what are you up to?*

I had no idea what I was doing.

I leaned my hands against the tiled sink and stared into the bathroom mirror, shaking my head in disgust.

I'd strutted in here like I had a plan. I had no plan beyond wanting to spend every second with her. As I'd been lying in bed last night, I'd replayed every moment of the weekend, and then I'd come to terms with my new obsession.

I was completely infatuated with Mia Emerson.

The beautiful ghost with the mesmerizing blue eyes who had haunted my dreams for so long had come to life, and I couldn't stop myself from returning to her doorstep each and every day.

I had no plan, but I knew I couldn't walk away.

I was a fool to think we could be friends, but I needed to try. I wanted to be everything and anything but friends with Mia, and the fact that she still sent me into a tailspin after all these years pissed me off. Even through all the agony and hurt, I still wanted her. Despite the fact that I blamed her for the hell of my existence, I still craved her like no other.

I was at war with my own emotions, and I had no idea which side would eventually win.

I'd spent so long curled up with anger and betrayal as my only bedmates that I didn't know if I knew any other way.

Tossing my work clothes into the duffel, I zipped it up and threw the bag over my shoulder. Now dressed in worn jeans and a white T-shirt, I was ready for manual labor. I hated wearing ties and dress shirts. I was the type of man who liked to get his hands dirty. *Give me jeans and a T-shirt any day.*

I'd spent half my childhood in the garage with my dad helping him fix things around the house. We'd both stroll in around dinner, covered in sawdust or grease, but we'd be grinning from ear to ear after a hard day's work. Those were some of my favorite memories as a child, and it had been why I went into architecture. I'd wanted to get dirty and create something. I had known I would have to go into an office, but I'd also be able to visit construction sites and wear a hard hat as I watched my designs become a reality.

But I'd deserted my dream and settled.

Being a salesman to uppity doctors is fun—said no one ever.

Opening the bathroom door, I dropped my bag in the living room and made my way to the kitchen. Mia was inspecting the food I'd brought. I figured she hadn't eaten, and even if she had, I hadn't. I'd put in twelve hours at the office, and I had barely stopped for lunch. I was starving.

"Burritos today?" she asked.

"Yep. I figured you haven't eaten, but if you have, I'll gladly eat both of those," I said with a grin.

She gave me a doubtful look as she pulled the two monstrous burritos out of the bag. "There is no way you could eat both of these."

"Oh, I bet I could."

"That's gross."

"I'm a guy. We're inherently gross," I said with a shrug.

She laughed, and the sound made me smile. I liked making her laugh. I always had. It had once been my goal to make her laugh at least five times a day. She had the best laugh.

We polished off our burritos. Well, she had eaten half

of hers, and I'd eaten the rest. She'd watched in slight horror as I'd downed one-and-a-half burritos without much fuss.

After cleaning up the small mess from dinner, we started in on the floors again. Mia had chosen a hearty oak flooring that went with the historical nature of the home. It was very similar to the original floor, minus the smell and damage.

We began in the living room and put down the under-layment. She watched as I cut and fit the pieces together. She would help when they needed to be taped together.

We did most of this in silence, but we did occasionally strike up a conversation about random things. She asked about my parents and how my sister had met her husband. I asked how she'd ended up in Atlanta, and I got a vague answer that involved something about a job.

"Mia, why won't you talk about your past?"

"What? I am. I just did."

I put down the cutting tool I was using and drew my gaze upward until we were eye level. "No, you skirted around the question and gave me a bullshit answer. Did someone hurt you? Are you running from something or someone?"

She shook her head. "No, it's nothing like that. There's just not much to tell."

I let it go, but I knew she wasn't telling me everything. She couldn't have been gone for eight years without some sort of story. Someone doesn't leave for that long without having a little baggage following behind.

We worked for several more hours, well past midnight, and we managed to get the floor put down in the living room. When the last board was locked into place, she jumped up and clapped.

"Oh my God! It's freaking gorgeous! It actually looks like a living room!"

"It does," I said. "We just need to put the trim down, and it will be done. But I'll wait to do that at the end."

"Thank you so much, Garrett. I don't know how I would have done all this without you."

"You would have ended up hiring someone," I said with a grin.

"Probably," she agreed.

We picked up the tools and cleaned up a bit. Both of us needed to get to bed. I was looking at getting only a few hours of sleep. I needed to get home, but that didn't stop me from dragging my feet as I headed in the direction of the door.

"How many days do you think we have left to finish it all?" she asked.

I picked up my duffel bag and rocked back on my heels, not wanting to leave. "Probably another week to finish the downstairs completely. That reminds me...I have a business trip in two days. I have to fly up to New York for a couple of days to meet with a few clients. I'll be back after that. I just didn't want you to wonder why I wasn't showing up," I added quickly, not wanting her to think I was expecting her to worry about me.

Would she?

Loser. I am a loser.

"Oh, okay. Have fun, I guess," she said awkwardly. "Are you going to be in the city for the weekend, too?"

"I hadn't planned on it. It's not really fun when you're alone. I've been there tons of times anyway with my family."

"Right."

"You've been to New York City, haven't you?" I asked.

"Yes." She nodded, looking down at her shoes. "When I was younger. My parents always had functions there, so we would stay at these beautiful, fancy hotels. My mom would hire a babysitter to stay with me while they went out to parties and formal events."

I gave her a hard stare. "You haven't really been to New York then. You've just been on the inside of fancy hotels. It doesn't count. You missed out on all the fun things."

She shrugged and gave me a small smile. "Maybe next time."

"Come with me," I said without thinking.

"What?" she asked, her eyes widening in surprise.

"Come with me. I won't be much good during the day when I'm working, but at night, we can hang out. We'll spend the weekend there, and I'll take you to all the places you missed out on as a kid."

She looked uneasy as her gaze appraised me.

"Just as friends, I promise. We'll even get separate rooms."

"Can we go to the Statue of Liberty?" she asked shyly, her eyes taking on a rounder appearance.

It reminded me of the girl I'd met in homeroom so long ago.

"Whatever you want, Mia."

Her smile spread into a megawatt grin, and my knees almost buckled. I'd spent years dreaming of that smile and the way it made my heart falter and kick-start into a gallop. Now, she was looking up at me with the same wide-eyed smile.

"Deal," she said.

I was done for.

Chapter Nine

"Don't pack those! Ugh, why do you even own underwear like that?" Liv asked in outright disgust as she threw my cute hot-pink-and-lime-green boy shorts on the floor. Then, she started rummaging through my top drawer.

Sam raised his head from his place on the bed and lifted an ear, but he quickly lost interest and relaxed back into the comforter.

"What is wrong with boy shorts?"

"Nothing—if they are covered in lace or crotchless. But these are neon and have words on the butt. Seriously, Mia? Did you shop in the juniors section for these?"

Yes, yes, I did. I chose to ignore that question to save myself the humiliation that would follow.

She continued to ransack my drawer in search of God-only-knows-what until I heard an excited, high-pitched noise escape her throat.

"Yes! These! Pack these!" she said, throwing several lacy thongs in my suitcase.

"Liv! This is not a sexy weekend away with my boyfriend. I will not need thongs."

"No, it's a weekend with your ex-boyfriend, who you secretly still have a thing for. Pack the thongs."

My mouth gaped open as I stared at her blankly. She grinned back and did that annoying thing with her hip that made her look like a teenager from the Valley.

"I-I don't know what you're talking about," I fumbled.

"Uh-huh. You're a terrible liar."

"Why is everyone so hung up on my love life? Why can't you concentrate on your own?" I huffed.

"Oh, I do—a lot," she said with a grin.

After coming home, I'd quickly figured out that my best friend had adopted a very casual definition of *relationship*. She'd said she hadn't found the right one yet, and she really had no interest in ever doing so, but she loved taste-testing and sampling the variety. She would do this often. The few weeks I'd lived with her, I'd done so with headphones and a pillow over my head. Her *samplings* would get pretty loud.

"We're just friends," I said adamantly.

"Right. About that—I thought he hated you."

I thought back on the last several weeks with Garrett since I'd arrived back in Richmond. It had been a constant roller coaster of hot and cold. I had no idea what was going on.

"He did. Maybe he still does. I don't know. But we're trying to be friends."

"Friends. Right," she said with sarcasm.

I threw a pair of boy shorts at her, and she ducked and screamed.

"Come on, would you help me? He's going to be here in a few minutes, and I'm not done yet!"

Her butt shifted into gear finally, and we managed to have everything packed right as the doorbell chimed, announcing Garrett's arrival.

"I'll go get it!" she sang. She hopped down the stairs toward the door with Sam following behind her.

I rolled my eyes as I lugged my suitcase behind me.

By the time I reached the foyer, Liv was already rattling off questions faster than Garrett could comprehend them.

"Where are you guys going? Where are you staying? Have you booked tickets to the Statue of Liberty? I hear it's hard to get tickets. Have you thought about restaurants?"

His eyes were starting to bug out of his head, and he nervously tugged at the back of his head as he looked around the room for sanctuary. "Oh, look! There's Mia! Looks like we've got to go! Don't want to miss our flight!" he said in one quick breath.

I giggled a bit under my breath.

"Hmm…okay. Well, you two have fun," Liv said, giving me a quick wink.

I avoided rolling my eyes, and instead, I gave her directions for Sam, pointing to the bag of food, his leash, and his toys that I'd laid out next to the door.

"Okay, okay, Mom. I've got it. Come on, Sammy Boy!"

Sam came wagging his tail, and she hooked him on the leash. Garrett helped her by lugging all of Sam's stuff out the door and into the car. A few weeks ago, I would have never known dogs required so much stuff. Within a few short minutes, he was back, and we were alone.

Garrett gave me an appreciative once-over and commented, "Nice dress."

I'd decided to forgo my normal summer ensembles of shorts and a tank top, and I'd gone for something a bit nicer since we were headed for New York City. I didn't want to stick out like a sore thumb. So, I'd put on a flowery sundress that came about mid-thigh and accented my slim waist. I grabbed a sweater on my way out and threw it over my arm. Airplanes were notoriously cold, and my internal thermostat was permanently broken. I was always freezing.

"Thanks," I answered shyly.

"You ready?" he asked.

I quickly nodded. Without asking, he grabbed my suitcase, and we made our way out the front door. I locked up as he packed the car, and we both hopped in at the same time.

I smoothed out the wrinkles in my dress and crossed my ankles nervously. I didn't know why, but every time we had been together in a car, his presence seemed to multiply. His scent filled the small space, and I felt like I was drowning in his woodsy, masculine essence.

"I have to go directly to a client's office before they close. I'll drop you off at the hotel and check us in first, if that's all right?"

"Yes, that's great!" I said with a little too much enthusiasm. *Calm down, Mia.*

He chuckled quietly. "Okay."

We drove in silence during the short distance to the airport, and then we checked in without much fuss. I bit the inside of my cheek when the woman at the front counter recognized Garrett from his many business flights. She flirted with his mercilessly, and she didn't give me the time of day until I had to hand over my ID. She gave it a passive glance and then handed it back before she continued her deep conversation with Garrett. He was polite and smiled, but I could see the loner in him was uncomfortable from all the attention.

"Nice to see you, too…" he started to say.

He looked at me in a panic. He didn't know her name.

Darla, I mouthed, catching her name tag out peeking out from under the lapel of her jacket.

"Darla!" he said quickly.

She gave a huge wave, and we exited in a hurry.

"Oh my Gawd, Mr. Finnegan, it's *so* good to see you again," I mocked, adding extra Southern sugar to my voice to mimic Darla's sweet drawl.

"Shut up," he said.

"She likes you."

"I didn't notice."

"Not your type?" I joked.

"No."

"No? So, what is your type, Garrett?" I asked as we passed through security.

What the hell was I doing? I didn't want to know his type.

He stopped dead, right in the middle of the morning rush of passengers walking in both directions. He turned and gave me a hard stare, one that gave me goose bumps.

"I don't have one—not anymore."

GARRETT

I'd been bringing Mia to this spot for a few months.

It was quiet, and the view was spectacular. The water from the river sparkled under the moonlight, and if we came at the right time, we could watch the fireflies spark and light up the night sky.

I hadn't planned on it being our go-to make-out spot, but I wasn't going to complain that it had worked out that way. I'd just turned sixteen, and freedom was now mine in the form of the car my father and I had painstakingly restored over the last year. I used that freedom to my advantage, and right now, I was enjoying that advantage to the fullest.

My hand slid up Mia's bare leg and slipped under her skirt to grab her shapely ass. She'd been mine for just over a year now. Over three-hundred-and-sixty-five days of this. My buddies had made fun of me for dating the same girl for so long, but they didn't know. They didn't have a Mia.

I groaned and steadied my eager hand. "This is where you usually tell me to stop," I whispered, leaning into the curve of her neck.

She leaned back, letting her long hair fan out beneath her on the blanket I'd spread out on the grass.

"I'm not saying stop tonight," she replied.

I gulped and tried to reply. It wasn't a very manly thing to do, but my hands were shaking, and I was trying to give her time to change her mind. We'd never gone past this point, and I didn't want to push her into doing something she wasn't comfortable with. I was sixteen and horny as hell, but for her, I'd wait forever.

"Are you sure? You know I'd never pressure you."

"We've been together a year, Garrett. Of course I know that. No more waiting. I love you. I know we're young, but I'll never love anyone like I love you."

Reaching down, she folded her fingers over my trembling hand and brought it up to the buttons of her blouse. "I'm ready, Garrett. I'm ready for you."

With shaky fingers, I removed her blouse. Slowly, like we

were cherishing every moment, we undressed each other with care. As we made love for the first time, she gave me her love and trust, and I knew I'd found my soul mate.

"I love you, too, Mia."

"Garrett," someone was saying, breaking through my fogginess of sleep. "We're about to land."

Soft fingers brushed my hand, and my eyes fluttered open to find Mia's piercing blue eyes watching me. Her fingertips were stroking the top of my hand, but she quickly stopped when I took notice of it.

"We're about to land. I'm not sure if you heard me say that," she repeated.

I nodded and sat up in my seat. I hadn't realized I'd fallen asleep. The flight between Richmond and New York City was short, so I couldn't have been asleep for more than thirty minutes. Still a bit groggy, I watched the plane touch down and taxi in toward our gate.

"Oh, I forgot to ask. Where are we staying?" Mia asked.

I watched everyone power up their cell phones. I didn't bother. Work could wait.

"I always stay at this small Irish hotel in Manhattan. It's right around the corner from Grand Central Station, and they have a great pub."

She became quiet, and her eyes shifted to the floor. I might not have been around Mia for several years, but I knew that look.

"What is it? What did I say? Do you not like pubs? Do you have a thing against Manhattan? We can stay someplace else."

Her smile immediately brightened and recovered all too quickly. "No, I'm fine. Sorry, I'm just a little tired."

Lie.

Like many things with Mia lately, I chose to let it go—

for now. If she didn't trust me to open up, I wasn't going to force it out of her.

We deplaned, and then we made our way through the busy airport and gathered our luggage. I hailed a taxi, and we were on our way within twenty minutes. Mia looked out the window curiously, looking at the tall buildings and endless streets of yellow cabs.

The cabbie dropped us off at the hotel, and I hopped out to pay. He helped us with our two suitcases, and I thanked him, tipping him generously for his trouble. Having already made the reservations in advance, we didn't have to deal with the awkward question of how many rooms. The person at the check-in counter just handed us our keys and told us our room numbers, assuming we were coworkers, and that was it.

Mia and I as coworkers? That would never happen. I wouldn't get shit done with her in the same building—right down the hall from me, having to listen to her laugh all day, knowing she was probably getting hit on by every male in the building.

I was having problems focusing with her being in the same city.

The elevator chimed, notifying our arrival on the twelfth floor. We exited and found our room numbers easily, only to discover they were adjoining. There was only one thin door separating us.

That would make for a good night's sleep.

She went into her room, and I went into mine. I had to change for my meeting. I wasn't one of those businessmen who dressed up to fly. I was sure some of them genuinely needed to because of schedule restraints, but I thought some of them just did it to look like assholes.

I pulled out my slacks, jacket, and dress shirt. I yanked

my T-shirt over my head and took a look at the once crisp white button-down that was now sporting several wrinkles, thanks to its cramped quarters in my suitcase. I refused to do garment bags. Chicks used garment bags, not men.

I guessed I was ironing today.

I set up the iron and brushed my teeth while I waited for it to heat up. I finished up in the bathroom and started in on the task of ironing my shirt. I was halfway through when a tiny knock came from Mia's side of the adjoining door.

I set down the iron and opened the door. I heard her suck in her breath as her eyes traveled up my bare chest.

Oh, right—the shirt, or lack of.

Her eyes lingered on my tattoos, and they paused on the script written on the underside of my right arm. The rest of my tattoos were scattered over my back and arms. They were things I'd randomly picked up along the way, but the one she had her eyes on now was special—and *mine*.

I spoke quickly to divert her attention, "Hey, what's up?"

"Oh, I was wondering if you wanted to go down for lunch. I mean, if you have time."

I glanced down at my watch and grimaced. "I'm actually running late."

She nodded and smiled, but I could see the disappointment in her eyes.

"I'll make it up to you tonight, I promise."

"Okay, no problem."

She looked lost and bewildered, and I felt like a jackass.

But I was not her boyfriend, and I needed to remind myself of that. It was not my job to make her smile and laugh, not anymore.

I closed the door and finished getting ready.

I thought about those sad eyes for the rest of the day.

Chapter Ten

MIA

I didn't know why I had been surprised when he said we were staying in Manhattan. *Don't a lot of people stay in Manhattan when they go to New York City?* I didn't know why I hadn't thought of that.

Why should it matter? It was a gigantic, huge city.

Yet, there I was, lying on the bed with my greasy leftovers from room service and a giant foldout map, looking at the streets of Manhattan.

"Three blocks," I said to no one.

Three blocks—that was the current distance between my parents and me.

The parents I hadn't seen in eight years. The parents who had never bothered to contact me in eight years since moving out of my childhood home without so much as a forwarding address.

I was stupid to come here. But when Garrett would ask me to do things, I found it hard to say no. When he'd started talking about doing the things I'd never done as a kid, I'd felt myself melting for Garrett Finnegan all over again.

I'd spent many weekends in this city as a child, but I'd never seen a single part of it. I'd never been to Central Park or gone ice-skating. I'd never seen the lights of Times Square at night or had tea at The Plaza—and I'd stayed at The Plaza.

Garrett wanted to make up for that even though it wasn't his place, and I wanted to let him. But now that I was here—staring at this map, knowing my parents were in the same city and sharing the same space—I wanted to run. It was what I was good at after all.

I needed to do something, anything to distract myself from the map sitting in front of me. I stood up, grabbed my purse and key card, and made a dash toward the elevator.

One taxi ride later, I ended up at the Met. I'd always loved art, and The Metropolitan Museum of Art seemed like the best way to spend the afternoon. It didn't require talking or interaction with others—just quiet observation. I could roam through each room as quickly or slowly as I wanted, enjoying each piece of art as I went.

Around the second hour of my visit, I came into a room filled with children on a field trip. They had a docent leading them, patiently asking them questions and answering theirs. They were very well-behaved for being so young. I quietly snuck behind them and immersed myself in the painting on the far wall.

"She's pretty," a little girl said to my right.

She was petite with long brown hair and a cute button nose. Her eyes were green, and she had the same uniform on as every other child in the room.

"Yes, she is," I said in reference to the ballerina in the painting.

"I want to be a painter when I grow up."

"You do? I think that's wonderful. Do you paint at home?" I asked.

"Yes, Mommy bought me all sorts of paints. She even got me an easel for Christmas!"

"Wow, you are a very lucky little girl! How old are you?"

"Seven," she answered, holding her fingers out to show me.

My heart lurched for a second, and I nodded. "You are very grown-up for your age."

"That's what my daddy says. He says I was born middle-aged. What does that mean?"

I snorted a bit, but I covered it up with my hand.

"I think your daddy just finds you very mature for your age."

She beamed, obviously understanding the meaning of the word *mature*.

Someone called the group, and the little girl said her good-byes, waving as she went.

Then, I was alone again.

I wasn't much in the mood for being alone anymore after that, so I headed back to the hotel. The taxi pulled up to the curb just as Garrett was walking up to the front entrance.

He looked handsome in his dark gray suit and teal tie. He had a laptop bag strapped over his shoulder and looked the part of sophisticated businessman. Just as he was about to enter the hotel, he turned and caught my eye as I was stepping out of the cab.

He didn't say anything. He just watched as I took the

few steps closing the gap between us.

"Hi," he said.

"Hi."

"Where did you spend your day?" he asked, tucking a strand of my hair behind my ear.

I didn't even think he'd realized he'd done it until my breath faltered. He hastily tucked his hands in his pockets.

"I went to the Met."

"Ah, good choice," he said, abruptly turning.

We both stepped forward and entered the hotel. We talked about the museum during our short elevator ride. He asked me several questions about which pieces were my favorite, and he told me his.

"So, you have something to make up to me?" I said as I slipped the card into my door to unlock my room.

"I haven't forgotten. Be ready in twenty, and wear something comfortable. We're walking—a lot."

He disappeared into his room, and I slipped into mine. I raced around, freshening up my makeup and brushing my hair. I slipped on a pair of comfortable sandals and kept on my dress. It was comfortable, and I liked how I looked in it. I grabbed a sweater and tied it around my purse before making it out my door just in time.

"Not bad," he commented. He was dressed down again, wearing dark jeans and a gray T-shirt. It clung to him and showed off the definition of his upper body.

I tried not to let my eyes linger too much.

"So, where are we going?" I asked.

We started walking down the streets of Manhattan.

"Well, you mentioned that you never left the hotel when you were a kid, so I'm taking you somewhere every kid has to go when visiting New York."

Twenty minutes later, we were standing in front of FAO Schwarz.

"Oh my gosh! Are you kidding me? We're going to a toy store?" I squealed, looking up at the massive store.

"Not just any toy store. This is *the* toy store. It's awesome."

We took the required cheesy photos with the live toy soldier standing at the entrance. I wondered how many photos that poor guy posed in each day.

Garrett wasn't kidding. The store was massive with two floors and an escalator in between. It was insane. We spent an hour or more on the first floor, squeezing stuffed animals and playing with toys that were much too young for us. I didn't think I'd laughed so much in my life.

We made our way upstairs and took a turn on the giant keyboard from *Big*. We were terrible.

Garrett went to go check out Legos, and I walked around. I stopped to check out something called Floam. An employee was doing a demonstration, and I was slightly envious that I hadn't had cool stuff like that when I was little.

Now, I sounded old.

I made my way away from the Floam and wandered into the doll section. It was huge. They had every doll imaginable from expensive-looking porcelain ones that must have been imported from foreign countries to the type of dolls found at Target. My steps faltered in the aisle that had the baby dolls. I stood nearly frozen in place and stared, looking at the tiny outfits and shoes, as my fingers grazed the soft fabric of a baby blanket.

"There you are. I've been looking all over—" Garrett's words evaporated as he came closer. "Are you crying?" he whispered.

I reached up with my fingertips and felt the wetness of tears.

"Hey," he said cautiously, pulling me into his arms.

It was the first time he'd held me in years, yet it still felt familiar and safe.

"I'm sorry," I said. "I don't know what's wrong with me."

"It's okay. Let's get you out of here and get some fresh air, all right?"

I nodded, not risking another glance at my surroundings. I didn't need another reminder of everything I'd lost. The man holding me was enough.

GARRETT

I took her out of the toy store, and her tears dried up rather quickly. She'd tried to hide them as if she were embarrassed by them.

I was just glad she'd stopped crying. I hated seeing her in tears.

As we walked down the street, I knew it would take more than a bit of fresh air to cheer her up from whatever had upset her in that store.

I'd only left her alone for a few minutes. When I'd found her, she looked destroyed. She had been staring lifelessly at the baby-doll accessories, her fingers grasping a tiny pink blanket like her life depended on it.

I couldn't figure out—and then, it dawned on me.

No, she wasn't allowed to mourn that. She couldn't.

It had been her decision.

I glanced over at her eyes, still rimmed in red, and I wondered if something else had happened to her in the years we were apart to make her react that way. Had she experienced some other sort of loss? The thought soured my stomach.

"Hey, I've got an idea for dinner, if you're up for it?" I announced, hoping to cheer her up and pull my mind out of the darkness.

She gave me a ghost of a smile and nodded.

I hailed a cab because it was now well into nighttime, and I didn't want her to have to walk while feeling upset.

Within a few minutes, we arrived at the place I'd whispered to the taxi driver.

Mia looked up, and she laughed. It was a genuine laugh, and I breathed a sigh of relief. She was coming back to me.

"Wasn't this place in a movie?"

"Probably several. There was a movie named after it actually."

She smiled. "I know. I loved that movie. It was about two people finding each other after so long. It was very romantic." Her eyes widened, and she immediately clamped her mouth shut.

I laughed. "Come on, let's go inside." I grabbed her arm, pulling her into the front doors of Serendipity.

The place was always packed. So, we waited our turn and made some plans for the next day. I had to meet a client in the morning, but I had the rest of the day free since I had originally planned on flying home afterward. I bought us tickets to the Statue of Liberty on my phone while we waited, and we planned on eating somewhere in Times Square for dinner.

Our table was called, and we followed the hostess upstairs to a small table in the corner.

"What's good here?" Mia asked me after we'd been handed our menus.

"I always get the frozen hot chocolate."

"Frozen hot chocolate? It's really a thing? I thought they just made that up."

"No," I said, pointing to the spot on her menu. "See? It's right there."

"So, do you order anything else?"

"Cake."

She looked at my deadpanned face and laughed. "So, we're going extra healthy tonight then?" she joked.

I grinned. "You could get pie if you want."

We ended up ordering a few desserts, and at my insistence, we each ordered our own frozen hot chocolate. Mia thought I was insane when they brought those huge suckers out, but I wanted her to have her own, so she could enjoy the full experience. She ate a few bites of each dessert and declared she was stuffed. I polished off everything else, and she watched in fascination.

"I don't know where you put it."

"I'll work it off," I said.

She caught me looking at her, and she blushed. I hadn't meant it in that way, but I definitely wouldn't mind giving it a try.

Damn it, Garrett. Stop.

Friends didn't sleep together.

But fuck, I wanted to.

"Thank you," she said.

I polished off the last bite of pie. "For what?"

"Taking me here…everywhere. Really, it's been a great day."

"Well, I wanted you to have some of the fond memories and experiences I had as a child, that every kid should have, when visiting New York. No one should come to a city like this and spend it inside a hotel room."

She sat across from me and silently played with the straw in her drink. "You always had the best family," she said wistfully, her eyes downcast as she continued to fiddle with her straw.

"Yeah," I agreed. "They're great. My parents used to bring Clare and me here whenever we came to New York. My dad would let us pick anything we wanted off the menu even if it was cake and pie," I said with a wink.

That earned me a small smile, but I knew her thoughts were somewhere else. We finished up, and I paid the bill. She tried to slip her credit card in there, but I refused.

"My treat. I insist."

She pouted but let me win.

We caught a taxi outside the restaurant, and I gave him directions back to the hotel. Halfway there, I changed my mind and asked him to take us somewhere else.

"What are you up to now?"

"Just trying to squeeze it all in," I answered. "Come on!"

She squealed and jumped out of the car when we pulled up to the Empire State Building. I loved this place, and I had hoped she would too. As an architecture major, I'd spent years studying buildings like this. It made my chest tighten in anticipation and warmth to see her giddy with excitement over something that was so near and dear to my heart.

Stop it Garrett. Friends, you're just friends.

"Oh my gosh, Garrett. I've always wanted to come here!"

"Well, here we are."

We bought our tickets and waited our turn to take the tight elevator ride up.

"Do you ever wish you were making buildings like this?" she asked.

I thought about it for a moment as the elevator went up the eighty-sixth floor.

"Yes. Maybe not quite like this, but I do wish I was still designing."

"Then, why don't you do it?" she asked.

I shrugged and chose not to answer. Frankly, I didn't have an answer. The market had changed in the last few years. There were more jobs now than there were a few years ago, and if I wanted to use my degree, now would be the time to do it. So, why didn't I?

The elevator came to a stop, and we were escorted out before I had a chance to ponder that question further. We walked out onto the observation deck and the entirety of New York spread out before us.

"It's beautiful," she said, taking in the panoramic view of the city.

I just stared at her. "Yes, it is."

I had always dreamed of proposing to Mia at a place like this—someplace worthy of her beauty and elegance. It would have been an engagement story she could have told her friends about. She could have run home, excited and full of bubbly glee, showing off the ring I'd spent months saving up for.

But sometimes, things didn't happen the way one had planned. At the time, none of that had mattered. It hadn't mattered that our engagement was a secret or that when I had knelt down, it had been in the wet grass on the banks of the river we'd dubbed our own secret spot. It hadn't mattered that the ring I gave her cost less the class ring I once wore. We had been happy and ready for anything.

Or at least, I'd thought we had.

Chapter Eleven

MIA

I heard him slip off to his morning meeting a few minutes after I'd woken up. The sun was just starting to break over the horizon, and I knew I was alone. I was still lying in bed, curled up with a pillow, staring at the wall next to me. I was trying to avoid the crumpled-up map sitting on the desk across the room.

The map that had kept me up most of the night.

The map that clearly showed the three blocks separating me from my parents.

I couldn't go.

I wouldn't.

But what if I do?

It had been eight years since I last saw them, since I'd heard their voices or seen their faces. The only reason I knew their address was because I was nosy, and I'd kept tabs on them after they moved. It hadn't been more than a couple of weeks after I left Richmond that my father announced the news he'd been offered a job in New York. They had quickly and quietly moved and never looked back. My father had tried to contact me once or twice, but I'd made it clear that I was done.

I'd been done being manhandled and bullied. They'd run my life long enough, and when I'd needed them most, they'd chosen themselves instead.

As I stared across the room at that tattered map, I tried to picture them in my mind.

Would my mother be just as perfect looking—never a hair out of place or a toe out of line? She'd carried herself like the Queen of Sheba and expected nothing less. Would my father still be conveniently absent, letting my mother make all the decisions so that he didn't have to? He had always allowed her to run his life, never standing his ground for anything—including me. He'd chosen her over me, pushing me away when she told him to, even though I knew he didn't want to leave.

I'd sometimes wondered how their lives would pan out without me in it. Would they even notice my absence? Would it matter that their only daughter wasn't around anymore? Or would things go on as normal?

I gave one last glance at the creased and crinkled up map that had become my obsession over the last twenty-four hours, and I let out a curse.

Thirty minutes later, I was showered and dressed. I walked down the street, doing something incredibly stupid. I turned around and walked back to the hotel half a dozen times. I had no doubt that I looked insane to the pedestrians around me.

When I finally made the decision to go through with it, I found the address easily. Like most of Manhattan, the apartment building was well-kept with an uppity doorman who looked down at me as he held the door. I slipped inside with a group of unassuming tenants.

My hands started shaking, and my palms were sweaty by the time I made it up to their floor.

I was so stupid. What was I thinking?

But still, I kept going.

The wide-eyed eighteen-year-old girl who had had her heart crushed by the two people she trusted most in the world needed to know.

I needed to know.

I needed closure, whatever it might be.

So, I continued my journey down the ornate hall, counting the apartment numbers as I went.

My parents definitely hadn't lost their love for flare. Everything was decadent. From the plush elevator to the exquisite hallways and right down to the gilded door knockers—everything screamed money.

At last, I found my parents' place. I took a deep breath, pushed the buzzer, and waited.

GARRETT

She'd been quiet all day.

Last night, as we'd waited for our table at Serendipity, planning everything out, she'd been excited. She'd peeked over my shoulder as I'd bought tickets for the Statue of Liberty, and she'd begged me to take her to the Hard Rock Café even though there were dozens of other restaurants that would have been much better.

But that was where the excitement had ended.

I'd gotten back to the hotel a bit later than I'd planned,

but it had still been early enough that we had time to pick up lunch and head out for our boat ride to the statue. After I'd changed and packed up my work clothes, I'd knocked on the door separating our rooms, and I'd gotten a faint reply. I'd opened the door and found her curled up on the bed, staring at a map of the city like it was the saddest thing ever.

"Hey, you okay?" I'd asked, coming forward to comfort her. I'd stopped myself because I hadn't known where the boundaries of our friendship were.

She'd looked up in a daze, and I'd thought that was when she finally realized I was in the room. She'd appeared startled and quickly shook herself out of whatever funk she was in. It'd felt like a slap in the face to watch her change moods so quickly, but I hadn't known what else to do, so I'd just gone with it. She'd jumped up and grabbed her things, and then we had headed out for the day.

We'd picked up a quick lunch at the pub downstairs, and she'd barely eaten. We'd ridden the subway, and she hadn't said a thing.

Even as the boat had pulled away from the harbor and we'd gotten our first glimpse of Lady Liberty, she had been eerily quiet. I'd tried to ask her what was going on, but she had just shrugged it off and cheered back up, posing for pictures and skipping ahead to read signs.

Dinner hadn't been any better. She'd pushed around her food and stared at the wall. I hadn't known what to do. Minus the woman sitting in front of me, the only experiences I'd had with women were brief drunken interludes. But even she was different than what I remembered.

Mia from years past would have come out and told me what was troubling her. She would have bled her soul to me the second it was hurting. I didn't know what to do when she was closed off and silent.

Finally, as we were walking back from the restaurant, I snapped. "Damn it, Mia! Please tell me what's wrong."

Her eyes became watery, and she pushed away the tears with her sleeve. "I visited my parents today."

That was the last thing I'd expected. As we entered the hotel and made our way to the elevator, I tried to come up with a reply.

"They live here?"

She nodded. "Yes, they moved here after I left… Richmond."

I had a feeling she had been about to say, *after I left you,* but I didn't press.

"Okay, so you visited your parents. Please explain to me further, so I can understand," I pleaded.

The elevator dinged, and we stepped out onto our floor. She fished out her key card, and I waited. She unlocked her room and stepped inside, and then I followed her inside. Our conversation wasn't over. I closed the door behind me, and she turned, becoming aware of the very small space between us.

"I haven't seen them in eight years," she said.

"Eight years, Mia? Why?"

I searched her face for answers, but she wasn't giving any.

"I wasn't perfect anymore," she answered.

Fuck friendship boundaries.

I took a step forward and pulled her into my arms. She came willingly, and I tried not to think about how perfectly she still molded into my body.

"Tell me about today," I said gently.

"She didn't recognize me," she said into my chest.

"What do you mean?"

"My own mother. She didn't recognize me. If she did, she pretended not to. The maid brought me in, and my mother looked up and said, 'May I help you?' She just stared blankly at me like I'd come off the streets, looking for a job."

"Did you say anything to her?" I asked as I stroked her hair.

"No, I turned and ran, so she wouldn't see my tears."

"Oh, baby, I'm so sorry."

I held her until all her tears dried up, and the sobs ceased, but even then I didn't let go. I couldn't. Now that I had her, I didn't want to lose the feel of her between my arms again. Her head turned upward, and our eyes met. Hers were still red, but they were the most beautiful eyes I'd ever seen. They were blue and translucent, like ocean water.

"Garrett, I—"

"Shh," I said.

I bent down and hovered, feeling her heart beating against mine, as I waited for her to push away. She didn't, and for the first time in eight years, I found heaven again as my mouth brushed up against hers. Our lips met hesitantly at first, and we kissed each other softly, like a reunion of souls. But soon, our impatience grew, and I needed more. My fingers dived into her hair and angled her mouth, so I could kiss her long and deep. She tasted exactly the same yet completely different. It was like having a favorite wine and trying it again several years later after it had aged a bit. She was still my Mia but bolder, fiercer, and sexier.

She moaned into my mouth, and I lost it.

Slipping my hands down to her thighs, I caught her knees and pulled her up around my torso as I walked us to the bed.

I was done being friends with Mia Emerson.

With her hands wrapped around my shoulders, we tumbled onto the mattress. She watched me as I slipped my hands under her dress and pulled it over her head. My dreams hadn't done her justice. She was stunning. Her breasts spilled over the edge of her lacy pink bra, and they were begging to be touched and licked. Reaching behind her, I undid her bra and freed it from her body. She squirmed and writhed underneath me as I attacked, rubbing each nipple between my fingers into a taut peak.

Bending down, I licked and sucked that perfect pink nipple until she was screaming.

"Oh God, Garrett!"

Hearing her say my name nearly made me come in my jeans.

In one swift movement, I reached over me and pulled off my T-shirt. I groaned as her hands found my chest.

Loving the way her hands felt on me, my hands found her waist and I lifted up off the bed and flipped us, loving my new view—Mia on top of me in a lacy pink thong.

I watched as she bent over and started kissing her way up my body. Her nipples brushed against my skin, and I felt myself growing harder with every single touch. She paid special attention to my tattoos, stopping to kiss the band around my left arm, the knot woven over my shoulder, and then moved to my inner arm.

"Stop," I said suddenly.

Her eyes focused on the script, and she read the words.

"*Until then*. What does it mean?" she whispered, her eyes now focused on me.

"Just drop it, Mia."

Her eyes shifted to my arm again and stayed. "What does it mean, Garrett?"

I exhaled and pinched the bridge of my nose to keep the emotions at bay. I didn't want to do this. Not now. Not ever. But there were some things you couldn't outrun.

I took a deep breath. "That day we found out…when you were crying in my arms, asking what we were going to do. I wasn't scared, not at all. You were carrying my child. The woman I loved was carrying my child. I didn't care how old we were or what people would think. I kissed you and said everything would be okay because I knew it would be."

She moved off of me, and I sat up. Both of us needed a bit of space. This was a conversation that we'd put off far too long.

"I always thought we would have a girl. I pictured her with your hair and my eyes. She'd be seven by now, Mia."

She nodded, and a stray tear fell from her cheek. I grabbed my shirt and got up, knowing this was over. All of it was over. We were living a lie if we'd thought this could be fixed.

She'd aborted our child without giving me a choice. She'd left me with nothing more than a note and a shattered, broken heart. I couldn't get over that.

I wouldn't.

"I got the tattoo to remind myself that despite your decision, I'd see my child someday."

She didn't say anything else, and I started to take my exit.

"Garrett," she said softly as I was about to close the door behind me.

I turned around and saw her looking up at me from the bed. She'd pulled the sheet up to cover herself.

"You were right," she said.

"About what?"

"The baby…was a girl."

Chapter Twelve

I should have waited.

We had a plan. We were going to tell them together, but I hadn't listened.

"What did you just say, young lady?" my mother asked, her voice taking on that authoritative tone I hated.

"I'm pregnant, and Garrett and I are getting married this summer."

I watched as the words settled, and her glare deepened. She still maintained her impeccable posture, sitting on the couch like she was expecting the royal court to arrive at any moment. My father paced behind her like a caged lion—or cowardly lion. He didn't bother to say anything. He never did.

"And just how do you expect to support yourself?" she asked.

"We've talked it through, and we're both still going to school. I'll take the second half of next year off to spend with the baby, and Garrett will attend part-time to pay for our apartment."

Her icy demeanor didn't change in the slightest. She showed

no emotions, no hysterics. "And school? How are you going to pay for school?"

My mouth gaped open, but I closed it without a single word springing forth.

"Oh, you thought we were going to pay for it? Well, that was before you decided to get yourself pregnant. If you choose this life, Amelia, you're on your own," she said.

"Mom, you can't do that! What about my trust fund?" My voice was rising, and my panic was soaring as well.

"Oh, I can, and I will. I will not support this embarrassing behavior, and neither would your grandfather, if he were alive. If you want a future that we pay for, you will end this, all of it, right now."

My eyes widened in horror as I stared into her stone-cold face, hoping she didn't mean what I thought she meant.

"You can't truly mean that?"

"I do. Do you really think that you and that boy can raise a child on your own? Do you really think you can afford to live and pay for college? Who do you think will have to drop out, Amelia? I might not like the boy, but he's loyal. Do you think he'll let you give up your dreams?"

We'd planned it all out. We hadn't gone into this lightly. We'd looked up housing costs and made budgets and goals. Garrett had even started looking for places he could contact for work after we moved, but everything hinged on our parents' support. We had briefly talked about staying local, attending a community college for a few years, but he didn't want to hinder my dreams of going to my first-choice school. He wanted me to have everything.

"I can see from your face that you know he wouldn't. Are you willing to destroy his life along with yours for this future you have planned?"

The life I'd envisioned and planned started fading...vanish-

ing. Garrett would give up everything for our child and me, including himself. There was no happy ending for us, not anymore.

"No, Mom, I'm not."

The scattered papers in front of me hadn't moved in thirty minutes. I'd been frozen in my thoughts, lost in my memories and haunted by my regrets for most of the day. I didn't think I'd done a single productive thing since I clocked in four hours earlier.

Leah breezed in from one of the labor rooms, looking far too good for someone in a pair of scrubs. She leaned over the counter with a wide grin. "Hey, heard you went on a trip. How was it?" she asked.

"Oh, it was, um…good."

"Good? That's all I get? I thought we were friends. Friends get more than *good*, Mia."

Where did I begin? Did I say it was an amazing two days? Yes, two days, not four. That was why I was at work on a Sunday afternoon when I should still be in New York.

I'd woken up the morning after the incident and found Garrett banging on the door. He'd told me to get dressed and that we needed to head to the airport. Something had come up, and we had to catch an earlier flight home. He'd briefly apologized in the cab for cutting our trip short, but that had been the only conversation we shared the entire way home. He hadn't needed to lie. I'd known there wasn't anything that had suddenly come up at home that needed his attention. He hadn't wanted to be around me anymore, and I couldn't blame him.

"We had a great time. He took me to a toy store," I said with a shy smile.

"A toy store? Yeah, that sounds like Goober."

"Goober?" I asked, intrigued by the nickname.

I'd noticed Leah had nicknames for almost everyone. She called her husband Hotshot and would sometimes refer to herself as Mrs. Hotshot with a goofy grin.

"Yeah, it's a nickname I gave him a long time ago when he was short, adorable, and annoying. Actually, most of those are still true—except for being short. He's like a tree now."

A flash of him bending down to kiss me in the hotel room came rushing back suddenly. There was always quite a height difference between the two of us, and I'd loved the way he would curl himself into me to steal a kiss.

I kissed you and said everything would be okay because I knew it would be.

When he'd kissed me again after so much time, I'd felt a part of my heart repairing itself. But I had been living a fantasy. There were some things that couldn't be forgotten.

"Well," Leah said, her eyes locking with mine, "if you need someone to talk to, Mia, I'm here. From the expression on your face right now, I know there's more going on, so please talk to someone. It doesn't have to be me, but I'm here, and I won't judge. I'm going to go check on my patients one last time and then clock out."

She turned away and disappeared down the hallway, and I was once again alone with my thoughts.

I was so tired of thinking.

After Garrett had silently dropped me off, I'd spent the rest of the weekend drowning in my own thoughts until I finally called into work to see if I could cancel my day off. I'd thought that at least I'd have something to do besides mope around the house. I hadn't even bothered calling

Liv to tell her I was home early, so she could bring Sam back.

As I'd waited for Sunday to come and work to follow, I'd just sat in my empty house and remembered. Memories could be the best and the worst part of living. The good kind could keep someone going, serving as a reminder to keep moving even when life was intent on dragging one down. The bad memories were like little reminders of everything everyone tried so hard to forget —reminders of failure, guilt, and periods of our past that were unchangeable. They clawed at every good memory, making them fade into the background until only pain was left.

Months after that fateful night with my parents, when my entire world had changed, I'd spent hours on the Internet researching grief. I'd read story after story of other women who had gone through the same thing I had. I'd learned I had a form of post-traumatic stress disorder, but I had felt too ashamed to seek treatment.

What would I tell the doctor?

I'm the reason my child isn't alive. I left my fiancé, and now, I can't walk down the street without crying.

Who would feel bad for me?

Eventually, the tears had started to ebb, and I'd found the strength to attend classes. School had become my obsession and coping mechanism. I'd paid for every single semester. Thanks to a generous scholarship from a small college out west and many student loans, I'd made it on my own. I had been done living under my mother's authority.

But it hadn't changed what had already happened. Bottling up feelings doesn't make them go away. You can't hide from your past—it always eventually finds you.

I should have never returned.

GARRETT

"You're quieter than normal," my sister said as she joined me on her sofa and handed me a glass of her homemade sweet tea.

Besides my niece and nephew, it was one of the main reasons I showed up here on a regular basis. Clare made a killer glass of sweet tea.

"Sorry. I'm just lost in my own thoughts."

She took a long sip from her own glass and watched me do the same thing. It was a lazy Sunday afternoon, and we'd just finished up having a late lunch. The kids were playing outside with Logan. Clare had cornered me on my way out and talked me into a drink and a nice brother-sister chat.

I should have known better.

"Hmm...it wouldn't have anything to do with Mia coming back into town, would it?"

It would have everything to do with Mia coming back into town, into my life, into my every thought.

"No, she's fine. It's not a big deal," I said, trying to brush it off.

"You're a terrible liar, Garrett."

"Am not."

"You so are! Remember when we were kids, and I asked you what happened to my goldfish from the state fair?"

"It died," I answered flatly.

"Only because you and your friends tried to see if a fish would actually get flushed down the toilet!" she cried.

"Well, I didn't actually think it would happen," I replied with a shrug.

"How is that possible?"

"Tim said it would swim against the current, like a salmon."

"Well, poor Goldie died because of your little experiment."

"I'm sure she made it out to the ocean," I encouraged.

"We live almost two hours from the ocean, Garrett!" This time, the loud voice was followed up by a punch to the arm.

"Ouch." I laughed. "Okay, the river maybe? Whatever. It was a fish, and I am a perfectly good liar."

"So, why don't you tell me why you are sitting on my couch when you should be flying home from New York?"

Shit. I didn't think about that.

"Something came up, and we needed to cut the trip short," I said quickly, trying not to remember the night that had sent me running back home, away from Mia and our past.

I'd dropped her off and left in a hurry, intent on ending this so-called friendship we'd started. No good could come from it. I'd been resolute in my decision. I'd even called a contractor to come in on Monday to finish the installation on her floors in hopes that my guilt at not finishing would be lessened.

Not even twenty-four hours later, I already missed her.

Clare huffed out a breath and stared down at her half-empty glass. She ran her finger along the condensation and made a little heart on the glass. "Look, I know that you are closer with Leah. I get that, and I've always been glad that you two were able to form such a close bond. But I'm still your sister. I'm here for you."

"I know, Clare, but this is shit I haven't told anyone."

"So, why not start with me?"

When something had been bottled up inside for so long, buried so deep, it took a long time to be able to dig it up again. I finished off my glass of tea and set it on the coffee table. I watched the ice start to melt. Clare didn't say anything and didn't pressure me. She just sat patiently and waited.

"Mia and I were supposed to get married."

I heard my sister audibly gasp.

She set down her tea and leaned forward. "What? When?"

"The summer after graduation."

"Why did I not know this?"

I looked down at my hands, remembering the night we'd gotten engaged. Lying on the blanket, I'd held her hand up in the air as we watched the tiny diamond twinkle and sparkle under the moonlight. She'd wanted to get me an engagement ring so that everyone knew I was hers. I'd told her that was unnecessary. She'd already marked every part of me.

"I never told Mom or Dad. I had planned to. We were going to tell them together, right after graduation."

Understanding spread across Clare's face as I looked up at her.

"But she left," she said.

I nodded. "She left town and never came back. I never heard a single word from her. She left me a note saying she couldn't go through with it, and that was it."

I remembered driving home in the pouring rain as the Southern sky went aglow with lightning. I could hear the roaring and grumbling of thunder as I'd parked the car in the front of my parents' house. My clothes had been soaked through from standing outside Mia's house, staring at that letter. It had still been in my hand. I'd held on to it the entire way home, fearing I'd lose the last thing I had of her.

I'd carried out our plans alone, hoping she would come find me. I'd thought she must have panicked, been frightened and run off, but she'd return to me still carrying that little miracle, and we would be happy.

She'll come back, I'd told myself. *She's just scared, and she'll come back.*

I'd told myself that every day until the baby's due date. I had been finishing up my finals at the school we were both supposed to attend, and I'd felt numb.

But she hadn't come back.

That day, I'd gotten the tattoo on my arm, and then the anger had started to settle in. It had stuck around ever since. I hated what she'd done to us and our future, yet I couldn't hate her. I'd tried, but it was like rejecting a part of myself.

Even now, I was protecting her—omitting some of the truth from Clare to keep Mia safe. Part of me wanted to throw Mia under the bus and tell my sister exactly what Mia had done, but I couldn't. I couldn't hate her, and I couldn't willingly hurt her either.

"Garrett, I'm so sorry. I wish you had told me sooner. I knew you were serious, but I guess I didn't realize how much," she confessed.

"You had a life of your own, Clare, with a husband and a new baby. I don't fault you for living it. And you can't feel guilty for not knowing what I didn't tell you."

She took my hand, and I pulled her into my arms. I'd

always be her baby brother, but she was a midget in comparison. I dwarfed her tiny frame.

"Do you think that maybe there's a chance that you two could—"

"No," I answered, cutting off her question before she had a chance to finish it.

"Are you sure? I saw the way you two looked at each other that night in the bar."

"We might still have chemistry, but it doesn't change the past."

"Forgiveness is a powerful thing, little brother," she said.

"Maybe for some people."

She sighed and gave me a squeeze, pulling back to gather our glasses. I heard the back door open, and the loud sounds of children rushed in. My two-year-old nephew, Ethan Oliver, took a flying leap into my arms and hugged me. He was named after my sister's late husband, but to give him his own distinction, everyone called him Ollie as a nickname.

"Care-wet!" he said, smashing my face together and laughing at the results.

"My name is Garrett, Ollie! Why does he always call me Carrot?" I managed to ask Clare.

She was also laughing at my mangled face. "He's two!" she said. "And besides, your name is difficult to say."

"Is not," I replied. I looked at him and smiled. "How do you say Logan?"

"Daddy!" he said cheerfully.

"Cheater."

I was about to ask him to say Declan when the phone rang, and Maddie ran through the house, shouting she would answer it. Clare had let her answer it a few times when a telemarketer would call, and now, she thought she was the official answering service for the house.

"No, Princess, I'll get it," Logan shouted, grabbing the phone seconds before Maddie could.

He was in the kitchen, but I could hear him as he cheerfully greeted my mom.

My stomach hit the floor when I heard him say, "Oh God, is he okay?"

I picked up Ollie and followed an equally frightened Clare into the kitchen. I grabbed her hand, fearing the worst.

Logan had just set the phone down, and he looked up at Clare and me with tearful eyes. "It's your dad."

Chapter Thirteen

"*I need to tell him. I need to say good-bye." The tears were falling from my cheek and splashing beneath me onto my suitcase as I packed.*

"No. He needs a clean break," she urged, pulling clothes from my closet and tossing them on my bed.

After I'd agreed to her plan, she hadn't wasted any time. I was leaving tonight.

"No need to linger," she said.

I would go take care of my problem, and she would make arrangements with one of the other many colleges I'd been accepted to, so I could move in as soon as possible. Until then, I would stay in our vacation home up north. Like a child, I was handing over my life to my parents.

I was a child, wasn't I?

"I at least want to write him a letter. He deserves that much."

He deserves so much more.

She looked as if she wanted to argue, but finally she nodded and left, giving me a few precious moments alone.

I sat at my desk, the same one I'd had since grade school. It was white with pink and gold accents. It matched my bed and dresser, and it looked like it was fit more for an infant than a teenager.

I pulled out the heavy stationary my mother had monogrammed with my initials. I never understood why she'd had it made. Who used stationary these days? I guessed it was useful for something.

I must have stared at that blank piece of paper for an eternity, trying to find the words to say good-bye.

How did I say good-bye when everything inside of me was screaming to stay?

This was wrong. My mother was wrong.

I needed to go to him and never look back.

Do you think he'll let you give up your dreams?

Her blunt words came crashing back, and I slumped back in the chair. How could I ask him to give up everything for me?

With a shaky hand, I began to write.

As I drove away that night, I said good-bye.

Good-bye to my home, good-bye to Garrett, and good-bye to my heart.

I woke up, sobbing.

I'd been doing this every night since he'd walked away from me in that hotel room.

Every night, I would awake, soaked in my own tears, shaking from my memories and drowning in my own regrets.

On Monday, I'd held out hope that our friendship might continue, and he would show up on my doorstep, like always, with a bag of food and a change of clothes, ready to tackle my floor. But he never showed, and instead, a truck of installers ready to finish my floor had greeted me.

Garrett had given me his answer loud and clear.

We were not friends, and whatever kind of relationship we'd started was over.

The dreams had gotten worse after that.

It was like losing him all over again. Only this time, he wasn't states away. He was right down the street, yet so far away.

I sat up in bed and checked the clock. *Two in the morning. Perfect.*

Sam lifted his head from the foot of the bed and looked at me. I'd given up on making him sleep on the floor ages ago. He hated the expensive doggie bed I'd bought for him, and I was too much of a pushover to force him to sleep on it. Besides, it was nice to share my bed with someone even if it was a dog. At least he didn't mind me tossing, turning, and waking up in hysterics.

If I didn't get a decent night's sleep soon, people at work would start realizing I was beginning to resemble a member of the undead more and more each day. At least Leah hadn't been at work. She would have called me out on it immediately.

I had large gray bags under my eyes, and my skin had gone pale. Thanks to a steady diet of Ben and Jerry's, I'd managed to keep my weight from plummeting. A girl had to take care of herself after all.

Since I'd done this crying ritual several evenings in a row now, I knew sleep wasn't happening for the rest of the night, so I got up and made myself a cup of chamomile tea. I snuggled with a blanket and a book on the couch. Sam jumped up in between my feet and groaned as I scratched him between his ears with my toes.

I'd just turned the page to start a new chapter in my latest paperback when my phone rang. I checked the time as I picked up my cell phone from the coffee table, but I immediately froze as I saw Garrett's name flashing across the screen.

Why was he calling me at three in the morning?

I quickly picked up, not wanting it to go to voice mail. "Hello?"

"Mia..." He sounded hoarse and distant.

"Garrett, are you okay? What's wrong?"

"My dad died."

He didn't say anything else, but I had heard the strain in his voice as he'd said the words, like just acknowledging them took immense physical strength.

"Oh God, Garrett. I'm so sorry."

"The funeral is tomorrow. I don't know if I can...I just don't know how to say good-bye."

"What time?" I asked.

"Ten in the morning."

My shift at the hospital started at eight, but I'd figure something out.

"Give me your address. I'll be over in the morning, and we'll go together."

"Okay."

He quickly gave me his address, and it confirmed my suspicions. Garrett lived less than a mile away from me.

"Try to get some sleep, okay?" I said gently.

He acknowledged, and we started to say our good-byes.

"Mia?" he said at the last moment.

"Yeah?"

"Thanks. I didn't know who else to call. I needed...I don't know. I just needed you."

I closed my eyes as I tried to steady my breath and erratic heartbeat. He was hurt and grieving.

Don't take the things he says to heart, Mia. Just be the friend he needs you to be.

"I'll see you tomorrow," I said before clicking End with a shaky hand.

GARRETT

This wasn't real.

At any minute, I was going to wake from this hell I'd been living in for the past few days, and everything would be back to normal. My family would be happy again, my mother would stop crying, and I wouldn't feel like there was this gaping hole in my heart anymore.

But I still kept waking up to find myself in this same fucking nightmare.

My dad was dead.

He'd been taken by a massive stroke at the age of fifty-eight.

It wasn't fair, and it wasn't right.

There was still too much for him to do, too much for him to see and experience. God needed to give him back.

"Goddamn it! Give him back!" I yelled, flinging the half-empty tequila bottle at my bedroom wall.

It exploded upon impact, shards of glass falling to the floor as amber liquid trickled down the bare white walls. The rising sun was just starting to cast its rays across the room as it ushered forth a new day—a reminder of something else my dad would miss. It was my first night back in my own bed since Logan had answered that phone call and all of our lives had changed.

We ran out of the house, hastily strapped the kids in the car, and rushed to the hospital. As we entered the ER, Logan disappeared, immediately switching into doctor mode to get more information. My father had been brought in unconscious but breathing, but my mother hadn't known much else. Clare and I found her huddled in the corner of the waiting room, clutching her handkerchief with wrinkled white knuckles.

"Mom," Clare called.

She looked up, and her eyes found us. They were red, and tears stained her cheeks. She jumped up and pulled us into her arms, and the sobs grew louder.

"We did everything we were supposed to do," she cried, referring to his last stroke that had put him into early retirement. "Everything the doctors told us to do after the last stroke, we did. Why did this happen? I don't understand. He was fine this morning. Then, he got a headache, and now..."

I didn't know what to say, so I held her. For as long as she needed, I held her.

Logan came out about an hour after arriving at the hospital and explained the stroke was fatal, and it was just a matter of time. His brain was hemorrhaging, and there was nothing that could be done. They'd given him morphine for the pain and kept him unconscious, but the rest would happen with time.

We were allowed to go in and see him one by one—to say good-bye.

I didn't want to say good-bye.

Less than twenty-four hours later, he was gone.

I still didn't want to say good-bye now.

The tequila bottle, now a beautiful mess of shards on the floor, sparkled under the sunlight, and the leftover alcohol bled down the wall, like tears.

"What the hell am I going to drink now?" I asked myself out loud, looking around the messy bedroom for something else to numb the endless stream of thoughts running through my head.

"I think you've had enough to drink," I heard someone answer back.

How much did I drink last night?

My head lolled to the side, and through the blur, I made out Mia standing in the doorway.

"How did you get in here?" I slurred.

"You left your door unlocked, genius."

"Did that on purpose," I said with more slurring.

She looked around and noticed the glass. She sighed and disappeared into the kitchen. She returned with a trash bag and made quick work of the mess. She obviously didn't appreciate the brilliant spectacle the sun was doing with the tiny glass fragments as much as I did. She also wasn't drunk, so there was that.

I silently watched her as she meticulously picked up each piece, vacuumed, and cleaned the wall. She vanished into the kitchen again and came back moments later with clean hands and an expectant expression.

"What?" I asked.

"Get up," she said.

"Why?" My head slumped back on my pillow, and I made no move to get up from my position on the bed.

"You're not showing up to your dad's funeral looking like that!" she exclaimed.

I looked up at her, and she was trying hard to be nice, but I could see she was annoyed. She probably hadn't expected this when she said she'd help me.

"I'm not going, so you can just go if you want," I said before slumping back down on the sheets.

"You're not going?"

"Nope."

After a few minutes of silence, I figured she had gotten sick of my behavior, and she'd left to save herself one more second of having to be around me. But as I glanced up, I found her standing in the exact same spot with her arms folded over her chest in that familiar pose she liked to take with me.

"Get up, Garrett," she commanded.

"No."

She took several steps forward until she was standing at the edge of the bed, hovering over me. The citrusy smell of her lotion invaded my senses.

"Get the fuck up."

At her bold words, my eyes darted to hers. She wasn't messing around. She was stone-cold serious. Well, two could play at that game.

I sat up so that we were nose-to-nose. I could feel her breath against my neck, and heat radiated off her body.

"I'm. Not. Fucking. Going," I punctuated each word as the anger seethed out of every pore on my body.

I was a ticking time bomb, and she was playing with fire.

Just when I thought she would match me and give me exactly what I needed—her screaming back and offering up a worthy opponent to channel my rage—she did the opposite.

She reached out, clutching my face gently, as she whispered, "What are you afraid of Garrett?"

"I'm not scared, damn it!" I yelled, pulling back from her tender touch.

"Then, what is this about? Because I know you wouldn't willingly bail on your family when they need you."

Her hand found mine, and I didn't think she understood the effect her touch had on me. Every single brush of her hand and lingering touch or taste of her lips was like taking a walk back in time. I would remember the first time she'd let me hold her hand at school or the shy smile she had given me when I taught her to ride a bike in my driveway. My dad had laughed at me, saying I had the worst game he'd ever seen, but I'd gotten her anyway. I'd been so excited to tell him that we were getting married, but I'd never gotten the chance.

"I can't go, Mia. I don't know how to be strong today," I said, feeling deflated. I gripped her hand like a lifeline.

"No one is asking you to be strong. Let me be the strong one today. Just hold my hand and find a way to say good-bye," she answered.

"Okay," I said in defeat.

She helped me find a suit and tie and politely stepped out of the room while I changed, but I quickly called her back in. My hands were so shaky that I couldn't button my own shirt. She gave me a sad smile and helped me with the buttons as I tried not to bend down and smell her hair. She was wearing a classy form-fitting black dress and heels. Her normally straight hair was curled and pinned back.

"Can you help me with my tie, too?" I asked, handing the dark blue silk tie to her.

She nodded and reached up to loop it around my neck. Our eyes met and held briefly before she quickly looked down and began working on the knot.

"There you go," she said, taking a step back to put space between us.

"Thank you. I guess it's time."

She nodded and took my hand as I tried to find a way to say good-bye to my father.

Chapter Fourteen

MIA

I was full of shit.

I'd told him I would be strong for him, but I honestly didn't know if I could be.

When I'd seen him broken and defeated, curled up on that bed like the world was closing in around him, I hadn't known what else to do. So, I had taken charge and fought for him when he didn't have the strength to do so himself.

As we walked into that church on this hot summer day, with his fingers curled around my own, I seriously doubted my ability to be all that he needed me to be. But I would give everything to try. Immediately after entering the church, we were greeted by an older woman with salt-and-pepper hair and a name tag that said Betty with the church logo. She gave Garrett a sad smile, recognizing him at once. He looked so much like his father that it was hard to miss the resemblance.

"You must be Garrett," she said, taking his free hand in greeting.

He nodded, and she offered her condolences to which he just stared at the floor and swallowed hard.

"We've set up a room over here," she said, pointing to the right of the sanctuary, "where the family can wait until it's time to enter."

I saw her quickly glance at our joined hands, and I didn't miss her eyes darting to Garrett's ring finger.

"Your friend is free to take a seat in the sanctuary until the service begins," she said politely.

"She stays with me. She is family today," he insisted.

We turned away, leaving the woman stunned and speechless.

Judgmental old bat.

The church Garrett and Clare's parents attended was large and modern with high ceilings and updated decor. Every church I'd ever been in always had a distinctive musty odor, but walking into this church felt more like walking into a performing arts building. It was huge.

We entered the room designated for the family and found them all gathered together tightly. Everyone was talking in hushed tones and passing around boxes of tissues. I suddenly felt out of place, like I was intruding on a private moment. Garrett must have sensed my hesitance because his hand tightened on mine, and I was suddenly reminded why I was there.

This day wasn't about me or how I might feel. It was about the man standing next to me. He needed me, and no matter what was going on between us, I would be there for him. I owed him that much. Regardless, I wanted to do this for him. I would do anything for him.

All eyes turned to us as the door shut behind us.

"Garrett," his mother said, rising from her seat to greet us. She pulled her son in a tight hug and stroked his hair, which I found endearing.

She turned toward me, and to my surprise, she also pulled me into a warm embrace. "So good to see you again, Mia. Welcome home. We've missed you."

She remembers me?

Before I had much time to contemplate that thought, everyone else in the family greeted us. Everyone, even the children, hugged me. Clare's daughter, Maddie, took to me immediately, asking who I was.

Most of us found seats while others made coffee or grabbed water.

Maddie sat down next to me and asked, "Did you know my Papa?"

My heart hurt that she'd lost her grandfather at such a young age. Grandparents were one of the best parts of being a kid. They loved unconditionally, spoiled their grandchildren rotten, and would let them eat sweets even if vegetables were skipped over. My grandparents made the early years of my childhood better. I never knew my mother's parents. They had died before I was born, but my father's parents were great. I always wondered what happened to my dad, having come from such an amazing set of parents.

"I did know your Papa. He was a wonderful man," I said.

"He always had M&M's in his coat pocket. Whenever I'd see him, he'd always share with me. They were always mushy from being in his pocket, but I liked them anyway."

"Well, now, you always have something special to remind you of your Papa, huh?"

She thought about it for a minute and shook her head.

"No, I don't think I can eat them anymore. They'll make me too sad."

"Memories of our loved ones shouldn't make us sad after they're gone. Happy memories should make us happy. Why don't you try to think of all the happy memories you had with your Papa every time you eat an M&M?"

She twirled her strawberry-blonde curls and contemplated my advice. Finally, she gave me a ghost of a smile. "Well, I do love M&M's," she said.

"And you love your Papa. It's perfect."

She cuddled with me for a few minutes and talked about her brother. He was currently running around the room, chasing Leah's daughter, Lily. They were both oblivious to what was going on. Their laughter and cries of glee were misplaced but a welcome change to the mournful atmosphere of the room. Sometimes, being so young must be a blissful alternative.

Garrett was in the corner, speaking with Leah, but his eyes were on me, and I wondered how long he'd been watching me.

The door opened, and the annoying woman from earlier entered.

"It's time, if you're ready," she said, giving her best sad, empathetic face.

Laura, Garrett's mother stood in front, and everyone paired off behind her. Clare went to Logan, Leah found Declan, and Garrett stood next to me. All the kids attached themselves to their parents, and we lined up. The other family members were already seated. Only the immediate family would be ushered in, and the fact that they had always included Leah made me love their family even more. The Finnegan's always welcomed everyone into their home with open arms, but Leah was special. Leah was family, regardless of blood ties.

Garrett's hand sought mine, and I turned to find him standing next to me with his eyes closed. He was breathing heavily through his mouth, like he was gearing up for a fight.

Taking a step, I moved in front of him and placed my hand on his erratically beating heart. His eyes opened and locked on mine.

"I'm right here, okay?"

He nodded, and I fell back into line. We took our first steps out of the room toward the sanctuary.

GARRETT

Every step we took closer to those double doors leading to my father lying lifeless in a casket made me want to turn and run even more.

Ever since Mia had left, I'd been surviving life by avoiding everything. I hadn't wanted to move on, so I didn't. I'd immersed myself in college. When that had been over, I'd become a workaholic, all so I could avoid having to deal with the fact that she'd left, and I'd have to find someone else.

I had used avoidance as my crutch for my entire adult life.

As I walked into that sanctuary and found so many eyes on us, I really wanted to turn and run. I could just get in my car and go anywhere just to avoid this new reality that was now my life.

My father was a well-respected man in our community, and seeing so many people attending his funeral should have made me proud, but it didn't.

It just made it real, and I didn't want to face it.

Curled up on my bed with a bottle of tequila had made it easy to forget what I'd seen in that hospital room. The alcohol had made everything dull and fuzzy. It had eased the pain and made the hurt go away.

"I don't know what to do," I said.

My sister clutched my hand outside my father's room in the ICU. "Just talk to him, Garrett. That's what I did." Her eyes were red and puffy from the tears she'd shed.

We were all saying good-bye. I had held out, hanging back in the hallway, until there was no one left but me. It was now or never.

Clare squeezed my hand one last time, and I took the remaining steps into the darkened room holding my father. The room beeped and echoed as the machines did their work.

Just one look at him brought me to my knees. The tears rolled down my face, and my chest heaved. Oh God, why?

There were tubes and wires everywhere. He looked nothing like the man who I'd seen just days earlier. This made it real. They'd told me he was dying, but seeing him made it a reality.

I was losing my father.

With shaky limbs, I managed to reach his bedside, and I took his lifeless hand. "Hey, Dad, it's me. Where do I even begin?"

I hadn't been able to say enough that day. How could I say good-bye to the greatest father in the world?

Sitting down on those uncomfortable church pews with my family brought everything rushing back with crystal-clear clarity.

There were programs and boxes of Kleenex laid out on the pews, and I had to move them to sit down next to Mia. She picked up a program and handed it to me. On the front was a picture of my dad. Dressed in his signature

Hawaiian shirt and khakis he loved to wear so much in the summer, he looked happy with a huge grin that took up his entire face.

Mia's grip on my hand never failed, and she leaned into me. Feeling her beside me anchored me in a way I couldn't explain. The feeling to run was still there, but with her here, I felt grounded. Every time I felt like the walls were collapsing around me, her steady hand was there to help pull me through to the other side.

My eyes focused on the casket and wouldn't budge. My mother had chosen a closed casket, and I was thankful. The last memory of my father was hard enough without having to see him embalmed and lifeless.

A minister I didn't know took the podium and began quoting scripture before speaking about my father. I guessed he knew my father. My parents had attended this church for a while, and my dad was a social guy. Everyone had loved him.

Everyone loved him—past tense.

I didn't like talking about my father in past tense. It made me angry.

Finally, the minister opened the podium to family members. My mom had mentioned this part to us last night. She'd wanted to give all of us the opportunity to speak about Dad if we wanted.

Logan was the first to take the podium. "Hi, my name is Logan Matthews, and I was lucky enough to call Thomas Finnegan, Dad. The first time I met him was about four years ago at one of their famous cookouts. I was scared to death. I was dating his daughter, and I was convinced he was going to kill me."

The audience chuckled a bit, and Logan gave a hint of a smile.

"He took one look at me, and I thought I was a goner. When he pulled me to the side and started grilling me, I thought for sure I'd never see Clare or Maddie again, and they'd find my body floating along the James River. Something I said must have convinced him I was good enough for them because he pulled me into a tight hug and welcomed me to the family...just like that."

The room was silent, and Logan was fighting back tears.

"Sometimes, the people who give us life aren't capable to take on the role of a parent, so we spend a lifetime trying to find someone to fill that gaping hole in our heart. Thomas Finnegan was that person for me. He was the only real father figure I've ever known, and I am so lucky that I had him in my life. He gave me the love of my life and a family. I will be indebted to him for the rest of my days."

He stepped off the podium, wiping tears from his eyes. After him, one by one, my family spoke. Clare said Dad had a tremendous heart. My mother recounted the tale of their fairy-tale wedding day, but she couldn't make it through, and Leah stepped in to help her. Leah's speech was much like Logan's, speaking of how he was the only real father she'd ever known. Her biological father was currently serving a life sentence for attempted kidnapping and abuse.

Soon, there was no one left but me, and I knew it was time. Mia squeezed my hand—her way of telling me it was okay if I didn't go up there, but for once in my life, I didn't want to avoid the hard stuff. I wanted my dad to be proud of me.

The distance between the front pew and the podium felt endless, and by the time I took my place behind it, my heart was rattling in my chest. I looked out to the audience and saw my family staring back at me with encouraging tear-stained eyes. Mia had slid over next to Leah, and they were holding hands.

"My father was always a man of words. Growing up, when we had math or science homework, we went to Mom, but if we had a paper to write, Clare and I knew to go to Dad for help. He always knew what to say and when. He had a knack for it, and he was this way with advice, too. In my sophomore year of high school, we were working on fixing up an old car, so I'd have something to drive once I got my license. We were always doing projects together, and unlike some teenagers, I never grew tired of hanging out with my old man. We'd talk about school and football. He'd ask about my friends and my girlfriend."

I glanced over at Mia, and her eyes grew a bit wider at my mention of her.

"I usually shied away from any girlfriend talk. I thought my dad was cool, but there were limits."

That earned me a laugh from the crowd, but I didn't join in. I wasn't doing stand-up. I was just trying to explain.

"As my sixteenth birthday grew closer, we were nearing the end of the car rebuild. One day, I found myself asking my dad a question. I said, 'Dad, how do you know if you're in love?' His head popped out of the hood and just about hit the top. He gave me an appraising look and finally said, 'It's pretty simple really. If you can't imagine your life without her in it, you're in love.'"

The wood of the podium was smooth and polished, and my gaze drifted down to it as I gathered my last thoughts. It was better than staring out at that quiet crowd.

"He left me alone for a while to finish up, and I remember sitting on the hood of that car, thinking about what he said." I took a strangled breath and choked out, "He was right, you know. Love is a simple thing—whether it's the love of your life or a father. Right now, I'm having the hardest time trying to imagine my life without him in it."

I should have ended on an uplifting note like the rest of my family had, but I couldn't speak anymore. If I did, I'd break down, and I didn't want to do that in front of an entire church full of people.

I took the stairs one at a time, and each one felt like another nail in the coffin—final and irreversible.

The rest of the funeral passed in a blur of sobs and tears. All I remember is Mia's warm hand in mine, and the immense feeling of peace it gave me. I didn't know what I'd do when she left tonight.

MIA

Garrett hadn't said a single word so far on the way back to his apartment from the funeral. He just blankly stared out the window, watching the leafy green trees pass by in a blur while I drove his car. The lines etched in his face and the dark grooves under his eyes explained what I already knew.

He was exhausted, both mentally and physically.

It had been a long day. After the funeral service, the family had driven out to the gravesite, and they had a private service. There was no big funeral procession stopping traffic and involving police. Just the family and minister were in attendance. Garrett had explained that his father wasn't big on showy ordeals, and he would have hated all the fuss. The service alone would have been considered over the top, but his mother had known the many people who had loved him needed to mourn. So, they'd gone with a large funeral and a quiet graveside service.

Not once through the entire day had Garrett allowed himself to cry, even as they lowered his father's casket into the ground. There were several times I'd caught him pinching the bridge of his nose or squeezing his eyes shut as if he was forcing the tears away. Why he wouldn't just allow himself to let go, I'd never understand. No one in his family would have judged him for that. Everyone in that room had cried, including myself, and it had been years since I'd seen Thomas Finnegan. He used to make me turkey sandwiches and sweet tea on Saturday afternoons when I'd sit in the garage, watching Garrett work on his car. He was still one of the most dedicated fathers I'd ever known.

"You missed the turn," Garrett muttered quietly, pointing to the street sign.

He was right. I was two blocks past where I should have turned.

"I'm sorry," I sighed. I had been so wrapped up in my own thoughts that I hadn't been paying attention.

I flipped us around at the next block and managed to get us parked and settled in front of his large apartment building a few minutes later. I didn't know how I got a parking spot right in front, but I thanked the parking gods for the gift. I quickly locked the door and handed Garrett his keys.

My car was parallel-parked about three blocks down. This was the joy of living in this area of town. It was always a game of hide-and-seek when it came to parking. Finding the right spot was a constant challenge.

"Why don't you come up for a bit?" he suggested. He shoved his hands into his pockets and watched a car pass by.

It wasn't quite nighttime yet, so if I left now, I

wouldn't have to walk to my car in the dark, but I was finding it hard to say no. I didn't want to disappoint him.

"Sure," I answered.

He let me lead as he trailed behind me. We took the two flights of stairs up to his apartment, and the entire way I felt his eyes on me. Even from behind, I knew his eyes were traveling every inch of me, and my skin prickled into goose bumps at the thought.

His door was the second to the right. I waited while he fished his keys out of his pocket and unlocked the door. He was pressed up so tightly behind me that I could feel every hard line of his body, and I swore I heard him inhale, like he was smelling my hair. My heart kicked into overdrive at his nearness, but then he took a step forward and opened the door. Relieved for the distraction, I followed and let my nerves settle.

No other man in my life could set my body ablaze like Garrett Finnegan. One heated gaze, and I was on fire. One single touch, and I was begging for more. When I was young, I'd never questioned it. He was my ever after, and I loved the way he made me feel. Leaving him, knowing everything I was giving up, had been the hardest thing I'd ever done.

But now, returning and finding myself still hostage to his touch, was the worst kind of agony imaginable. Knowing my heart belonged to someone I couldn't have felt like walking through life with half of my soul missing.

I dropped my purse on the kitchen counter separating the tiny kitchen from the equally small living space. The entire apartment was pint-sized. With Garrett's six-foot-plus size, he looked like he was standing in the middle of a hobbit hole.

"Have you lived here long?" I asked, noticing the absence of wall art or decorations.

There was a black couch pushed up against the far wall with a small end table standing next to it. The end table was littered with black-and-white drawings. Some were shoved into notebooks and others were stacked into messy piles. Now, I knew what Garrett did with his free time.

"Since I moved back from college," he answered.

I chalked his lack of decorative skills to the fact that he was male, but it felt like he'd never really settled, or he'd refused to.

"Do you want a drink?" He shuffled through a cupboard and pulled out a bottle of whiskey.

I cocked my eyebrow, remembering the state he had been in this morning when I arrived.

He quickly defended himself. "One drink," he clarified.

"Okay, but no whiskey. I don't know how you can stand that stuff."

I gave a sour face, and the corners of his mouth curved into a slight smile. It was the first time I'd seen a hint of one all day. He turned back toward the cupboard and pulled out some rum and orange juice from the refrigerator.

"I don't have pineapple juice, but orange juice will be a good stand-in," he said.

Malibu and pineapple was my favorite drink, and he still remembered.

He began mixing everything and chuckled to himself. "Do you remember the first time we got drunk?"

"Ugh, yes. You stole a bottle of whiskey from your parents' liquor cabinet, and we sat at the river with Olivia and whoever she was dating."

"You ended up puking your guts out into the river that night," he said.

"You held my hair, and I kept telling you to go away because I was mortified of you seeing me get sick."

"I would have gladly held your hair back any day," he replied as he handed me my drink.

It wasn't the last time he'd held my hair while I got sick.

"Hey!" Garrett greeted me with an enthusiastic grin, "You ready for lunch?" With his green eyes blazing, he looked young and vibrant.

"Yep, let me just drop this stuff off in my locker!"

I twirled around the lock, and I had to start over several times when Garrett kissed my cheek, flicked the pendant around my neck, or tickled me.

"We will never get to eat if you keep doing this!" I teased.

He immediately stopped but had a devilish grin on his face.

"Can't have that. Man's gotta eat. In fact—" He took my backpack without letting me unload it, and he threw it over his back. He grabbed me around the waist and hoisted me up and over his massive shoulders.

"Garrett! Put me down!" I screamed.

"Nope. I'm hungry, and we need to eat," he said, slapping my ass.

"Oh my God!" I said when I heard everyone in the hall laughing and cheering.

He didn't set me down until we were all the way into the cafeteria. His shit-eating grin said he'd loved every single second, and to be honest, I had, too—minus all the blood rushing to my head.

"Come on, babe, let's get some food."

As soon as we hit the line, my stomach rolled. The instant smell of pizza, french fries, and hamburgers made me nauseous.

Cafeteria food wasn't the best to begin with, but I usually could stomach it without much fuss.

"Hey," Garrett said, cupping my chin. His emerald eyes were filled with concern. "You okay?"

"I don't feel so well all of a sudden."

"You want me to get you some crackers or water?" he suggested.

Just the mere mention of food was making me gag. "I think I'm going to be sick."

I ran for the restroom, passing everyone who'd just cheered for us in the hallway, and I made it just in time. My stomach unloaded everything, yet I was still gagging and heaving.

Suddenly, someone was behind me, holding me and protecting me.

"Shh...it's okay," Garrett soothed.

I was clammy and sweaty from being sick. I flushed the toilet, and we walked out of the stall, so I could wash my hands. A freshman looked over at us and saw Garrett, and she quickly scurried out.

"Flu maybe? Do I need to take you home?"

I shook my head, finally coming to terms with what I'd been fearing for weeks. It wasn't the first time I'd been sick.

"Garrett...I haven't had my period in two months."

While his parents had still been at work that afternoon, he'd held me, and we had cried together as we waited those three minutes for that stupid stick to tell us our future. It was called a pregnancy test, but it should really be called a crystal ball. *Gaze into it, and it will tell you your future.* When it had come up positive, I hadn't known what to do, but Garrett had.

Sitting on Garrett's couch, I found myself staring into an empty glass. I didn't even realize I'd finished it.

"Don't go," Garrett said.

I looked up and found him moving toward me. He sat down on the couch and took my glass before setting it down.

"I saw that look in your eye and knew you were thinking of leaving. Please don't."

"Garrett…"

"I just don't want to be alone, not tonight. Look…" he said with a sigh. "Ever since you came back, I've been trying to push you away. Every time I push, I find myself right back on your damn doorstep, so I push harder, and I'll be damned if I don't find myself right back where I started. The harder I fight it, the stronger the urge to give in becomes. It's exhausting, and I'm fucking tired. So, for one night, please…help me forget about all the shit going on in my life, and let me finally fall asleep with you in my arms again. Help me forget."

I stared into those green eyes and knew I'd never be able to say no.

"Okay."

GARRETT

I was a fucking moronic fool, but I couldn't let her leave.

I'd spent the entire day touching her, feeling her beside me, and the thought of not having her next to me anymore left me feeling cold and restless.

I knew I was just delaying the inevitable, but avoidance was something I'd mastered a long time ago, and right now, I was going to use it to my full advantage. I didn't want to think about the consequences of what having her in my bed would do to me—what I would be like after she was gone and I was alone again. I didn't want to worry about the loss I would feel when I couldn't feel her soft skin under mine anymore even if was just her fingers.

Nope, I was avoiding it all and doing a pretty good job —or at least pretending to.

We ordered a late-night pizza and spent some time going through my piles of drawings. It was something I'd never shared with anyone, but I shared it with her.

"These are really good," she said.

"They're all right."

"Garrett, you should be doing this every day," she urged.

"And what about you, Miss Accountant?" I countered.

"I'm not an accountant anymore."

After we cleaned up, she made a call to Liv and asked if she could check on Sam. I didn't hear the rest of the conversation because she ducked into the bathroom, but I did her say, "Shut up, Liv!" a few times, so I was sure Miss Prescott had an opinion about where Mia was spending her evening.

As she was finishing up her phone call, I padded into my bedroom and slipped into a pair of loose-fitting sweats. Mia had seen me naked many times over, but I figured dropping my pants in front of her wouldn't give her a good impression of my intentions for the evening— not that I would mind if she offered.

Jesus, Garrett...get your fucking head on straight.

I was just slipping a T-shirt over my head when she came in. She took in my change of clothes and looked down at her black dress.

"I don't have anything to wear," she said.

"I have a T-shirt you can change into." I pulled open a

drawer and handed her an old college T-shirt. Then, I sat down on the bed and waited to see what she would do.

Her eyes drifted down to the shirt and back to me. She took in my casual position on the bed, realizing I wasn't making any attempts to vacate the room for her privacy. She hesitated a moment longer and then swiveled around in the direction of the bathroom.

I wasn't sure if I was more relieved or bummed. I wasn't positive I'd be able to handle watching her strip down bare in front of me right now, but seeing her flee at the thought of getting undressed in front of me still hurt.

Mia returned no less than two minutes later with her black dress tucked in her hands. She nervously stopped at the doorway and looked around as if she were unsure of how to proceed.

"Come here," I murmured.

Her dress fell to the floor at the door, and she came to my side as I sat at the foot of the bed. Against my better judgment, my fingers reached out for her, curling around her bare leg and up her thigh.

Her breath caught, but she didn't stop me.

"Garrett..." she started to say.

"Shh...just allow me this. Just for tonight. We'll go back to being friends tomorrow, but tonight...just help me remember."

I could see the split decision swirling in her steady gaze. I knew this decision would end me. I knew I'd most likely never recover from a second blow to the heart by Mia Emerson, but I'd just lost my father. I wasn't sure there was much of a heart left.

Finally, she nodded, and I had my answer. My hand slipped higher under the ratty T-shirt covering her body until I found the edge of her panties. I curled my hand around her ass and pulled her down, letting her legs spread open so she was straddling me. Our eyes met, and I knew this was no favor she was doing for me. Her eyes were heated and filled with desire. She wanted this as much as I did.

Lifting the T-shirt she no longer needed, I threw it to the floor and found those perky round breasts I'd become reacquainted with in New York. I fisted one in each hand, and I took my time sucking and savoring each nipple until she was writhing so hard in my lap that I thought I might explode from the friction.

It wasn't enough. I needed more. I needed all of her. Eight years of starving for the one thing I needed most in the world had left me a shell of a man, and now, I was finally feasting again.

I wanted it all.

My mouth made a scorching trail up through the valley of her breasts, and I trailed kisses along her neck until I found her lips. She moaned into my mouth as my tongue found hers. My hands snaked around her body, leaving a fiery path over her soft skin. I gripped her ass and pulled her closer positioning her exactly where I needed her to be. She moved and wiggled her sexy little body right on top of my hard cock, and I groaned in pleasure. Her hands found the hem of my T-shirt, and I helped pull it up and over my head. She tossed it on the floor, and her hands went to my chest, tracing every hard line and defined edge.

I closed my eyes and tried to memorize the feel of her touch on my body, knowing it would have to last me a lifetime. Tomorrow, reality would come back, and I would remember why this would never work.

But tonight, she was Mia, and I was Garrett, and that was all that mattered.

With one arm under her back, my other grabbed her behind the knee, and I flipped us onto the bed. Her hair fanned out on my sheets, reminding me of the way it had looked under the hot August sun on lazy summer days at the river. Her hands never left my body, and she traced every inch of my stomach, chest, and arms. Her fingers curled into the waistband of my sweats and tugged. Never breaking eye contact with her, I slid them off my body.

No words were said as I slid my fingers into her panties. I nudged a single finger inside her slick core, wet from her own desire. She moaned and bucked. I added another digit, fucking her with my fingers, as my thumb found her clit.

"Garrett…" she moaned.

Hearing her say my name made me want to hear it again and again, but I wanted to be inside her. I wanted to feel her pulsate and spasm around me as she screamed out my name.

She cried out from the abrupt absence of my fingers.

"I need to be inside you, Mia."

She looked up at me with hooded eyes, but she didn't say anything.

"Say yes, Mia. I need to hear you say yes."

"Yes," she breathed.

I didn't hesitate. I reached for the small nightstand next to my bed and pulled open the drawer. I blindly searched around until I found what I was looking for. Mia didn't say a word about the supply of condoms in my nightstand. I didn't divulge any information either. This was not a night about sharing our past or creating a future. This was only about the present—here and now.

After ripping open the condom with my teeth, I sheathed myself quickly. I peered down at Mia, who was watching in heated fascination. I bent down and kissed her, fusing our mouths together, as my fingers ghosted down her lush body, stopping at the edge of her panties. I slid my fingers under the waistband, and then I broke our kiss to remove the last piece of clothing off her body until all I was left with was Mia.

She was even more breathtaking than I remembered.

This would haunt me until the day I died.

She pulled me down and wrapped her legs around my body. I felt my dick at the slick entrance of her core. One thrust, and I would be home again. I cupped her chin, stared into the eyes of the woman I'd gave my soul to when I was nothing but a child and silently told her everything I wanted to say but would never be able to again.

I love you. I'll always love you.

She gasped as I entered her, and in that instant, I felt my heart restart, firing and kicking into gear as it found its missing piece. Pausing to savor the moment, I kissed her again and felt her hands grip my shoulders.

Our kisses, like our lovemaking, became impatient, making up for lost time. Soon, I was devouring her, slamming into her, as she cried out my name over and over again.

"Garrett! Oh God, yes!" she cried as her nails dug into my back.

"Say it again," I growled.

She cried out my name one last time as she climaxed, spasming and squeezing my cock like a vise, which sent me over the edge into my own spiral of pleasure.

I spent the rest of the night trying to make the evening

last forever, so we wouldn't have to leave that bed. If I could keep the sun from rising, I would never have to give her up. I worshipped her body—sweet and slow, hard and fast, over and over—until we both passed out from exhaustion.

But I was no miracle worker, and even I couldn't outwit the sun.

Chapter Sixteen

MIA

I awkwardly juggled the plate of freshly baked goods and casserole in my hands and tried to press the doorbell.

What if she was just being nice at the funeral and wasn't really happy to see me?

Was there still time to run?

I looked at the huge mound of food in my hands and glanced between my car and the door.

No, I was an adult. I could do this. This was what respectable people did when someone died. They showered the family with food and sympathy. I would not run with my cowardly tail between my legs just because I'd run out on her son eight years ago without so much as a phone call afterward.

Garrett.

His name flashed through my mind like a tidal wave, bringing back glimpses and memories of our passionate night together. I could still feel his touch on my skin, his warm breath on my cheek as he'd whispered in my ear, and his quivering body as he'd rocked deep inside me.

It had been a few days since I'd snuck out of his apartment in the wee hours of the morning, leaving his tender touch into the eerie solitude of my own home. I'd fled his bed, rather than face him. I couldn't bear the thought of him saying the words I knew I deserved to hear. He didn't want me and never would. Our night was just that—one night—and it would never be more. So, I'd thrown on my dress and run.

I hadn't heard from him since. My floors were done, so there wasn't any reason for him to come by. I didn't know why I'd expected anything different. We'd tried to be friends, and we had ended up in bed together.

The door I'd been staring at finally opened, and I found myself face-to-face with Laura Finnegan.

"Mia? Is that you behind all that food?"

I laughed a bit. "Yes, Mrs. Finnegan. I came by for a visit. I hope you don't mind. I guess I should have called."

She waved her hand and hushed me, inviting my pile of food and me inside. "Don't ever think you need an invitation to come over here, Mia. You're like family—no matter how long you decide to stay away. And no calling me Mrs. Finnegan, you hear?"

"Yes..."

She gave me a stern look and waited.

"Mom," I finished.

She grinned in satisfaction.

Her kindness humbled me. Garrett had obviously never told her about what had happened between the two of us. If he had, she would hate me.

"Much better. Why don't you help me put that stuff away, and then we can catch up?"

I nodded, and we headed for the kitchen. It was weird being back in Garrett's childhood home. It was the same but completely different. The kitchen had been thoroughly remodeled and renovated. It now appeared more modern and updated. There were pictures of Garrett and Clare's family everywhere, including Clare's first husband who had passed away. Knowing I hadn't been around to help Garrett through the death of his brother-in-law hurt. I knew he and Ethan had been close, but I was glad Clare had found love again.

"Now, what did you bring me?" she asked.

"Well, I brought some muffins from this place Leah had told me about—Phil's. I told the owner I was a friend of hers, and he loaded me up with so many muffins that I thought I was going to double over. He threw in the casserole for free. I didn't cook any of it, so you're safe. I'm a terrible cook." I was a babbling, nervous mess.

Laura smiled and gave me a wink. "Phil is such a sweet man. He's got a soft spot for Leah. It would drive Declan mad if Phil wasn't as gay as they come. Leah mercilessly flirts with him for free muffins and coffee."

She put the casserole in the fridge, and I saw several others in there. Then, she pulled out two muffins for the two of us and placed them on pretty floral plates. She brewed some fresh coffee, and we took our matching floral mugs and muffins into the living room.

I took a nibble and then drank a bit from of my cup before I got the courage to ask, "How are you doing?"

She sighed and took a long sip of coffee, holding on to the cup for warmth. Outside, it was blazing from the late summer heat, but inside, there was a lingering chill from the overworked air conditioner. I held my cup as well, savoring the heat.

"It's getting easier to come to terms with it each day. The loss, however, hasn't lessened. I've been told it never will. It just gets easier to deal with."

I nodded. "That sounds about right."

"You sound like you speak from experience," she said, meeting my gaze.

"What? Oh, I, um…was just agreeing."

"Hmm…so, tell me about yourself, Mia. What have you been doing? Where has life taken you?"

"Oh, well, um…there isn't much to tell," I floundered, picking apart pieces from my muffin.

"I don't believe that. Surely, you have something special to tell. Or someone maybe?" she asked, her tone even and supportive. She took a sip of coffee and then remained quiet. She genuinely wanted to know about my life.

"There was someone, but it wasn't right. I wasn't right."

"Hmm…" she said again.

We continued to nibble on our muffins and sip our coffees. I looked around the room and noticed the small changes that had been made. New furniture had been purchased, and pictures had been added. Clare's and Leah's children had been added to the mantel as well as wedding photos. Time had moved on while I was away.

"He's been waiting for you," she said, pulling me from my thoughts.

"What?"

"Garrett has been waiting for you to come back to him."

I set my muffin down on the small table next to the sofa. My heartbeat had just kicked into high gear, and I didn't want to risk spilling anything on what looked like brand-new carpet. This was not how I'd expected this visit to go.

"No, I don't think so."

"He might not come to me like Clare does, but I'm still his mother. I know him better than he thinks I do."

Tears stung my eyes, and my voice quivered as I said, "I never meant to put his life on pause."

"Oh, sweetheart," she said, rising from her chair to sit with me on the couch. "I'm not accusing you of anything. Love can often be strange, and sometimes, it doesn't always take the path we expect it to. Whatever or whoever took you away from us, from him, it doesn't matter now. You're here now. Make it count."

"I don't think this can be fixed or forgiven."

"It can. If it's true love, you can move past this," she encouraged, taking my hands.

I stared down at them as I let the tears flow freely down my cheeks. "You don't understand. You don't know what happened."

She squeezed my hands and I looked up to find her looking at me with those warm green eyes that were so much like her son's. "I do."

"No, you—"

"I do. I've always known," she said.

I gasped and tried to pull away, but she kept a firm hold on my hands.

"I found the note in Garrett's room a few weeks after you left."

My head fell forward. I was too ashamed to look at her. "You must hate me."

"I could never hate you, Mia. You were faced with an immense choice, one beyond your capacity to handle as an eighteen-year-old."

"I chose wrong, so wrong," I said.

"Whatever you chose, it led you to this moment, sweetheart. Don't let another opportunity pass you by. Stop living your life in regret."

I fell into her arms and sobbed. I cried for the child I never knew and the life I lost because of it. I mourned the loss of possibilities because of my poor decisions, and I cried for the kindness I was being given from a woman who should hate me. I'd ruined her son's life.

"Since that day I said good-bye to Tom, the only thing that gets me up in the morning is the fact that I know we spent every day of our lives together loving each other as much as we possibly could. If I didn't have that, I think I'd lose myself to regret and grief."

She stroked my hair as my tears dried up. Our coffee had long since gone cold, but neither of us cared. The sun was setting and casting rays of light on the mantel. Out of the corner of my eye, I saw a picture frame catch the sun's reflection. It was Garrett in a cap and gown on the day of his college graduation. He was smiling, but it didn't reach his eyes.

That was supposed to be our graduation day, our accomplishment.

So many lost moments.

So many regrets.

How could we move forward when we were both still stuck in the past?

GARRETT

Sweat poured down my bare back as I wiped my brow and pushed my parents' lawn mower back into the shed.

Correction—my mother's lawn mower.

Would it ever get easier?

He'd been gone almost two weeks, and I couldn't bring myself to take his cell number out of my list of contacts. Clare and I still called this our parents' house, regardless of who lived here. For the life of me, I couldn't walk into the living room without expecting my father to be sitting in his favorite chair, ready to ask me about work or read a story to one of the grandchildren.

But he wasn't here, and as I locked the shed and walked back into the house where my mother now lived alone, I felt more lost than ever.

My father had been my rock in life, my mentor and guide, the one I turned to when I needed advice or strength. Even after Mia had left and I shut down and closed myself off, he had still been the person I went to when I needed an outlet.

Now, he was gone, and after a week of silence, so was Mia.

I didn't know why I'd expected anything different. It was what we'd wanted and needed—no attachment beyond one night. In one moment of weakness, we'd reached out for each other to remember, and God, had I remembered.

Her skin had jump-started my heart, her kiss had ignited my passion, and every single touch had reminded me that my soul would never belong to anyone else but the woman beneath me. Mia owned me and always would. The rest of my life would be a game of trying to find someone who would never quite measure up to the woman I'd lost. Was it even worth trying? Would it be cruel to pursue someone, knowing I'd never be able to give her anything more than a lukewarm companionship?

No answers came to me as I grabbed a freshly laundered towel from a basket near the laundry room. I used it to wipe away the sweat still left on my body from outside. My dad had always been the one to take care of the immaculate lawn. Now, I would have to do it or find someone to take over because there was no way my petite mother was taking charge of that task.

I meandered into the living room, avoiding the empty chair in the corner. I lifted my shirt from the back of the couch and threw it over my head. Taking a look around, I found my mom in the kitchen, trying to make sense of all the food, flowers, and gifts that had been dropped off over the last week. Every inch of countertop was covered.

"Here, Mom, let me help you," I offered.

She nodded, and we started making stacks and piles. Desserts went into one pile, flowers went on the kitchen table, and cards went in another stack to be taken to Clare so that she could write thank-you cards.

"I can write the thank-you cards," my mother objected.

"So can Clare," I countered. "You've done enough. Let us help."

"I just don't want anyone thinking I'm ungrateful."

"No one is going to think that, Mama."

She smiled. "You haven't called me that in a long time."

"What? Mama? Yes, I have."

"No, you haven't, not since high school."

"Oh…well, it wasn't on purpose," I said, scratching my head.

"I know, sweetheart."

We continued to make headway through everything, and I stole a muffin from a giant stack. My midday mowing in the middle of summer had left me starving.

"Mia brought those over yesterday," she mentioned, pointing to my muffin as I shoveled it in.

"Mia was here?" I said between bites.

"Mmhmm."

"Why?"

"To offer her condolences and to spend some time with me."

Confused, I looked around, like I expected her to suddenly appear and explain herself. "But why?" I asked.

"What do you mean, Garrett?"

"Why would she come see you after—" I started but stopped myself.

"I have no ill will toward that girl, Garrett Finnegan. I loved that child, and I still do. That hasn't changed, no matter what happened between you two."

I grumbled under my breath and continued to pick at my muffin. It was still delicious, and that pissed me off.

"You need to find a way to move past your anger," my nosy mother said.

My eyes flew up to hers. She'd set down the cards she was going through, and she was now looking at me with that motherly expression that made me feel like a small child again. It was the same expression I'd seen over and over throughout my youth, the one that told me I was being stubborn and needed to get over myself.

Well, I had news for her. I might be stubborn, but I had grounds this time.

"Mom, you don't understand—"

"I do," she interrupted.

"You couldn't possibly."

"No? I couldn't possibly understand how difficult it might be for a young woman—still a child herself and probably under great pressure at home and elsewhere—to make a monumental life decision?"

How could she possibly know anything?

I looked into her eyes, the same eyes that had been staring back at me since birth, and I knew she was calling my bluff. She knew.

"How did you find out?" I asked quietly.

"You were never good at hiding things, Garrett," she answered.

"The note."

She simply nodded. "I wish you had come to us. I knew you were hurt and grieving, but you wouldn't talk to me. I was afraid if I said something, you would lash out and tell me I didn't trust you. I was so scared, Garrett."

"She aborted our child, Mom," I whispered.

"She was eighteen, Garrett. Have you ever asked her about it?"

"No, I can't. I don't want to know the details. I couldn't live with that," I said, shaking my head.

I squeezed my eyes shut, trying to block out the memories of finding that note and realizing Mia had made that monumental decision—without me. I'd had no idea of where she was, no way of saving that little life Mia and I had created. She had taken that away from me.

"The two of you need to talk about this—maybe not now but soon. I saw the way you looked at her at the funeral. Whatever you think you can't forgive, you can."

I shook my head. "I don't know how, Mom. I love her, but every time I see her, all I see is the past."

She gave a faint smile and reached for my now empty hand. "Reach into the past and remember the reasons you fell in love. Hold on to that, son, and cherish it. Then, you must start moving forward again."

Chapter Seventeen

GARRETT

*L*etting out a huff of breath I'd been holding since the purr of the engine had died down at the curb, I pushed the doorbell and waited.

How many times had I found myself back at this exact spot, standing on Mia's doorstep, after I'd sworn I would never return?

How many times did I have to stare at the front of this door, waiting for her face to appear, to realize I'd keep coming back, week after week, day after day?

An enthusiastic bark from inside came barreling toward the front door, and I heard a familiar giggle.

"Hold on, psycho!" Mia laughed, her voice carrying.

She flipped the lock and pulled the door open to find me on the other side, holding flowers like a dork. As her eyes took in the gargantuan bouquet I was balancing with the bag of groceries, I stole a moment to sweep my gaze down, focusing on her every delectable inch. My fingers twitched to touch her again.

"Um…hi," she said awkwardly.

"Hey," I responded, finally meeting her gaze.

She looked at me expectantly and shifted on her bare feet.

Oh, right, the flowers. "My mom wanted me to drop these off for you," I said, handing over the flowers. "She has about a million bouquets sitting around the house, and she hates the idea of them going to waste, so I've been playing delivery boy for most of the afternoon."

"Oh," she replied, realizing this was probably the only reason for my visit.

"I, uh…also brought groceries if you're interested in dinner?"

Her eyes lifted, and I flashed her a quick grin.

"Okay," she agreed, stepping aside to let me in.

The smell of her citrus-scented skin invaded my senses. I'd spent hours that night in my bedroom licking and kissing every inch of her body in an effort to commit it to memory. My memories hadn't done it justice, and my body instantly wanted more.

Sam jumped up and down at my invasion into the house. He'd taken a liking to me ever since that day in the shelter, and the feeling was definitely mutual. After giving Sam his proper greeting, we wandered into the kitchen, so I could drop the bag of groceries. Mia started rummaging through her cupboards for a vase.

"Oh…looks like you've already gotten a flower delivery today," I said, noticing a large bouquet of roses on the kitchen table. I fingered a soft petal between my fingers, and then I noticed a card wedged among the many multicolored buds.

"Um…yeah," she replied.

"Who's Aiden? And why does he want you back?" I asked, feeling jealousy beginning to boil in the pit of my stomach. I didn't even know who the guy was, but I didn't like him. He wanted Mia to leave?

"Oh, um…Aiden was my boss. He really misses me and wants me to come back. He's trying anything to get me return to my old job. It's crazy really," she answered with a hesitant laugh.

I eyed her suspiciously for a moment as she began to arrange the flowers in a vase.

What was she hiding? And why didn't she trust me enough to tell me?

Like all mysterious things Mia had done these days, I let it go.

It shouldn't be my problem.

We'd agreed on one night, and regardless of what my mom had thought, there were some things even love couldn't forgive. Despite my best efforts to stay away, I couldn't. Mia had a pull on me that was undeniable, but I would control how far it went.

Leaving the flower subject alone, I walked to the kitchen counter and helped with the groceries.

"What are we making?" she asked.

"Nothing fancy. I just picked up stuff for spaghetti and salad."

"Okay, sounds great. Let me get the pot for the pasta."

That was when my torture began.

She bent forward, wiggling, as she strained to pull out the correct pot from her tiny cupboard wedged in the corner of her ancient kitchen. I should have saved myself and looked away, but I couldn't. My eyes were glued to her.

Did she know her ass was practically hanging out of her shorts?

"Found it!" she exclaimed.

I turned to adjust the hard-on I was now sporting.

"Oh, we're going to need a colander, too! That's up here!" she said, pointing to one of the higher cabinets.

She rose on her tiptoes and began reaching and struggling to grab it. Her shirt rode up, and I caught a glimpse of that honey-colored skin I'd spent hours licking and sucking.

"You know, let's go out!" I said suddenly.

She lowered back down to her feet and turned. "What?"

"We always eat in when I come over. Let's just go out for a change." *Otherwise, I'm going to die.*

Twenty minutes later, we were seated at a local place a couple of blocks down from Mia's house. It was one of the many perks of where she lived. She could literally walk to almost anything. Of course, the thought of her walking alone didn't settle well with me.

The waiter came and took our order, and then he scurried away to let us enjoy our drinks. She slowly sipped on her wine and played with the rim of the glass.

"Why didn't you become a teacher?" I asked. I needed

to know how the girl I had known became the woman before me.

"After…after everything that happened, I didn't think I was worthy."

Her honest answer shocked me, and I remained quiet for a long time, trying to gather my thoughts.

Had she really been punishing herself this entire time?

"The children of the world deserve great teachers, Mia," I finally said.

She nodded. "They do. I'm just not sure I'm one of them."

Giving her a half-grin, I replied, "How do you know until you try?"

I took a swig of my beer and grabbed a roll from the basket the waiter had brought over. She watched as I pulled it apart and buttered it. I smiled as I set half of it on her plate and the other half on mine.

She reached for it and asked, "What about you? Why aren't you out doing what you love?"

Because I would have to have a working heart left for that, I wanted to reply.

"I tried after school, but there weren't any opportunities, so my pretty face landed me a job in sales." I flashed a wolfish grin in her direction.

She rolled her eyes at me. "Well, what about now?"

I didn't have an answer for that, but before I had a chance to make one up, we were interrupted.

"Mia?"

She turned her head at the same time I did, and we both found ourselves facing Brent Malcolm. She smiled brightly and politely rose out of her seat to give him a hug. He held her a bit too tightly for my liking, and I had to resist the childish urge to throw a roll at him.

"It's so good to see you," Mia said, returning to her seat.

"It's been too long. Can you believe our high school reunion is just around the corner?" he said, flashing a white toothy grin.

I fucking hate this guy.

"I haven't really thought about it, but I guess you're right!" she replied.

"And, Garrett!" he said. "So good to see you, man!"

I nodded, and we shook hands.

"Well, I guess I really missed my opportunity back then, huh? I can't believe you guys are still together," he said, obviously fishing for information as he glanced down at Mia's ringless finger.

"He's harmless, Garrett. He's just a flirt. He flirts with all the girls," Mia said.

"I don't buy it, Mia. He pays special attention to you, and I don't like it."

"Just let it go, babe. I belong to you and no one else."

Two weeks later, I'd put my fist to Brent's face after hearing him talk about Mia in the locker room. Mia hadn't talked to me for two days, thinking I'd overreacted. I never told her about the locker room, not wanting her to know what he'd said, but he'd deserved it, every goddamn bit.

"Oh, um…actually, we aren't together anymore. We're just friends now," Mia said sheepishly.

Brent's eyes perked up, and he met my hard stare and smiled. My fists tightened under the table as his pearly white smile turned toward Mia.

"Well, how about that?" he said.

He looked around. For what, I didn't know. *Probably his wife, knowing him.*

"I'd love to catch up some more, but I'm out celebrating with a few of my buddies. I just finished my MBA," he said with a grin.

Smug bastard.

"Let me give you my phone number, Mia, so we can get together later and catch up privately."

"Oh, um…sure," Mia said before giving a polite smile as her eyes met mine.

Just friends?

No, we were definitely not just friends.

Mia was mine.

MIA

Garrett's eyes had barely left the piece of paper with Brent's phone number since he'd walked away. The waiter had come with our food, and I didn't think Garrett had done more than shovel a few angry bites of chicken parmesan into his mouth. He'd just pushed the rest around his plate.

I was afraid to touch it. *Do I leave it on the table? Or quietly tuck it into my purse before we leave? Do I want to see Brent? No, not really, but it seems rude to leave it on the table. What if he sees it when he's leaving?*

Garrett and I finished our dinner in silence. He handed over his credit card to the waiter, and we waited for him to return. I took the last sip of my wine and wished I had more. I could use a little more liquid courage right now to gather up the courage to ask what was going through that man's head right now.

Finally, the waiter reappeared, and Garrett angrily scribbled his name on the receipt. I grabbed my purse, and I knew he was waiting to see what I would do. It made me angry, so I grabbed the paper off the table and slipped it into the front pocket of my purse. His eyes flared, and he lunged forward, taking my arm. After escorting us quickly out of the restaurant, he kept the quick pace down the block toward my house. His hand slipped possessively around my waist, and his fingers curled into my hip.

"You're angry," I whispered.

His fingers dug further into my hip. "No, Mia, I'm livid," he answered.

"Why?"

He stopped, forcing people around us to shift their walking patterns, as we stood, frozen, in the middle of the sidewalk. I looked around, afraid of making a scene, but he cupped my chin until all I saw were his intense green eyes.

"Why? Jesus, Mia." He dropped his hand and stalked away.

He was almost a full block ahead of me until my street appeared, and I caught up.

"You're not my boyfriend, Garrett. You can't tell me who I can and cannot see," I said. I had no idea why I was pushing this. I had no intentions of seeing Brent, but it angered me that he thought he had a say in it.

I pushed ahead of him, climbing the steps of my front porch, and I reached for my keys. He was right behind me, and he pushed his hand into my purse and then pulled out the piece of paper I'd shoved in there at the restaurant.

"I don't need any reminders, Mia. Every fucking hellish day of my life reminds me that you are no longer mine. But this? This is who you want now?" he asked, holding up the piece of paper.

I stared at him blankly with my keys in my hand. He

took a step forward, which caused me to take a step back. When my back hit the wood of the front door, he took another step until his body brushed against my hips, and I shuddered.

"Is it?" he whispered.

I didn't answer, so he pushed harder. Letting the scrap of paper fall to the ground, his now free hand slid up my bare thigh until it found the button of my shorts. I steadied his hand, and his heated green eyes moved up my body and met my own.

"Someone could see us," I warned, reminding him of our current position on my porch.

"Good. Maybe Brent will hear you screaming my name from down the street."

Garrett made quick work of the button and zipper, and I moaned when his hand slipped under my panties and found my flesh.

"Tell me who you want, Mia," he demanded as his fingers danced along my clit.

I whimpered and pushed against him, and he rewarded me by thrusting two fingers inside me. I trembled as the pressure began to build.

"Say it, Mia."

"You. I only want you."

His mouth slammed against mine, his tongue plunging and sweeping against my own in a punishing rhythm. His fingers continued to work in and out of my body, making my body pulsate and throb with every mastered thrust. Just when I thought my knees might buckle, the orgasm took swept through my body, sending me into an endless wave of pleasure. I sagged against him, breathing heavily. He kissed my forehead and cheek. Then, he pulled the keys from my hand. I hadn't realized I was still holding them. The dog was barking, and I hadn't even noticed.

Shit, an entire army could have probably walked by, and I wouldn't have noticed.

Garrett reached behind me and unlocked the door. He picked me up, letting my legs wrap around him, and he carried me inside, kicking the door closed behind him. Sam, unfortunately, did not get the greeting he was used to as we both stared into each other's eyes.

I bent down and kissed him, no longer caring what any of this meant. His fingers threaded my hair as the kiss grew urgent.

"I need you, Mia. Fuck, I'll always need you," he confessed.

I kissed him again, and that was the only answer he needed.

I stayed wrapped in his embrace as he walked up the stairs until we entered my bedroom. Letting my legs slowly slide to the floor, I found the hem of his T-shirt and lifted it over his head. My hands brushed over the tanned lines of his chest, and I placed tiny kisses to his belly button. He watched as I did this while he ran his fingers through my hair.

Eventually, he decided he'd had enough attention, and his hands bunched the fabric of my tank top. He pulled it off from my body, exposing the lacy purple bra underneath. I wiggled out of my already unbuttoned shorts, so he could admire the matching panties.

His eyes swept over me, making me blush. "You better not have bought those for anyone else."

"I might have purchased these the other day while thinking of you," I confessed.

He pulled me into his grasp and devoured me, his

possessiveness taking over once again. His hands were everywhere as he led us to the bed. The backs of my knees hit the edge and I gently fell onto the soft mattress. I scooted backward until I was lying in the center with my knees up and my legs spread while I sported a huge grin.

"Damn," he cursed.

He made quick work of his clothes, dropping his shorts and boxers to the ground, as l tried to keep the drooling to a minimum. I was trying to maintain a sexy stance, and drooling would definitely kill that image.

"Do you have a condom?" he asked, suddenly stopping to look around.

The possibility of me having a condom lying around seemed to make him suddenly very conflicted.

"No," I answered.

He let out a breath of relief.

Jealous oaf.

Of course, a second later, his eyes flashed back up to me, naked on the bed, and he reconsidered that earlier bit of relief.

"I can't get pregnant," I said.

"Oh, you're on the pill?"

"Yeah, something like that," I answered.

As he crawled up the bed and hovered over me, I felt my heart leap in my chest. It had done that a lot since finding Garrett in that farmers' market.

His eyes met mine, and he smirked. "Straddle me."

"What?"

"There seems to be a few things I'm fuzzy on still, and I might need some reminding. I need you to straddle me."

I laughed and watched as he lay down. I straddled his waist, but he shook his head.

"Higher," he commanded.

I looked at him, and he just nodded. So, I scooted up higher to his chest.

"Higher, Mia." His voice had lost its playfulness.

Widening my legs, I straddled his shoulders, but he grabbed me around the waist and hauled me higher until I was above his face.

"Garrett, no! I'll smother you."

Embarrassed, I tried to squirm off, but he held me firmly, and with one lick of his tongue, I was moaning.

"That's it," he said against my tender flesh. "Now, ride my face, Mia."

Despite my inhibitions, I did. I grabbed the top of my headboard and moved. Slowly at first, I thrust my hips as he licked and then twisted his tongue in my core. With each moan, his passion grew, which only made my hips go faster. His hands roamed up my hips and down to my ass until I felt my core tightening, and everything exploded. I screamed out his name and felt him grab me around the hips before flipping me onto my back. He kissed me hard, and I could still taste myself on him.

His eyes were wild and frenzied. "No more telling people we're friends, Mia. You're mine."

I cried out as he entered me without warning. Every thrust was hard and exquisite, like he was rebranding me as his from the inside out. He pushed my knees forward, adjusting the angle, so he could penetrate even deeper. I could feel my body tightening and squeezing him as I climbed higher toward another climax.

"Oh God, Garrett," I cried.

"Come for me again, Mia. Scream out my name."

I did. As the world grew hazy again for the third time tonight, I screamed his name over and over through as my body continued to shake and fall apart. He cried out mine seconds later as he released into me. It was a miracle the cops hadn't shown up.

We spent the night naked, cuddled in each other arms, and the last thought I had before drifting off to sleep was that I hope he was still holding me when the sun rose the next day.

GARRETT

For the first time since I watched her walk away from me that fateful day with her dark brown hair shining in the sunlight as she carried my hopes and dreams with her, I awoke, not fearing the day ahead.

No horrid dreams had chased me in my sleep, reminding me of the life I'd lost. I was peacefully nudged awake by the sunrise breaking over the horizon, and I felt more refreshed than I had in years. Spending an entire night dream- free and not without waking up, shaking and covered in sweat, could do a lot for a guy.

I felt like I could run a marathon.

But there was only one thing I wanted to do.

Find Mia.

My hands searched the sheets but came up empty, and my eyes opened to find myself alone in the room. Only her sweet smell was keeping me company. Through the paper-thin walls of Mia's historic home, I heard the refrigerator open and footsteps downstairs. I quickly threw on my boxers and searched around for my shirt, but I couldn't find it anywhere.

I shrugged and then jogged quietly down the stairs in search of my missing prize.

She was there, humming and singing to herself in the kitchen, as she was cracking eggs and then making coffee.

Her hair was pulled to the side in a loose braid, and she was in my shirt. My dick twitched at the mere sight of her in my clothes. I didn't know how I'd stayed away for so long, but now that I had her, I couldn't stop touching her. I wanted my hands on her every second of every day just to make sure she wasn't a figment of my imagination.

I stepped into the kitchen until my chest brushed her back, and I snaked my hand around her waist.

"You stole my shirt," I said against her hair.

She turned in my arms, and her eyes took in my naked chest. Her lip curved into a smile. "Yes, and look how well that worked out for me."

Reaching behind her, I pushed away the bowl of egg mixture she'd been working on, and I hoisted her up onto the counter. She yelped out in surprise as I spread her legs and stepped between to close the gap between us.

"I was making you breakfast." She stuck her lip out in an attempt to fake a pout.

I caught it between my teeth as my hands worked their way under the T-shirt she'd stolen. Shit, she could have it. It looked a hell of a lot better on her. But for now, it was going on the floor.

Her fingers made heated pathways along my abdomen. Like a forest fire consuming everything it came in contact with, I felt out of control, and Mia was my kerosene. After nuzzling her neck, I left a trail of kisses down her collarbone and over her breast until my mouth closed over that tiny pink bud. I sucked and licked, causing her to cry out, as my hand massaged her other breast. I repeated the process until I had her panting and begging for more.

She leaned back on her elbows on the counter and looked up at me. Her half-lidded gaze almost knocked me to the floor as she wrapped a leg around my waist and pulled me closer.

"You want me to fuck you on the counter, Mia?"

She nodded, but I wanted to hear her say it.

"Then, tell me," I commanded, running my fingers under the waistband of her panties.

She bit her lip, making me almost lose my cool demeanor. I loved it when she bit her lip. I'd once taken her under the bleachers after a football game because she'd bitten her lip too much and distracted me during the game.

"I want you, Garrett," she whispered.

"You want me to what?" I countered.

Mia had been raised in a very rigid house. She'd uttered her first curse word in my presence at the age of fifteen. It had taken hours and a dare to finally get her to do it. She'd been terrified that her mother would somehow hear her from ten miles down the street.

"Fuck me," she said quietly.

"What? I couldn't hear you."

I bunched up her panties in my hand, waiting for her next response. I was playing the man-in-charge role well, but inside, I was dying. I needed to be inside her so damn bad that I was nearly vibrating, but I wanted to hear her scream it.

"Fuck me!" she cried.

In one swift motion, I ripped the panties from her body and slid the boxers from my body.

I slammed into her. "Like this?" I said through gritted teeth.

"Yes, God, yes!" she screamed.

I spread her legs wide and pulled her ass as close to the edge of the counter as I could without risking her falling off. She was still propped up on her elbows so that she could watch. Our eyes locked as I relentlessly pumped into her body, giving her everything I had.

But it wasn't enough. I needed more. Wrapping my arms under her body, I pulled her up so she was facing me. Now we were touching everywhere. My hands roamed her waist, her breasts, and over every other inch of skin her body owned. Our lips fused together, and my tongue merged with hers, thrusting into her mouth, as my body continued to pound into her.

Her body gripped my cock like a glove, and I knew I wouldn't last much longer. Just when I felt my balls tighten to the point of no return, she cried out as I felt her body squeeze my dick like a vise, and I was gone. I spilled into her, feeling like I'd just run that marathon I swore I could have done when I woke up.

We had worked up quite a sweat.

My forehead found hers, and I tried to find my breath again. She bent down and her lips brushed my chest, and she kissed it as she clung to me.

"Garrett, what are we doing?" she whispered.

I'd known this was coming. She'd fallen asleep in my arms last night, and while lying awake, tangled in her sheets and nuzzled against her, I'd tried to prepare.

"I don't know, but I don't want to stop."

Her eyes lifted and met mine.

"I honestly don't know what we are doing, Mia, but I know that I can't walk out that door and go back to whatever we were doing before. I just can't. I don't know where this will take us, but I know one thing. I can't seem to move forward in my life without you in it."

Her gaze dropped once more, and her forehead fell against my chest. "You deserve better, Garrett, so much better," she murmured.

I lifted her chin. "I don't want anyone else, Mia. This turn in our relationship doesn't mean it's an instant fix for all past transgressions. I don't know how to forgive you…"

She tried to look away, but I kept a firm grasp on her chin.

"But the difference now is that I want to. I want to forgive you. Let me try."

Tears fell down her cheeks, and I carefully caught them with my thumbs and whisked them away.

"No tears, baby. We'll figure this out," I said with an encouraging smile I hoped she bought.

I was playing it by ear as much as she was, and I was probably just as scared. I had so much to overcome if we were going to make it through to the other side of whatever stood between happiness and us.

"So, what happens now?" she asked after the tears dried up.

I bent down and handed her back the shirt I'd thrown on the floor. "We take it one day at a time. Right now, you're going to make me breakfast because I'm starving from that workout you gave me," I said with a wicked grin. "Then, we're going to go do whatever the hell you want for the rest of the day."

She slipped the shirt over her head, and I silently

mourned the absence of her breasts from my view, but it was nice to see her back in my shirt. I slipped back into my boxers and helped her off the counter. I held her in my arms a bit longer.

"Don't you have to work?" she asked, glancing at the clock.

It was just after seven in the morning on a Wednesday.

"Yes, but I think I just came down with the flu, and it's bad. I'm gonna need a day off, maybe two."

She looked stunned as she hit me on the arm. "I'm appalled, Garrett Finnegan! Playing hooky? I thought workaholics didn't take days off."

Sliding my hands underneath the T-shirt so that I could feel her bare ass again, I laughed. "I think I've been a workaholic long enough, don't you? Besides, I've never taken a sick day before. I want to see what all the fuss is about."

"Hmm…well, lucky for you, I don't have to work for the next two days," she said as her fingers danced along my chest.

"I know. I checked with Leah."

Her eyes widened, and I chuckled.

"You checked up on me?"

"I did. I wanted to see when you'd be home, so I could drop off the flowers. We had a nice chat."

She looked horrified, and I couldn't help but grin from the torture I was putting her through.

"What did she say?"

"She said…"

"What, Garrett? Tell me!"

"She said you need to make me breakfast."

I got a slap on the ass for that one, which I thoroughly enjoyed.

After Garrett called in sick, I made him a sorry excuse for eggs, and we retreated upstairs. He proceeded to take full advantage of my shower, making sure the door was wide open. He made a show of sliding his boxers down his firm ass as he waited for the water to warm. I finally caved and jumped in with him. We emptied the hot water tank while finding innovative ways to pleasure each other in the tight space. When I dropped down in front of him and took his hard length in my waiting warm mouth, he cried out my name and fisted my hair until he was shaking and shooting his release into the back of my throat. I gave him a grin and licked the tip clean before I climbed up his body. He pressed me against the wall and showed me his gratitude in many inventive ways.

He carried me out of the bathroom, wrapped in a fuzzy green towel, and he took time drying my hair and body, like I was the most precious thing in the world. He did it with such care and sensitivity, and I was nearly sobbing by the time his fingers left my skin.

I didn't deserve any of his tenderness, any of his soft words or care, but I was taking it anyway. I was the worst kind of person. I was selfish and untrustworthy, but I couldn't walk away again. A life without this man wasn't living, and I'd spent too long living half of a life. Now that I'd felt what it was like to breathe again, I couldn't fathom going back. I would hold on to him even if I didn't deserve to.

There was so much he didn't know, so much I should explain.

He deserved to know everything. But where should I begin?

"Where's that lotion you always wear?" Garrett said against my ear after lying down next to me on the bed.

As he caressed my skin, I smiled, feeling a little giddy that he'd noticed the lotion I still wore. It was the same brand I'd worn since I was fifteen, and I'd never changed it.

"Mia, did you know that you always smell like oranges?"

I smiled but covered it up quickly as I turned in my seat to address him.

Garrett Finnegan did strange things to my body that I'd never experienced before. Whenever I was around him, my heart fluttered. It went beyond a crush, and the thought scared me.

"It's my lotion. Does it bother you?" I asked hesitantly.

I'd bought it at this fancy store my mom had taken me to. I'd fallen in love with the fresh smell, and I'd secretly thought he would like it, too.

What if I was wrong and he hated it?

Oh God, did I smell awful?

"No, it makes me want to lick you."

"You're blushing," Garrett said with a grin.

"I was thinking about that time you told me you wanted to lick me."

His grin widened, and he pushed me down farther on the bed, so he could stretch out above me. "It drove me crazy. I'd sit in class and feel like I was swimming in it. It made my mouth water and my dick hard." His nose moved down my neck as he left a path of kisses. "It still does, and now, I want to rub it all over your body."

He hadn't been kidding. He spent an hour rubbing the orange-scented lotion over every inch of my skin, paying special care to my breasts and the inside of my thighs. He rubbed his circles closer and closer to my core until I was begging him to touch me. By the time his fingers touched my clit, I was so wet and ready that I nearly exploded on contact.

It took us half the day to eat breakfast, shower, and drive over to Garrett's, so he could change.

"So, what do you want to do for the rest of the day?" he asked before shoving a ham sandwich in his mouth.

Besides last night in the restaurant, the man never stopped eating. After he'd changed, he'd placed a soft kiss on my nose and then sauntered into his tiny kitchen where he whipped up two ham sandwiches.

"Oh, did you want one?" he said between bites.

I laughed and jumped in to make my own while answering his previous question. "I don't know. Why don't you pick the activity for the day? It is, after all, your first sick day. Better make it count," I said with a wink.

He'd finished off his sandwich and moved on to a bag of chips as he thought for a moment.

"Hmm…are you sure you want me to decide?"

"Yep," I answered.

"Okay, but you can't complain."

"I trust you."

"Good. We need to stop back at your house for a bathing suit."

A bathing suit? How bad could that be?

It was bad, really bad.

"Rafting?" I squeaked, looking at the tiny building with the large rafting sign displayed.

We'd broken off the main road and turned down a

lone beaten path toward the James River. I'd figured we were going swimming or floating but not rafting.

"You know I don't do rafts!"

"No, you just haven't gone before," he corrected.

"Yes, because I'm terrified!"

"Why?"

"Because the river moves, Garrett. It *moves*. I don't want to be in a tiny inflatable boat, floating down the river, with no ability to turn around!"

He laughed and cupped my chin. "You're being irrational."

I folded my arms over my chest. "You're being irrational," I said, acting like a five-year-old.

His laugh turned into a smirk, and it was infectious. I couldn't help but grin back.

"Fine," I agreed. "But if I die, you're going to feel really bad about it."

"You're not going to die, baby. You'll have me, and for fuck's sake, it's the James, not the Grand Rapids!"

My stomach fluttered every time he called me *baby*. Besides renaming me Mia, it was what he always called me, and hearing him fall back into it so easily made my heart swell.

"Come on, let's go inside," he urged.

"Okay." I was rewarded with a huge grin, one I hadn't seen in ages, and it made me incredibly happy to be the one who had made him smile again.

With everything he'd been through in the last few weeks, he deserved to smile again.

We both hopped out of Garrett's car, and he came around the back to walk by my side. His arm went casually over my shoulder, and I naturally melted into him, the two of us falling into a natural rhythm.

The door chimed as we entered the small rafting company. A few other customers milled around, waiting for the scheduled tour to begin. There was a small store set up with snacks, drinks, and a few rafting supplies.

Garrett looked down at my flip-flops and frowned.

"What?" I asked.

"You are going to lose the flip-flops in the water." His eyes traveled around the store until he found a rack displaying water shoes.

"I'm fine," I tried to argue.

But he hauled me over to the rack and started sorting through the shoes. He didn't need to ask me what size I wore. He remembered, picking up a size seven in black and pink.

"Which color, baby?"

I started to disagree, folding my arms over my chest in protest, but he just rolled his eyes and bent down on the ground. He lifted my foot up on his muscular thigh, forcing me to balance on one foot.

"Pink or black, Mia?"

I let out an exasperated sigh, but its effectiveness was lost when my lips curved into a goofy grin.

"Fine. Pink."

"Good choice. Very girlie."

He slipped my flip-flop off, and he began to help me put on the water shoes. He pulled the tag off, so he could pay for them whenever the store clerk decided to show up. He'd just finished putting on my right shoe when the store clerk, who was clearly not worried about theft, finally decided to make an appearance.

He was tall and lean, and as he turned around to greet everyone, I heard Garrett mutter a curse under his breath.

Brent's eyes caught mine, and he instantly smiled.

"Well, long time no see. Hello, Mia." His eyes briefly met Garrett's in greeting. "Garrett, good to see you again."

Garrett didn't say anything in return. He just continued to stare at Brent like he was the devil incarnate.

"So, here to take a trip down the James?"

"Uh…yes," I answered.

"Good, I'll be your guide."

Crap.

"I thought you were in graduate school?" Garrett said with a menacing tone.

My fingers found his and weaved around them. I was hoping my touch would keep him from killing our rafting instructor.

"I am, or was. I just completed my MBA. I'd taken a few years off in between to work for my dad, but I figured it was time to spread my wings." His white toothy grin grew—along with his arrogance.

Brent's family came from the same social circle as mine. I'd known him far longer than Garrett, having attended social events with Brent since I was in grade school. His dad was a major player at a corporate bank, and Brent had wanted nothing more in life than to follow in his father's footsteps.

"So, why are you here?" Garrett motioned to the run-down rafting business, which was about as far from the stuffy banking world as one could get.

"Oh, well, I love the river, and it's a great way to stay in shape and meet beautiful women," he said with a wink.

Garrett's hand tightened on mine.

Brent pointed at our joined hands. "I thought you two were just friends?"

I opened my mouth to answer, but Garrett beat me to it.

"A slight oversight, which has been corrected—permanently. In fact, did you happen to hear anything last night as you were stepping out of the restaurant?"

My eyes widened, remembering his heated words as his fingers had grazed my core.

Maybe Brent will hear you screaming my name from down the street.

Garrett and Brent shared angry stares that were about to escalate, and I had no idea what to do.

"Well, it's probably for the best anyway. It's not like I could take you home—not after your parents made such spectacles of themselves, fleeing town with their tails between their legs."

My eyes flew to his. The light flirty glow he'd greeted us with was now replaced with ice and menace.

"What are you talking about?" I asked softly.

"Oh, come on, Mia. Everyone knew. A teenage girl can't puke her way through the last few months of high school and have it go unnoticed. When you bailed right after graduation, the rumors only got worse. That's why I was so surprised to see you two together yesterday. I figured he was done with you after that."

I felt nauseous. Everything in my stomach suddenly wanted to defy gravity and purge out of me. This couldn't be happening. It was my secret—mine and Garrett's. Now, I find out that everyone had known. If that were true, Liv would have said something. Wouldn't she?

I heard the crack seconds before my eyes recognized the force of Garrett's fist colliding with Brent. With little effort, Garrett quickly had Brent pinned to the wall.

"Listen to me, you piece of shit," Garrett said with gritted teeth.

Everyone in the store was now eerily silent, afraid to make a peep.

"You're going to apologize to Mia, and you're going to do it quickly."

Brent began to protest, but he quickly changed his mind as Garrett tightened his grip.

"I'm sorry."

"I'm sorry what?" Garrett pushed.

"I'm sorry, Mia. I'm sorry for saying what I did," Brent said.

Garrett released his hold on Brent, and he slumped to the floor. Garrett's eyes found mine, and he was instantly by my side, wrapping me in his arms. We vacated the store. Tears I hadn't realized were there were streaming down my face.

"Shh…baby, it's okay. It's over."

He helped me into the car and even fastened my seat belt. Once he was strapped in and the engine roared to life, he looked over and gently swept away my tears.

"We didn't pay for my shoes," I said quietly.

He gave a hint of a smile, and his eyes softened. "Consider them a parting gift from Brent."

I didn't think we would be going rafting anytime soon.

Chapter Nineteen

He'd held me all night, soaking up my tears as they fell onto his chest. His arms had encased me in warmth, and I'd never felt more precious.

When we awoke this morning, he wanted to call in sick again, but I was adamant. I would not be the reason for the demise of his career. He'd already taken one day, a first for him. If he took another, I was sure they'd send out a search party or a HAZMAT team.

"But I can't leave you like this," he'd said.

I could tell he had been conflicted.

"I'll be fine, really. I have Sam. There is also ice cream in the freezer and plenty of horrible daytime TV to keep me occupied."

His eyes had searched mine, and he'd finally relented. "Fine, but I'm not working a minute past five. I'll be home right after, and we'll order a pizza or something. We can watch one of those horrible chick flicks you used to love."

I'd smiled, realizing he'd referred to my home like it was ours. I didn't think he'd even noticed it, and I definitely wasn't going to point it out, but it had made my heart flutter, seeing how easily we had fallen back into place.

We were so different. Eight years had changed us both, yet we were still the same.

I'd offered to make him breakfast, but he'd wanted me to stay in bed, saying he would much rather have that vision in his head for the rest of the day.

After a long, lingering kiss that left me dizzy, he was out the door, and I was alone.

For about ten minutes, I seriously contemplated going to work, but then I realized I didn't have a job where I could do that. Shift work didn't allow me to just pop in and work whenever I wanted. I couldn't be a workaholic like Garrett even if I tried.

I took a long, hot shower, letting the hot spray work my muscles until the water turned cold. I spent a ridiculous amount of time rubbing lotion into my skin, remembering the way Garrett's fingers and hands had massaged and moved along my body.

Once dressed, I dried my hair and threw it up into a ponytail, and then I checked the clock.

One hour.

That was all that had passed.

Damn. This is going to be a long day.

I needed to find something to do to keep my mind off of yesterday. *Why did I ever think Brent was nice?* I should have known better.

Everyone at school had known I was pregnant, which means everyone knew what I eventually did. It didn't take a genius to put it together. Girls didn't run away to have babies anymore. It wasn't the fifties. Girls ran when they wanted to start over, and I'd run.

I'd run, which meant I hadn't been around to deal with any sideways glances, stares, or whispers. Had Garrett had to endure any of that? Had he known about the rumors, too? If it were only me involved, I honestly wouldn't have cared if everyone knew. *Let them drag me through the mud. But Garrett?* I didn't want anyone thinking for a second that he'd forced me into a decision I didn't want or that he hadn't been there for me.

That was what hurt the most about people knowing. I'd always hoped that I had protected Garrett by disappearing.

Letting out a huff of breath, I realized I was doing a terrible job of distracting myself. My trusty four-legged sidekick and I headed downstairs, and I started searching around the kitchen for something to eat for breakfast. Besides the small amount of pasta fixings Garrett brought over the night before, I was out of almost everything. I seriously needed to make a run to the grocery store.

I pulled out a box of cereal and opened the fridge.

No milk. Great.

As I was grumbling to myself, my doorbell chimed, and Sam and I ran to the door to answer it.

Standing with a glorious bag of groceries was Liv.

"You brought food!" I exclaimed.

"Yep, nice to see you, too."

"You brought food!" I clapped my hands together and took the bag from her. My mood immediately fell when I saw the contents. "What the hell is this crap?" I asked, making my way back into the kitchen.

Sam pranced and wagged his tail in reaction to our visitor. He and Liv had developed quite a deep bond since he'd stayed with her a few times. She'd jokingly told me that Sam was the only male she'd ever given her heart to.

"It's food," she answered blankly.

"This is not food—unless you're a rabbit."

"That is people food, real people food. It's vegetables, flax seed, organic muffins, and cage-free eggs."

I made a gagging noise that earned me a slap to the ass.

"I brought you groceries!" She pouted.

"You brought me hippie food. Sometimes, a girl just wants a milkshake and a hamburger."

"Well, he didn't exactly specify an order when he called." She was pulling out groceries I couldn't even name and putting them away.

"Who called? Garrett called you?"

Her lips curved into a smile, and she nodded. "Mmhmm…"

"He called you this morning?"

"Yes. He said you had a rough night, and he didn't want you to be alone all day. So, he asked if I could come over and spend the day with you. He quickly added that he'd eaten you out of house and home, so he told me to bring sustenance."

I felt a little blush, and I tried to hide the smile consuming my face.

"Oh my God!"

"What?" I tried to feign innocence.

"After that phone call, I thought maybe you guys were rekindling, taking it slow. But holy shit! You're doing the nasty with Garrett Finnegan again!"

I snorted out a laugh, and she began jumping up and down in triumph.

"I knew it! Now, spill!" She pulled a few brown muffins sprinkled with oats out of a container. They looked like they could take out a window with a single toss.

She handed one to me on a plate, and I gave it a doubtful look.

"What do you want me to say? Fine, yes, we're sleeping together."

I was right. The muffin was harder than a baseball. I slipped it into the microwave and waited for it to warm.

"Okay, but what does that mean?"

Hearing the ding, I pulled out my breakfast and grabbed some butter from the fridge. Liv gave me a judgmental look but didn't say a word. If she was going to make me eat this shit, she would have to deal with me slathering it in butter.

"I honestly don't know. He's made it crystal clear that we are not seeing other people, but I don't know much beyond that. We have a lot to work through."

Liv decided to forgo tea and had coffee with me instead. We took our breakfast into the living room and sat down on the couch while I worked up the courage to say what needed to be said.

After another sip of coffee, I finally asked, "Liv, when I left after graduation, were there rumors about me?"

Her eyes met mine, and she took the time to set down her plate and coffee.

"Is that why Garrett sent me over here? Is that why you were so upset? Mia, what happened?"

I let out a lengthy breath of air that I'd been holding in, and I told her how we'd run into Brent at the restaurant and Garrett's anger over the phone number.

"That's kind of hot," she said.

"Pay attention!" I snapped. I couldn't help but grin though. I continued on from there, telling her about Garrett's plan to get me on a raft.

She laughed at the thought until I got to the part about Brent basically telling me I was trash.

"That dirty rat bastard!" she yelled.

"Liv, it's fine. Garrett took care of it. Now, please, answer my question. Were there rumors?"

"You left so suddenly. You know there were bound to be a few."

"And before I left?" I asked.

Her eyes shifted, and I could tell she knew something.

"Liv, please tell me."

"I didn't believe a single word, Mia. Yes, everyone thought you were pregnant. A freshman heard you throwing up in the restroom and then crying with Garrett. Someone else saw you run out of class a week later. I tried to tell them that it was nothing, but it was high school."

She'd stuck up for me. The entire time, she'd defended me.

"They weren't rumors, Liv. It was true," I confessed.

"What?"

"I was pregnant."

"Oh my God, Mia. Why didn't you tell me? I would have been there for you." Her hands found mine and gripped them tightly.

"We didn't tell anyone, not even our parents."

"Is that why Garrett proposed?" she asked.

I smiled, remembering that happy memory when he'd asked me to marry him. I never once felt like he had done it out of duty or responsibility. His eyes had met mine, and I'd seen nothing but love shining through.

"That's why we moved it up so quickly, but he wanted to marry me, regardless of the baby."

"But something changed?" she asked hesitantly.

"Don't they always? I was young and easily swayed by my parents. I told them, thinking they'd support me. God, I was stupid. My mother convinced me that I would ruin Garrett's life by going through with it."

"So, you ran."

I nodded. "So, I ran."

"Does Garrett know why you left?"

"No, it doesn't matter."

Her hands squeezed mine. "It does matter. Don't you think he deserves to know everything?"

It was a question I'd thought about so many times.

But I'd always come to the same answer.

"It doesn't change the past."

GARRETT

"I am so fucked," I said to no one as I surveyed the amount of unfinished work on my desk. That was just the paper. I still had a ton of emails, reports, and a dozen other things to go through.

I'd never been so far behind in my life. I was always the go-getter, the man who finished first and asked for more. Looking down at the clock on my computer, it registered that I'd been in the office for almost four hours, and I'd accomplished nothing.

Not only was I behind but now I was lazy, too.

And the kicker was that I didn't care, not one fucking bit.

I was just sitting in my chair, counting down the minutes until I could run for the elevator and leave.

So, this was what the rest of America felt like?

It was boring.

For the first time since starting my job, I realized it was nauseatingly boring. I'd always hated it, but I'd just been too busy to care.

My phone chirped, and I checked it. A text from Liv appeared, saying she'd just arrived at Mia's and she was feeding her.

I smiled, glad that Mia wasn't alone and was being taken care of. I hated the thought of her being by herself today after what she had gone through.

I could have killed Brent Malcolm with my bare hands. I always knew he was a jerk, but yesterday, he'd proven he was a Grade A asshole. Not being one to listen in on high school gossip, I'd never known the rumors floating around about Mia. Had I known, I would have protected her as best as I could.

A knock on my office door pulled me out of my thoughts, and I found Kara walking in. Her pencil skirt and tight blouse did nothing for me as she neared, but I suddenly wondered what Mia would look like dressed like this.

Is this how she dressed for work in her old life?

I couldn't picture my Mia in an office, working files and pushing numbers.

My Mia.

It had been less than two days, and I'd already fallen back into my old ways.

"Hey, Kara."

"Hey, just came in to check on you."

"Huh?" I asked in confusion.

"You were sick, and I wanted to make sure you were feeling better."

Oh, that. Visions of taking Mia on the kitchen counter came to mind—her body reacting to my every touch, shattering as she pulsated around me.

Best sick day ever.

"Right. I feel much better, thanks." I might have thrown a little cough in there for effect.

"Great!" she said brightly. Her hands folded together, and she lingered. "I was also wondering if you wanted to grab a bite to eat."

"What? Now?"

"Well, it is lunchtime."

Her eyes were hopeful, and she bit her lip as she waited for my answer. When Mia did this, it would drive me to my knees, but I felt nothing seeing Kara do the exact same gesture.

"Kara, I don't want you to get the wrong idea. I'm seeing someone."

"Oh." Her eyes were downcast, and the look of defeat was clearly written all over her face. "Is it serious?" she asked.

I answered honestly, "She's the one."

Her eyes softened, and she smiled. "I'm happy for you, Garrett." She sounded genuine and sincere.

"Thank you, Kara,"

"Do you still want to grab some lunch? Friends only, I promise," she asked, throwing her hands up in defense.

I laughed but declined. "Actually, there's someone I'd like to visit."

Twenty minutes later, I had a bag of food, and I was once again knocking on a door. Lately, it seemed to be my thing.

Declan opened the door this time, and I heard Lily yell in glee.

He grinned. "That better be for me." He pointed to the huge bag of greasy food.

"Sure, but you've got to share."

He shrugged and invited me in.

"Leah's not here, if that's who you are looking for. She had to work."

"Nope," I answered, as I walked through the double doors, " I came to see you actually."

I followed him into their massive kitchen and pulled out the food as he set out the plates. While I placed the food on the plates, he set Lily down. She was now happily eating Cheerios in her high chair, blowing raspberry with her tongue.

"So, the food really was for me," he said with a grin, "Nice."

We made quick work of our food. Being men, we didn't talk much as we ate. We just shoveled food and washed it down.

Once I was sure I'd eaten an entire cow and a field of potatoes, I broke the silence. "Can I ask you something?"

"Are we going to have a heart-to-heart, Garrett? Because Leah will be home in, like, an hour, and she can totally take care of that shit."

I grinned. "What I need to ask, only you can answer."

"Okay, shoot."

I took a deep breath. "Were you ever able to forgive Connor's mother?"

Leah and Declan's oldest child was his from a previous relationship. Declan hadn't known Connor existed until a couple of years ago when Leah met Connor in an ER after his mother had been killed in a car accident. They had managed to put two and two together several months later. Heather, his ex-girlfriend, had chosen to keep Connor a secret from Declan.

Declan leaned back in his seat and stretched his neck, obviously giving himself a moment to think it through. "Eventually, yes, but it took a while. What she did was wrong, but it didn't make her a bad person."

"Even though she betrayed you?"

He nodded. "I didn't say it was an overnight revelation. It took a while. But we all have to make tough decisions, and when faced with extraordinary circumstances, even the greatest of us can choose wrong."

I let his words sink in. I'd never allowed myself to step into Mia's shoes. I'd never wanted to. From the time she'd left, it had been all about me—my feelings, my wounds, and my pain. I'd never stopped to think about her feelings, her wounds, or her pain. How much had she suffered over the years?

"What is this all about, Garrett?"

I told him everything. I told him about Mia and my love for her. I explained the pregnancy and our shock but elation.

"Becoming teenage parents hadn't been our plan, but we were going to make it work—together." I explained. Declan silently listened as I finally came clean about my past. I told him about the note that had destroyed me and how conflicted I'd been since Mia's return.

"And now?" he asked.

"I don't know, but I can't lose her again."

"Then, you've got to let it go, man. Love is pure. Don't let something like doubt or anger work its way in and taint it from the beginning. You'll never recover."

"I want to, more than anything. It's always been her. I just can't seem to find a way to get past it."

Lily chose this moment to bang on the tray of her high chair, sending Cheerios everywhere. A few landed in my hair, and Declan laughed.

With a light smack to the head, he gave me my answer. "Stop looking behind you, moron."

Chapter Twenty

Liv had spent the entire day making me laugh, reminding me what an amazing friend she was. I'd had other friends along the way since I left home, but none had been like Liv. She could read my mood with a single glance, hear my thoughts through my expressions, and know what my heart was saying even if I didn't.

After the great breakfast debacle, I convinced her that a walk would be nice. If we happened to find some edible lunch along the way, it would be even better.

We picked up sandwiches at a small cafe and spent the rest of the afternoon meandering through different stores. I picked up a new skirt and a pretty pair of earrings. Liv tried on practically everything her eyes saw, but she walked away only with a scarf. When I asked her what she was going to do with a scarf in the middle of August, she just smiled.

I suddenly didn't want to know.

After we walked back to my house, she said her good-byes, and then I ran upstairs and changed into my new skirt. For once, I wanted to look nice when Garrett showed up. Whenever he had come knocking on my door, I had answered it in cutoff shorts or yoga pants. I was feeling kind of slobby.

Barely fifteen minutes past five, Garrett came barreling through my front door—no knocking this time—lugging plastic bags from the home improvement store. Dressed in worn jeans and a dark T-shirt that tightly hugged his body, I wondered just how long he'd been away from work.

Before I got the chance to ask, he dropped the bags in the middle of the living room and swept me up into his arms. His mouth took mine in a fierce kiss as he dug his hands into my hair and pulled me closer.

When we finally broke apart, I was breathless.

My voice was ragged as I asked, "What was that for?"

"I missed you," he answered with a grin.

"You just saw me this morning!"

"Mmm…I know, but I have lost time to make up for, and you look amazing."

This time, when his lips touched mine, they were gentle. His mouth moved with mine, slowly tracing the soft fullness of my lips with his tongue. He pulled back, only to reach up and place a tender kiss on my forehead, and I melted. It was such a small thing but so significant in its symbolism.

"Why do you always kiss me on my forehead?" I asked, feeling a little silly every time he did so.

"I like to remind myself how perfect we are together," he answered with a shy smile.

"And kissing me on my forehead reminds you of this?"

"When we stand face-to-face and I pull you into my arms, you fit perfectly, like you are meant to be there, and I've found my missing puzzle piece. I remember the first time I held you and I bent down to kiss your forehead, I thought, Perfect.*"*

His green eyes found mine, and in them, I saw the boy I'd left coming back to me. The anger he'd become so accustomed to was starting to bleed away, and I only hoped I wouldn't hurt him again.

Then, you should tell him now, a voice in my head urged.

I quickly dismissed it, too swept up in my newfound bliss.

"Thank you for sending Liv over today. It was nice not to spend the day alone even if she did make me eat rabbit food."

He chuckled, and I poked his ribs.

"Ouch! It couldn't have been that bad."

"No? There are still some baseball muffins in the kitchen if you're hungry. Why don't you go try one?"

"No, I'm good."

"Wuss," I muttered.

"No, I'm just smarter than you."

I poked him in the ribs again, and he laughed.

"So, what's with all the bags? I don't see any food this time."

His exuberant grin sent my pulse racing as he reached down and picked up the bags he'd dropped on the floor. He motioned me over to the couch, and we sat down. He started pulling out paint swatches and tile samples.

"You're remodeling a house?" I asked.

"No, we are. I couldn't focus at work today, so I took a half day and went shopping."

I merely stared at him, completely tongue-tied.

He let out a nervous breath. "I wasn't here to help you

with the floors, and I hate that my anger got in the way of that. I'm sick of looking in the past when it comes to us. Wherever we're going, we need to be headed there together, and I can't do that if I'm constantly thinking about all the what-ifs and lost moments we could have had."

My lips parted, and I tried to interrupt him, but he stopped me, placing his finger on my lips.

"Let me finish. I know there are obstacles and road-blocks in our future, but the point to all of this is that we are creating a future, right?"

I nodded, unable to speak. A future with Garrett was all I'd ever wished for, and my heart ached in want from hearing the words.

"So, let's start doing it. We always wanted to fix up a house, and yours could definitely use it."

"Hey! I love my house." I pouted.

Chuckling, he touched my fingers, weaving our hands together. "I love your house, too, but it's definitely a fixer-upper. With a bit of work, it could be great." His eyes softened, and he smiled. "It just needs a bit of time and love, like us."

Yes! I wanted to scream it, but I held it together. He wasn't asking me to marry him. He just wanted permission to throw some paint on the walls.

"Okay, so where do we start?"

"Wherever you want. We can paint the walls and retile the bathrooms. Hell, we can even give you a new back-splash in the kitchen, if you want."

I looked around my house. I'd been living within these walls for two months, yet it didn't feel like home yet. There were no pictures on the white walls, and I had very little furniture. Nothing made it feel mine.

"I want to paint…every single wall."

He pulled out a huge metal ring that had every color imaginable hanging from it. Dangling it in front of me, he said, "Pick a room and a color!"

We ordered a pizza and spent the rest of the evening hunched over the rainbow of colors, pointing out all the various shades we loved and hated.

"Orange for the bedroom?" I asked with a bit of amusement.

"Yes, it's perfect."

"And why is it more perfect than this tranquil blue I picked out?"

"Because that room always has a lingering hint of orange leftover from your lotion, and I've always thought orange looks good on you."

"I'm not going to be wearing the bedroom," I reminded him.

"No, but I plan on you being naked in there most of the time, so it will be the closest thing to clothes your skin sees in there."

My breath caught at his smoldering words, and I suddenly didn't care if the room was hot pink with purple polka dots.

"Orange it is," I said quickly.

His face broke out into a smug grin. "I think we're done for tonight."

I nodded in agreement. "Yes, definitely."

"Race you to the bedroom?" he challenged.

"Deal!" I yelled, taking off in a run toward the steps.

By the time we got to the top of the stairs, neither of us cared who would win.

For the last three weeks, Mia and I had done nothing but paint. Mia had wanted every room a different color, and at first, I'd had serious doubts about her plan. But as we'd finished each room, the paint seemed to bring more and more vibrancy to the old house, resurrecting new life into the drab walls and bringing a renewed, fresh energy with every hue.

The house hadn't been the only thing benefiting from the color enhancements. With every flick of the paintbrush, I'd found myself falling deeply and permanently in love with Mia. I'd never stopped loving her, even when I wanted to hate her. As the anger had melted, I had been able to turn away from the past, and I had fallen harder.

During our epic paint project, we'd painted the master bedroom a burnt orange. As soon as the paint had dried, I'd shown Mia just how serious I was about keeping her naked. I'd stripped her bare and kept her occupied in bed for almost an entire weekend.

Next, we had tackled the other two bedrooms. We'd painted them various shades of tan since Mia hadn't decided what she wanted to do with them. The house was massive. It was the perfect size for a family, but it almost swallowed Mia whole. She had more space than she knew what to do with.

We'd moved downstairs after that, painting the kitchen a rich golden yellow that brought sunshine to the old cabinets and appliances. I couldn't wait to take a sledgehammer to some of these walls and make her a kitchen she'd be proud of. I'd mentioned that we needed to do some major repairs in there, but she had just shaken her head and said something about one step at a time.

She'd be singing a different tune if she was the one actually cooking in there.

After the kitchen, we'd moved into the office. To protect the brand-new floor, we'd laid down wall-to-wall plastic and taped it to the floorboards. Mia was not the neatest painter, and after watching her wield her paint roller like a psychopath, I didn't trust her not to ruin the floor.

As I stretched my aching back and yawned from the lack of sleep, I found myself grinning. I was physically exhausted from the marathon painting, but I'd never felt better.

"What are you grinning about?" Mia asked, catching me mid thought.

"Just thinking how I feel like an eighty-year-old man, but I couldn't be happier about it."

A tender smile touched her lips. "I don't know why we keep staying up so late. It's not like we're under a deadline."

I nodded in agreement, but I knew why we'd stayed up into the wee hours of the night, painting and talking, when we both had jobs and responsibilities the next day. We couldn't get enough of each other.

Every new minute I had with her felt like I was erasing one I'd lost.

I hadn't put a single hour of overtime in at work for a month. I'd managed to get my head back in the game, and I'd started getting shit done, but I wouldn't do more than I was required to anymore. I was now officially a retired workaholic. I'd reformed to a full-time minimalist. As soon as it reached five o'clock each day, I would practically fly out of the office. I'd cook a meal for us, or we'd run out for something down the street, and then we'd be back at the house, painting. I'd edge the walls with a paintbrush and listen as she spoke. She'd roll the paint up and down the wall, paint flying everywhere, and finally talk about her life.

At last, I had a rough outline of the life she'd had after me. I could at least picture her sitting in a classroom at the small private college she'd attended in Oregon. I had a vision now of her graduating and moving to Atlanta to begin her career.

She'd told me about some of her friends and how much she missed them. I'd suggested we take a trip there and visit, but she'd immediately turned me down.

Excitedly, she'd said, *It's okay. I'd rather go do something else. We should go to the beach!*

She'd opened up to me, yet I still felt she was hiding pieces of her life, and I didn't know why.

I looked around the half-painted room with boxes piled high and a small desk in the center.

"What are you going to do with this room?" I asked.

Mia surveyed the space as she turned. "I think I'm going to finally set up that clunker of a computer I have and use it to enroll in a few courses."

"As in college courses?"

She smiled and nodded.

"What are you going to take?" I asked, full of happy anticipation for her.

"I don't know yet, but I know I don't want to work in the hospital for the rest of my life, and I definitely don't want to go back to accounting."

"Get your teaching credential," I said suddenly.

"What?"

"It was always your dream to teach. Don't give up on that," I urged.

"But what would I teach?" she asked.

"Teach music. You'd be great at that."

"I don't know," she answered quietly.

She would be an amazing teacher. She was patient, encouraging, and loving. I knew the past kept her from doing what she loved, but we were learning to move on, and I wanted to see her happy.

"Oh, I'm supposed to ask you," she said moments later. "Leah and Declan are hosting an end-of-the-summer party at their house next weekend. They wanted to know if we could go?"

I turned with my brush in hand and asked in an amused tone, "So, now that you two are chummy, I don't even get a call?"

"Did you just use the word *chummy*? Maybe you weren't too far off with that eighty-year-old comment!"

"You better take that back," I warned, holding my paintbrush out toward her as I advanced.

She backed away and laughed. "You wouldn't!"

"Oh, don't tempt me, Mia."

I could see the mischief in her eyes seconds before she turned to dart away from me. I reached a hand out to pull her into my grasp, catching her easily.

"No!" she squealed as I dangled the paintbrush over her.

"Take it back." I laughed.

She looked at the brush and squirmed in my grip. "Sam will attack you. He'll defend me."

I looked over at Sam, who was looking at us with upturned ears and a waggling tail.

"Yep, he looks ferocious."

I thought about giving her a last chance, but now that I'd started the game, I really wanted to finish it. Taking my brush that was covered in a lovely shade of steel gray, I ran it down the length of her arm.

"No, Garrett!" she yelled, trying to get a hold of the brush.

My strength was no match for hers, and no matter how hard she tried, she couldn't get me to let go of her.

Suddenly, my hand went slack around the brush as her hand found its way to the front of my shorts. She palmed me, rubbing her fingers up and down, and I grew harder with each touch. As her hand reached around to grip me properly, I let go of the brush, splashing paint all over my legs. Mia yelled in triumph. I'd been duped, and now, I was covered in paint while sporting a rock-hard boner.

"You'll pay for that!"

She laughed and shouted as we both dove for control of the brush which had landed somewhere around my ankles. In the end, I was the victor and had Mia pinned to the ground. . Straddling her, I dangled the brush in the air above her while trying to decide the best punishment.

"Now, where shall I begin?"

"You're seriously not going to paint me, are you?" She wiggled beneath me, still hoping to win back the brush.

"Keep squirming, baby. I like it. Yes, I think I am going to paint you…but not with a brush."

I dropped the brush on the ground and reached for the tray of paint Mia had been using. I pulled it closer and dipped my index finger into the gray liquid. I lifted her shirt.

"Take it off," I instructed.

A little less resistant now, she complied. With a flick of my fingers, I unsnapped the front of her bra, exposing her breasts.

"You're not going to paint on my boobs, are you?" She laughed.

I gave her a wolfish grin but said nothing. I wasn't going to paint that specific area. I just enjoyed the view.

Her stomach sucked in as the cool paint made contact with her skin. I trailed my finger down to make a straight line. I got more paint and repeated this process until I spelled the word *mine* across her abdomen.

Her lips quirked up as her eyes raked over my creation. "Possessive much?"

"Fuck yes. I'd tattoo that on your ass if you'd let me."

"I'm not sure my ass would be the best place. No one would ever see it but you, so it wouldn't do much good."

"Good point." I grinned. "Let's just get it tattooed across your forehead. I'm sure it won't be weird."

She snorted, which gave way to a full-out laughing attack. The sound was infectious, and I couldn't help but join her.

"So, do I get to paint you?" she asked.

"Only if you stay half-naked."

"Deal, but you have to lose your shirt, too."

I let her up as I removed my shirt, and we switched positions. Her legs straddled my hips, and I groaned as her body made contact with the part of me that was aching for her. Her delicate fingers dipped into the paint, and she studied me as if she were looking at a canvas. She bent forward, and I felt her breasts brush against my chest as she kissed a path down my body. She worked her way back up my stomach, tracing the lines of my abs with the back of her hand. She left traces of paint everywhere her hand touched. It was like a Mia roadmap.

Her eyes settled on my chest, and the paint made contact with my skin. I watched her trace the letters of her name over my heart. As soon as her finger lifted after the last curl of the A, I fisted my hands in her hair and devoured her in a fiery kiss. She instantly responded, moaning into my mouth, as our tongues moved together.

We couldn't shed our clothes fast enough, uncaring of the wet paint covering our bodies. As we came together and my body moved in hers, the only thing I cared about was making sure she never left again.

Mia hadn't needed to paint her name on my heart. She already owned it. She always had.

Chapter Twenty-One

"Wake up," Mia whispered in my ear.

Sleep gave way, and my eyes opened. I groaned, burying my head in the pillow.

Her faint laughter made me smile. Fingers made their way up my bare back, and I felt her lean over me.

"Hey, wake up."

"No." I yawned and reached around to pull her into my arms, so I could go back to sleep.

Soft lips touched mine, and I opened my eyes to find her smiling at me.

"Why are you awake? It's the weekend. Weekends are made for sleeping," I said. Giving her naked body an appreciative glance, I added, "And fucking."

She gave me a slightly amused expression and rolled her eyes. "I'm hungry. You need to feed me."

"Why is it my turn?" I grumbled.

"Because I made breakfast yesterday. It's only fair. Plus, I suck at it."

"Can't get out of bed. Too warm."

I pulled her closer and nuzzled my head against her shoulder. I didn't want to leave this spot, even for food. We could order food eventually. I'd be perfectly happy being naked with Mia during the entire two days I had off. I couldn't remember the last night I'd spent at my apartment. Every time I had gone back there to grab clothes, it'd felt small and confining. I'd race through my drawers, pulling out whatever my hands touched first, just so I could get out of there quickly.

"It's summer. That's a horrible excuse."

"I just don't want to."

Her leg slid up mine. *That got my attention.*

I lifted my head and found her giving me her best rendition of the pouty face and I knew I was going to cave.

"Okay, fine! But we're taking a shower first—a really long, sexy shower. Then, you're making me coffee."

She agreed, and I carried her from the bed into the bathroom where we spent much too long doing things other than washing.

I was a big fan of shared showers.

Leaving Mia to dry off in the bathroom, I went into the bedroom to find her lotion. I'd made a habit of always being around when she put it on, so I could take over, but I had no idea where she stored it when I wasn't slathering it all over her body. She always pulled it out of some magical female hiding spot, and I had yet to figure out where that was.

Not wanting to bother her, I checked the top of her dresser and the highest drawer, knowing she stored a few things in there. Then, I looked in the top of her antique vanity. Finally, I decided it must be in the nightstand.

Pulling the drawer open, I found it lying on top of a stack of old photos.

The lotion suddenly forgotten, I picked up the large pile and started thumbing through. There were pictures of us from every single school dance, football games, and even the two of us with my parents.

I squeezed my eyes shut at the sight of my father. I had finally found solace through my turbulent journey with Mia, and he wasn't here to see it. He'd loved her like a daughter and struggled when she left so suddenly. When I'd refused to give answers, he'd retreated from me for a while. I thought he'd assumed something close to the truth, or he had known it from my mother and had been hurt that I didn't come to him.

Not wanting to lose myself in mourning again, I moved on and enjoyed seeing the younger versions of ourselves staring back at me.

After another couple of goofy dance pictures, I stumbled on something else entirely, and I froze.

It was an ultrasound picture.

I'd seen the many Clare had done throughout her two pregnancies, so I knew exactly what it was the moment my eyes settled on the grainy black-and-white image.

I immediately felt rage at the thought of Mia becoming pregnant with someone else's child, but I stilled the instant I saw the date. It was almost exactly eight years ago.

A tidal wave of confusion hit me, and I couldn't look away from the tiny image in front of me.

So many ultrasounds look like little blobby lima beans or blurry nothings, but this? I could see her.

My child, my daughter.

Why does she have this?

"Hey, am I going to get breakfast anytime soon?" Mia said jokingly as she walked out of the bathroom.

I heard the gasp of air fill her lungs seconds before our eyes collided.

Regret, fear, and despair plagued her beautiful features, and I immediately wanted to soothe them away, but I had to know.

"What is this?"

"An ultrasound of our daughter," she answered quietly, confirming what I'd already figured out.

"I don't understand."

She pulled the ties of her robe tighter and joined me on the bed. I hated that she felt insecure around me now. I didn't want her to feel that way, but I needed her to explain.

"I've never told a single soul about that picture. In fact, up until I saw you standing there in that farmer's market, I hadn't looked at it in years. Psychologists say bottling up feeling and emotions can be destructive and emotionally damaging, but sometimes it's the only way you can survive. And that's what I did—each and every day. I survived. I hid that sonogram photo and every memory I had tied to it as deep and far away as possible. But, then you showed up and everyday since, it's like a little piece of my wall has crumbled."

"I don't even understand why you have this."

She didn't even seem to hear me and just continued, like she was purging her deepest, darkest secret.

"I found it when I was unpacking—kind of by accident actually. It was a few days after we first ran into each other and I opened a box I didn't recognize and there was this stack of photos. I couldn't resist. I went through each one, remembering our life together and the dreams we had. And then I found it. Oh God, Garrett, I'm so sorry," she said, defeated.

Please Mia," I pleaded, taking her hand, "Help me understand,"

She finally looked at me hesitantly but agreed. "I never wanted to leave you. I made the mistake of telling my mother the night of graduation. She manipulated me and used you as a weapon, saying you would never amount to anything with a baby and wife tied to you. She told me I was selfish for stealing your dreams—that I would waste both of our lives with my careless decision. She knew exactly what to say to make me run and leave you."

I exhaled, letting out a breath I thought I'd been holding for eight years. Knowing she hadn't been secretly planning and plotting behind my back as I got down on one knee and asked her to marry me gave me a tremendous feeling of relief.

"I knew anything less than the horrible letter I wrote you would send you running for me, so I cried and screamed and finally sat down to write it. I felt my heart die with every false word. I could never stop loving you."

I reached up and caught a tear as it slid from her cheek. That explained why the letter had been stained with tears but so icy in its wording. She hadn't meant a single word of it.

"Your mother was wrong. A life with you would never be a waste, no matter where we ended up. You were my dream, nothing else," I said.

"I know. I, unfortunately, realized that too late."

"It's never too late, Mia," I said.

She turned away and continued, "I was so angry with her. I knew she was manipulating me, but her words struck a chord, and I was paralyzed with fear. I followed her directions and went to this horrible clinic four hours away. She didn't even go with me."

I always knew her mom would never win Mother of the Year, but I never knew just how bad it had been.

"What about your dad?" I asked.

"Like always, he just stood back and let her run the show. He gave me a brief hug before I left, but that was all."

My eyes fell back to the picture and the tiny shape in the middle. "Is that where you got this?" I asked, holding up the ultrasound picture, which was creased and well-worn from obvious handling.

"Yes. When I arrived, papers were thrown at me, and I was shoved into this tiny waiting room with other women who looked exactly like I did, scared out of their minds. When they finally called me back, I met Carol. She was a nurse, and she was very kind and loving. Her gentle nature calmed me, but even after the panic settled, I still knew I didn't want to be there."

She hesitated, and I waited. I always thought hearing her side of the story would make me angrier. I thought knowing the gory details would be too much, and I would be better off in my blind ignorance. But hearing her tell her version of that night made me love her more.

She'd left me but only because she'd thought she was doing the right thing.

"When Carol saw the uncertainty in my eyes, she pulled me aside and asked if I was sure I wanted to go through with it. I nodded, knowing my mother expected it, but Carol still saw through me. She asked if I wanted an ultrasound. It wasn't required, but sometimes, it helped make an iffy decision more firm, one way or another. I agreed, and she took me and prepared me for the test. I don't think I took a breath the entire time I was in that ultrasound room. I knew there was a baby in there. I'd seen my stomach change and grow slightly, but seeing her on the screen made it real. I wiped away my tears as Carol printed that picture for me, and then she left me alone to make my decision."

Frozen in place by her words, I managed to ask, "What did you do?"

"I walked out."

MIA

"You walked out?"

"Yes." I nodded.

His eyes were swimming with disbelief and utter confusion. "I don't understand."

"I couldn't do it," I choked out. "I ran out of that clinic and called my mom in hysterics, screaming that I'd never give up my child," I turned to look into his eyes. "Our child."

"I won't do it, Mom!" I screamed into the phone.

She had obviously expected this, or she just had no soul because her tone lacked any emotion whatsoever. "But what about Garrett, Mia? I thought you were doing this for him."

"No. Getting rid of our child will never be the answer, Mom. Garrett and I will figure it out together—with or without your support—but I will not do this. I'm coming home."

"You came home?" he asked quietly.

"No," I said, the tears creeping down my face as I relived that horrible day. "My mother told me to go to a motel for the night. She said she didn't want me to drive late at night. I couldn't believe how quickly she had caved. Little did I know, she had already been planning their move, and she needed a bit more time to finalize everything."

Garrett nodded. "I remember returning to your house a couple of weeks after you left. I'd already yelled and screamed at all your friends, begging them to tell me where you were, and your parents were my last hope, but they were gone."

"My parents actually had the move in the works before I dropped the pregnancy bomb on them. After that, they simply sped everything up. My mother was convinced that she would be ostracized by her friends if they ever found out."

"Why didn't you ever come back?" he asked.

"I was going to. I couldn't wait to call you and tell you how sorry I was and how foolish I'd been. After I checked in at the motel, I started to feel sick, and then my sickness turned into blinding cramps. I finally caved and called the front desk for help. Then, they called for an ambulance."

"You miscarried."

It wasn't a question. My eyes met his, and I watched him grieve before me, tears rolling down his face. I crawled into his lap, and we held each other.

"I'm so sorry, Mia. I should have been there. You shouldn't have been alone," he choked out, gripping the fabric of my robe like a lifeline.

"It was my fault. I was alone because I ran away. I lost the baby because I ran away."

He pulled back and sought my gaze. "No, none of that was your fault, Mia. You couldn't control that. The world just wasn't ready for her."

"The doctor said it was my fault," I sobbed.

"What?"

"They rushed me inside the hospital, and the ER was

a madhouse. It was packed, and there weren't enough doctors for the number of patients. Because of my condition, I was seen right away though. The doctor who saw me strolled in and asked what I was doing so far from home. I didn't want to lie, so I told him about the clinic, and my last-minute dash out of there. He said I probably miscarried because of the stress I'd put myself through."

"Is this why you ran? Is that why you never came back to me?"

"It was my fault, Garrett. I destroyed everything, and I didn't deserve you anymore," I whispered. *I still don't deserve him.*

With conviction, he cradled my face between his palms. "I don't care what that sorry excuse for a doctor told you, Mia. None of this was your fault. Do you understand?"

I didn't answer, so he pressed on. "Look at me. I will not let you carry this burden on your shoulders anymore, Mia. Let it go."

"I can't," I said.

"Yes, you can." He placed a tender kiss on my forehead and silently cradled me in his arms. "Why didn't you tell me? All those times I stormed out of here, angry with you over what happened, you could have come out and told me the truth."

"No matter how it happened, it doesn't change the outcome. Whether or not I chose to walk out of the clinic, I am still the reason our child died."

"Baby, you can't keep punishing yourself. We both have to stop living in the past, and we need to learn to move on, but we can't do that if we're still being tugged backward. Please, let it go."

I nuzzled my head in his chest, feeling safe and protected. "I don't know how," I answered honestly.

"Can I show you?" he asked.

Lifting my head, I nodded. He smoothed down my hair, letting his fingers run through the damp strands. His head bent down, and he kissed my cheek, lingered over my collarbone, and hovered at my lips.

"You let me love you, every day, forever," he whispered.

When his lips finally touched mine, I felt every raw emotion he felt being transmitted through our kiss. Love, compassion, desire, and devotion all tangled together as his mouth moved against mine. He untied my robe and slipped it off my shoulders. He kissed the hollow of my neck, and trailed kisses along my collar bone. The towel at his waist disappeared to the floor as he laid me back against the pillows.

"I love you, Mia. I loved you when we were barely old enough to know what true love was. I loved you when you left me, and I've loved you every day since. No matter what happens in our lives, that will be the one constant. I will always love you."

I should have stopped him. As his fingers grazed my skin, leaving a blazing trail in their wake, I should have steadied his hand and told him everything. The story wasn't finished, and I tried to form the words on my lips, but I couldn't bring myself to say them aloud.

Would he treat me differently, pull away, or worse...leave?

Unable to bear the thoughts swirling in my mind, I let his touch linger and intensify, as I remained silent, keeping my secret safe for another day.

He took me slowly, making each thrust surge through

me like a crashing wave. I wrapped my legs around him, needing to feel him closer, and I savored the sensation.

"I love you, Garrett," I cried as my orgasm took over, and my body shook.

As soon as the words left my lips, his mouth took mine in a fierce kiss. His pace quickened, and moments later, he cried out my name as he came.

Rather than feeling like we were making up for the time we'd lost, we spent the morning cuddled in each other's arms as we planned a future, instead of dwelling in the past.

Chapter Twenty-Two

"You know, we can just pick something up at the grocery store for the party," Garrett reminded me for the tenth time.

I was attempting to bake, and it wasn't going well. I was a terrible cook, and baking definitely fell into that category. As batter flew from the mixer, he surveyed the disaster in my kitchen. He gave me a lazy grin, and I powered down the mixer.

"No, I want to make something from scratch. I want your sister and Leah to like me."

His smile grew wider, and I could sense he was holding back his laughter. His eyes flickered with amusement, and his entire body quaked as he tried to hold himself together.

"What?" I asked, folding my arms over my chest with a bit of annoyance.

"You have chocolate batter all over your face."

The deep masculine laughter he'd been keeping at bay

came barreling out as soon as my eyes widened in horror. We only had an hour left until we had to be at Leah's house, and I still had nothing to bring. I had no perfectly baked brownies, no chocolate chip cookies—nothing. I just had a bunch of weird lumpy-looking batter.

Garrett sauntered forward and pulled me into his arms, grasping my hips with his strong, firm hands. "You don't need to stress, baby. Leah already loves you. She's told me a dozen times, and she's threatened bodily harm if I hurt you. And Clare just needs to get to know you. She barely remembers you, but she couldn't be happier for us."

"Okay, but are you sure you don't want someone else with a bit more culinary expertise? I mean, at this rate, you might die from starvation before our second wedding anniversary." The words had slipped out of my mouth, and I sucked in a sharp breath as soon as they had been uttered.

We'd talked about the future, and I thought that meant our future would be together, but that didn't mean he wanted to marry me.

He had wanted to once, but maybe he'd since changed his mind.

He still might after I finally come clean.

My panicked eyes turned up to his, and he only smiled.

"There's no one else I'd rather have than you, bad cooking and all."

I exhaled, and my knees went wobbly. Garrett had a gift of knowing exactly what to say to make my heart take flight. It had been free flying for weeks now.

"So, you're saying I am a terrible cook?" I joked.

He angled downward, his lips hovering over mine in a sly grin. Feeling him this close to me made my shaky knees feel weaker.

"The worst." He laughed as he placed playful kisses all over my lips and cheeks.

After a brief, playful make-out session in the kitchen, involving Garrett licking every bit of batter off my cheeks and chest, he finally saved the day by taking over.

Within fifteen minutes, the brownies and the first batch of cookies were baking in the oven.

I stared in wonderment. I was completely amazed and astonished that he could accomplish so much in such a small amount of time—and with no mess. "How did you do that?"

"I followed the directions on the box. Baby, it's not that hard."

I folded my arms and sulked. "For you maybe."

Within the hour, everything was baked, cooled, and packed up. I'd run upstairs and managed to make myself look presentable in a pretty floral sundress that brought out the subtle red highlights in my dark locks and the blue of my eyes.

"Forget brownies. I want to eat you," Garrett growled as I joined him back downstairs.

"That can be arranged…later," I teased.

"Not funny."

"Come on, we need to get going, or we'll never make it."

His eyes lingered, taking in every curve of my body in my brightly colored dress. "I'd be okay with that. I don't think they'd miss us too much."

I rolled my eyes as I took his hand and pulled him toward the door. He dragged his feet but reluctantly came, making sure to grab the goodies by the door before we left.

I'd never been to Leah and Declan's house. Since Leah

and I had become such close friends, I tried not to think of her husband as a famous movie star, but when we pulled up to their driveway, it was difficult. Their house was massive and beautiful. It had perfectly landscaped lawns and flower beds, a beautiful brick exterior, and a white picket fence. A large wide lot gave them privacy and room to let the children run.

After we made our way up the walkway, Garrett didn't bother knocking at the front door. He just turned the knob and walked in like he owned the place. I guessed family could do that. Leah and Declan's house was regal and sophisticated from the outside, but once we entered, I immediately felt at home. Inviting, warm colors and soft, plush fabric made the large spaces feel intimate and cozy. Children's artwork hung from the walls, and toys were shoved in every corner in an effort to keep things tidy. It screamed family, and I could see bits of my new friend scattered everywhere.

"Hey, Goober!" Leah greeted us as we entered the kitchen.

She was putting the final touches on a salad, and Clare was drinking a glass of wine while sitting at the counter.

"I really hate that nickname," Garrett grumbled, causing the three of us to burst out laughing.

"I think it's adorable." I placed a sweet kiss on his cheek.

The gesture didn't go unnoticed by Leah and Clare, and I saw them share a quick grin of satisfaction.

"Garrett, the guys are outside, pretending like they know how to use a grill. Why don't you go out there and help them?" Clare suggested.

He gave me a sideways glance, and I smiled in approval even though I wanted to hurl. I'd become comfortable and close with Leah. I could handle her blunt personality and witty humor. Clare was a wild card, and I didn't know how she would react to me without Garrett around.

"Okay, but be nice," he warned.

Leah and Clare put on their best innocent faces. Garrett only grunted in response, shaking his head, as he made his way out of the kitchen. He slipped out the sliding glass door, and I heard a bunch of manly greetings follow. I stood quietly and pretended to be highly interested in the curtains and beige wall color.

This is not at all awkward.

"You think we're going to interrogate you, don't you?" Clare asked, amusement flickering in her emerald eyes.

"Kind of," I answered honestly.

"Oh, please," Leah answered. "We just wanted to thank you."

Shocked senseless, I managed to ask, "Why?"

"For giving us our brother back," Leah answered. "Since you returned, he's found his way back to the living. He smiles, he laughs, and he's not holed up in his office twenty-four hours a day."

"But aren't you mad that it was my fault he became that way in the first place?" I asked.

Both Leah and Clare spoke at once, but Clare took the lead. "We all make decisions, Mia. I don't know what led you away from my brother, but I do know he chose to live the way he did. No one made him put his life on hold and wait for you. That was his own decision. It was painful to watch, but in the end, I think it was the right one."

"All that matters is that we have you both back," Leah added.

"Thank you."

They both nodded, and Leah laughed. "Okay, now that we have that out of the way, let's hug it out and then uncork some more wine!"

We ended up huddled together, laughing and hugging and shedding a few tears.

I knew how much these two had gone through with the death of Clare's father and how much they still must be hurting. Garrett would put on a good face, but there were still times I'd catch him looking sad and distant, and I would know he was thinking about his father. I would try to be there for him as much as possible for I knew it wasn't easy—for any of them. Yet, here they were in the midst of their grief, embracing me as one of their own, and I couldn't thank them enough.

Garrett came in and found the three of us in tears.

"Hey, I told you to be nice! Why is she crying?" he asked, coming quickly to my side.

"Happy tears," I simply said.

"Oh. Well, good. I wasn't looking forward to kicking Leah's ass."

"Because you know I'd win," she shot back with a wicked grin.

"Damn straight. You're fucking psycho."

GARRETT

Spending time with my family with Mia by my side only made our new bond even stronger in my eyes. She was cementing herself into my life, laughing and crying with my sister and Leah and joking with the guys. She'd sat down and spent time with my mother, and when I saw them hug toward the end, my chest tightened with overwhelming emotion.

The entire day was filled with emotions as we had our first family event without my father. Leah and Declan had done a wonderful thing for our family by offering to host the end-of-the-summer party. It was something my parents had always done, and we'd all known my mom wouldn't be able to go through with it on her own. Each of us felt the loss of my father everywhere. There was a silence where his boisterous laugh used to fill the entire backyard when he'd tell a joke or chase around the grand-kids while growling like a grizzly bear. His absence was like a gaping void, reminding us of what we'd lost.

As each of us sat down to eat, everyone had become eerily quiet. The children still made noise, but all of the adults had fallen strangely silent.

"I know this is difficult," my mom finally said, breaking the silence, "but this is exactly the way he'd want us to carry on. Life without him is so very hard, but we all still have each other, and that needs to be celebrated."

Everyone agreed, and eventually, the dinner took a turn. We were soon talking and filling the backyard with laughter again. It sounded different without him there, but life had to move on even if we weren't quite ready.

Later on, we all started saying our good-byes. We thanked Leah and Declan for taking the reins and contin-uing our family tradition at their house. We knew this was the first of many family traditions we'd have to reevaluate now that Dad was gone.

"Maybe we can have the next family get-together at your place," Leah whispered in my ear before giving me a secret grin.

I shook my head and rolled my eyes. She'd never stop meddling with Mia and me, not until the ink was dry on our marriage license and she'd escorted us to our honeymoon suite. I wasn't even sure she'd stop then.

As Mia and I headed home, an idea came, and I suddenly turned down the next street.

"Where are we going?" she asked.

"Somewhere we haven't been in a long time."

It took a bit of time to find. I got turned around several times, and all the streets looked the same. Eventually, I found it and parked. We both got out of the car, and I grabbed an old blanket from the trunk before we quietly walked down the beaten trail to the place where it had all started.

"It hasn't changed," she said softly, taking in the panoramic view of the river.

I laid the blanket down on the soft earth. "Some things don't," I reminded her, wrapping my hands around her waist to draw her hips closer to mine.

She nuzzled up to me, and I softly kissed her forehead.

"Do you think we would have made it?" she asked.

"What do you mean?"

"If things hadn't happened the way they did and we'd done everything we said we were going to do in high school. Do you think we would have survived?"

I tilted her chin upward, and she stared back at me.

"I think we can survive anything," I answered. Gently cupping her head, I kissed her lips softly.

This time, when I made love to her next to the river bank we used to call our own, I knew just how precious she was. The first time I'd told her I loved her was at this very spot, but I hadn't realized just how far I had truly fallen. Letting my hands and mouth slide over every inch of her body, I worshipped her, knowing exactly the depths of my love. I'd lost her once, but I would never lose her again. She was my life.

We took our time leaving that night, redressing each other slowly. We watched the moonlight dance across the rushing water, and then we quietly folded up the blanket and made our way back to the car. I opened the car door, and she moved to get in, but then I stopped her. I had this overwhelming need to kiss her at this spot, just one last time. My hand cradled her head as I brought my lips to hers.

"I love you, Mia," I said softly.

"I love you, too, Garrett—always," she vowed.

I held her hand as I drove back to her house. I hoped it would become *our* house one day. It was large enough to last us for years, and as we spent more and more time fixing it up together, I felt like we were finally fulfilling one of those dreams we'd had as kids.

"So, you can fix cars. Can you do anything else?" she teased.

I rolled out from under the car. She watched me from across my parents' garage as I stood up and wiped the grease from my hands. I threw the towel down, took a few steps and quickly cornered her.

"Oh, I assure you, I can do all sorts of things," I said with a cocky grin.

"You're evil, Garrett Finnegan!" She laughed. "I was being serious."

"So was I."

She raised her eyebrow and gave me a look that said I was being ridiculous.

"Okay," I said, throwing my hands up in surrender. "I can do all sorts of things with my hands."

She laughed and smacked me on the head.

"Ouch! I was being serious! It's not my fault you keep

thinking dirty thoughts of me. I was talking about fixing things. My dad always asks for my help around the house, so I've gotten pretty good at being handy."

"So, you'll be able to buy me a big, old house and fix it up one day?" she asked with a big grin on her face.

"No, we'll buy the house and fix it up—together."

Her eyes softened, and she gave me a small kiss. "Deal."

"Why are you so quiet over there?" she asked.

I pulled up to the curb. "Just remembering when you asked me to buy you a big, old house and fix it up for you, like you were a princess."

"I am a princess," she insisted. Her mouth twitched as she tried to keep a straight face.

We got out of the car.

"Is that why you wanted to paint your bathroom pink?" I joked.

"It was not pink. It was a dusty red!"

"Baby, it was pink."

"It was not!" She laughed.

Our laughter halted when we reached the porch. The front door was unlocked, and the lights were on inside.

"Did you leave it unlocked?" I asked, knowing she never did.

Mia was many things, but reckless was not one of them.

"No, I didn't. Maybe Liv came by and left it open? She has a key."

Liv would never have been so careless, and she certainly wouldn't have left the lights on. That was a criminal offense in her mind. I pushed over the plant that covered Mia's hidden key and found it missing. I suddenly felt uneasy, and I had an overwhelming urge to throw Mia over my shoulder, turn, and run.

"Go get in the car, Mia," I turned around and whispered.

"No, it's my house. I'm going with you," she insisted, folding her arms and giving me the Mia equivalent of the death stare.

I weighed my options for a half a second and seriously contemplating the throwing over the shoulder routine, but knew I'd be flayed alive for it. So instead, I pushed forward, pulling her behind me for protection. She could complain about equal rights all she wanted, but I was still sticking her behind me.

We entered slowly and quietly. Sam met us at the door, wagging his tail and panting with excitement.

Some guard dog you are.

I looked toward the kitchen and saw nothing. We rounded the corner to the living room and found our intruder. The man rose from the couch as we entered, and his eyes immediately focused on me, narrowing as if he were sizing me up. He looked nothing like a burglar with his expensive clothes and country-club looks, but I wasn't taking any chances. I turned to tell Mia to run, but she was frozen in place at the sight of the man invading her living room.

"Aiden?" She said it so soft, it was almost a whisper.

"Amelia," he breathed out in relief.

I pivoted back around to her in utter confusion. "Is this your boss?" I asked, remembering the name from the bouquet of flowers she'd received.

As I watched her face morph into pure horror, I realized the truth. This was not her boss.

"Mia, who is this guy?" I asked, trying to keep myself from leaping across the room to tear him apart.

He was staring at her with a look of pure adoration

and affection. There was emotional history there. My fists tightened at my sides, and I instantly saw red. I didn't want anyone looking at her that way.

"Who am I?" he asked, his eyes brimming with anger. "I'm her fiancé. Who the hell are you?"

I felt physical pain from his words, and my hand flew up to my chest as my heart convulsed. I turned to her for some sort of sign that this was a joke, but all I saw were tears. Her silence told me everything I needed to know.

"Who am I? I'm no one," I answered before walking out the door.

Chapter Twenty-Three

GARRETT

Fiancé.

The word had rattled around in my brain like a runaway ping-pong ball since the night I ran out of Mia's house almost a week ago. It was like a broken record on an endless loop, repeating over and over in my head, until I thought I might go mad from the constant repetition.

That singular word would be my first thought when I woke up with sweat dripping down my back from once again reliving the terror of losing her in my sleep. That horrible word would silently torment me as I buried myself in work, desperately trying to forget the past three months of my life. Drifting off to sleep, it would be the last thought I had along with the image of her tear-stained face following me when I'd walked out her front door.

She'd tried to call me. Hell, she'd tried to contact me by using every modern means of communication there was, but I hadn't responded to a single one.

She hadn't run after me that night, begging me to come back inside and swearing it wasn't true.

No, she'd let me go and stayed with him—the fiancé.

She'd lied to me. For three months, she'd done nothing but lie to me.

Yet, my traitorous heart ached for her, and my body begged to be near her again.

I'd stormed out of her house that night and sped down the street, anger surging through every molecule in my body, and I'd just driven with no particular destination in mind. I'd driven until I found myself in the empty parking lot of the cemetery where we'd buried my father just a few weeks earlier.

I'd pulled myself out of my car and absently walked the short distance to my family's plot where my father's grave was now, still freshly packed with dirt and marked with a temporary nameplate. My brother-in-law, Ethan, rested nearby.

I didn't know why I had gone there. I had just wanted to be close to my father. I'd knelt down on the soft, dewy grass next to where his body was buried, and I'd listened to the crickets chirp and frogs croak while I'd silently screamed inside.

Now, a week later, I was sitting at work, and I still felt exactly the same. My phone vibrated on the top of my desk, shaking me out of my thoughts. I leaned back in my office chair and picked it up to see another text message from Mia.

Please, Garrett. Call me. Let me explain.

I ignored it, just like I'd ignored all the others, as I shoved my phone in my desk drawer.

By eight o'clock, my back was aching from sitting in my chair too long, and my eyes were starting to cross. Pretty much everyone else in the office had already left. I shut down my computer and picked up the empty Starbucks cup from earlier. I added it to the pile that had accumulated in the trash can throughout the day.

I'd become him again—the old Garrett, the workaholic who survived on caffeine and coasted through life because he was too afraid to slow down and try to enjoy it.

Without her, I didn't know any other way. Without her, I was nothing.

I took the long way home, taking side streets and turns I didn't have to, just so I wouldn't have to spend any more time than necessary in that dark, empty apartment.

I hated it there. It was too quiet. Every tiny sound, curse, or utterance seemed to be sucked into those claustrophobic white walls. My sheets still smelled like her, and as much as I needed to, I couldn't bring myself to wash them. I'd lie in my bed, night after night, drinking in that sweet citrusy smell, torturing myself, until sleep would finally pull me into its hellish embrace.

After delaying the inevitable as much as possible, I pulled up to the curb and walked the short distance to my apartment. The sounds of my feet hitting the stairs echoed throughout the hollow space as I made my way upward. I fished out my keys and unlocked the door, pushing it open with my foot. There, sitting on my couch and flipping through channels like she was competing with someone for a speed award, was Leah.

"How the hell did you get in here?" I asked rudely.

"You gave me a key. Remember, Goober?"

"No."

"Well, you did."

She flicked the TV off and remained seated as I dropped my keys on the counter. I pulled out a bottle of whiskey from the top of the refrigerator and poured a decent amount of the bottle into a glass from the cabinet.

"Dinner?" she asked.

I joined her in the living room with my substantial glass of amber-colored booze. "Yep," I answered stoically.

Her eyes swept over me in an appraising fashion, obviously taking note of the new look I was sporting. Her eyes lingered over my disheveled hair and three days' worth of stubble.

"You look like shit," she finally said.

"Well, thanks. Love you, too." I took a long sip from my glass and let the liquid slowly burn down my parched throat.

"When was the last time you ate?"

I raised my eyebrow and shook my head. "Are you my mother now, Leah?"

"Well, when you're acting like a child, what do you expect me to do?

"I am not acting like a child!" I shouted. The force of my anger caused my drink to slosh forward, dripping down the glass and onto my hands.

Leah cocked an eyebrow and folded her arms, but she remained quiet.

"Mia and I broke up," I said, the words feeling like gravel against my throat.

"I know, although storming out of her house without so much as a parting word isn't much of a breakup, Garrett."

I should have guessed as much. "Is that why you're

here? You think you can kick my ass into shape and make everything better, Leah?"

"Yes. I was the chosen one to come over and try to knock some sense into you," she confessed.

"Look, you don't understand—" I started to explain, but she held up a hand, quickly cutting me off.

"She told me everything, Garrett."

"What?"

"Mia told me everything—the pregnancy, engagement, how she ran off, and the life she had before she came back."

"You mean, the fiancé she failed to mention," I bit out angrily. I took another swig from my glass, but all I got was ice. *Damn, that hadn't lasted long.*

"Did you ask her if she was engaged, Garrett?" Leah asked rather pointedly.

I walked back into the kitchen for a refill.

"I didn't have to. He was standing right there, and it's not like she ran after me when I bailed."

I unscrewed the cap from the half-empty bottle and bent the tip toward my glass, but I was stopped. Tiny fingers wrapped around the bottle as judgmental blue eyes bored into me.

"Now, you're starting to piss me off," I said, pushing off the counter.

I dumped my glass into the sink where it joined several others. There were no plates, just lonely empty glasses. I guessed it had been a while since I'd eaten. Whiskey and coffee had become my new staples.

"Good. At least you'll be feeling something other than sorry for yourself!"

I swiveled my head, the alcohol now doing its job of

making everything feel loose and numb, and looked at her. "She fucking destroyed me!" I roared. "Again!"

Feeling weak, I braced myself against the counter and hung my head in defeat. I felt Leah's warm touch as she rubbed my back.

"You need to talk to her, Garrett. Give her a chance. Please. There are so many things you don't understand, so many things that aren't my place to tell you. You can't end a relationship like this, Garrett. This is your life. Don't walk away from something based on assumptions and miscommunications. You both deserve more than this. So, please, go talk to her."

I lost the will to fight her, so I agreed. If she thought this would fix everything, I was happy to prove her wrong.

In the morning, I'd be knocking on Mia's door for the last time.

This time, I was saying good-bye.

MIA

I'd let him walk away.

I had just stood there as he stormed out the door, leaving me and my mangled heart behind.

Over the last week, I'd spent every waking minute reliving those nightmarish moments. I'd been joyously happy in those brief seconds before we stepped in my house, laughing and joking with Garrett after we'd spent a beautiful night at the river, and then everything had shattered when we found Aiden standing in my living room.

I should have known he would come for me after the endless phone calls, the flowers, and then the letters I'd refused to acknowledge. Without bothering to open them,

I'd shoved them in a box that I hid in the back of my closet. Maybe if I had read them, I would have realized his intentions.

I'd been so angry with Aiden as I watched through blurry, tear-filled eyes when Garrett ran out of the house, believing I was the worst sort of person on the planet.

"Why did you say that?" I screamed.

"I don't know, Amelia. I saw you with another man, and I panicked. I'm sorry," Aiden answered, his brow furrowed as he slumped down on the couch.

"We are not engaged," I hissed.

"Only because you ran out on me the night I proposed."

Folding my arms over my chest, I huffed out in frustration, "And you figured that was a maybe?"

He flinched at my harsh words, and I regretted them at once. Aiden had never been anything less than charming, wonderful, and giving. He deserved so much more than a woman who ran out on a romantic proposal and never returned.

"I didn't know what to think. You just disappeared."

I hung my head in shame as more tears etched a path down my cheek. "I'm sorry, Aiden. I just...I'm sorry. I couldn't accept."

He nodded, leaning forward to run his long fingers through his short dusty-blond hair. His dark brown eyes met mine, and he took a ragged deep breath.

"Why, Amelia? Why? Is it because of him, the guy that was here?"

Even though my head had screamed for me to go to Garrett, I'd spent the entire evening with Aiden, talking until the sun came up. I'd needed him to understand me—the real me, the one I'd never shared with him. So, for the first time since I'd met him, I'd opened myself up and told him everything.

I'd met Aiden right after college and found him to be

funny and easy to get along with. He was a few years older than me, and he'd been just starting his career in law while I had been just starting mine in accounting. He had been completely immersed in his career, and from the beginning, our relationship had been casual. He'd told me a wife and kids weren't in the cards for him, and those were terms I could happily agree to.

After losing Garrett, I had given up on the idea of marriage. It wasn't something I wanted with anyone else. So, when Aiden had asked me to move in with him a year later, I'd agreed, knowing it would be the furthest our relationship would ever go. I'd thought I would never be pressured for more. I would never have to share more of myself than I was willing.

Over the last year though, things had changed. Aiden's career had settled. He had become a partner in a firm, and he no longer needed to prove himself by working to death. When he'd started looking at me differently, tenderly, I'd known we were headed for trouble. His fingers would linger on my ring finger, and I'd find him stealing glances at me when he thought I wasn't looking.

The night he had proposed, he'd pulled out every stop. He'd rented out an entire restaurant, lit hundreds of candles, and decorated every surface with flowers. It had been every woman's fantasy—every woman but me. To me, it had been a nightmare. The only proposal I'd ever wanted was an impromptu declaration of love on a river bank with a tiny diamond ring and a boy who had stolen my heart when I was still a child.

I want you to be my wife, Amelia. I want you to be the mother of my children. Please, do me the honor and make me the luckiest man alive, he'd said. With a wide-mouthed grin, he'd dropped to one knee.

I'd been frozen stiff from the shock until I'd finally burst into panicked tears before running out of the candlelit restaurant. With shaky hands, I'd gathered as many things as I could from our apartment, and I'd spent the night at a friend's house. Even though she hadn't understood my reasoning, the next day, she'd gone over and packed everything else for me while Aiden drilled her on my whereabouts. She hadn't given in, and eventually, she'd made it out with everything I owned.

I'd left the next day, getting behind the wheel and driving to an unknown destination. When I'd realized where I was headed, I'd pulled into a shabby motel for the night, and I'd emailed Liv from my phone, not expecting her to respond. It had been eight years of radio silence. I had deserted my best friend without any explanation. I hadn't deserved a response, but being the person she was, Liv had welcomed me into her home with open arms.

I'd left Aiden with no explanation. I couldn't blame him for the length he went to find me. I should have never ran, but running had always been what I did best and now I had to fix it. It had been unfair and careless of me, and over those few hours after I watched Garrett walk out, I'd tried to make it up to him. There had been so much I'd never told him.

He'd known where I was from, but that was the extent of it. He hadn't known anything about my family or the type of home I was raised in. Aiden hadn't known the life I had before. For him, I was a completely different person. I was Amelia. Strong, independent and emotionally stable. After I left home, I bottled so many things up, thinking that by doing so, I was making a better life for myself and the new people in it. Aiden didn't know about Garrett, the baby, or the consequences of my actions from that part of my past.

I'd falsely let Aiden believe that my heart was still mine to give, and for that, I would forever be sorry. When he'd left the next day, feeling destroyed and rejected, I'd told him he deserved better than a woman who wouldn't be able to give him her whole heart.

He'd only given me a slight smile, shaking his head, as he'd said, *Oh, Amelia, I didn't deserve you.*

I'd spent the next few days desperately trying to reach Garrett, but my calls and texts had gone unanswered.

I feared my decision to stay and finally tell Aiden the truth, rather than running off to explain things to Garrett, had cost me everything.

After sloshing around at work for several days, Leah had finally thrown down the gauntlet and demanded information. She'd pulled me into an empty birthing suite, and I had finally told her everything. I'd cried until my eyes were bloodshot, and I couldn't make a single syllable without hiccuping. She'd been everything I expected Leah to be—compassionate, caring, and blunt.

"You've got to stop waiting for him to come to you and go get him, Mia," Leah said.

I blew my nose for the tenth time. So attractive.

"I can't. What if he throws me out?"

"That's a risk you have to take, but you won't know until you go over there and do it. Fight for him, Mia."

She'd persuaded and convinced me that I needed to stop waiting around. The longer I did so, the more damage I could be doing. I'd agreed wholeheartedly and walked out of the hospital, ready to fight for the man I loved and the life I thought we deserved.

Twenty minutes later, I was sitting in my car at the

curb of my street, not his, feeling like the biggest kind of coward. I killed the engine, slowly pulled my keys from the ignition, and stepped out of the car. The distance between the street and my house felt wider, and by the time I reached the house, I was gasping for air.

What was I doing? Was I giving up?

Was I that scared of what I'd done, what I'd hidden from him, that I was unwilling to even face him?

My fear had held me back, and now sitting in my house, a week after he'd left, it was still keeping me anchored within these walls, unable to move forward. All those emotions I'd kept bottled inside for so long? They were making a comeback in the most hellish of ways and I suddenly felt like the weakest person on the planet.

I knew what I wanted, but I couldn't seem to get past my own insecurities to take it.

Once again, the only obstacle in the way of my own happiness was myself.

Chapter Twenty-Four

GARRETT

My feet felt like lead weights as I dragged my unwilling body out of the car and toward the walkway leading to Mia's front door. I'd walked those steps so many times now that it felt like I had worn my own personal path down the center. Every interaction, both good and bad, since I'd found her standing in the street at that farmers' market had begun with me walking down this old concrete pathway, and now, it would end with one final trip.

I didn't want to be here. With every step propelling me toward that bright red door, my heart jerked and sputtered, and I faltered just a bit more in my stride. My body was in turmoil, and even though I continued moving forward, my heart was screaming for me to turn around and run because we both knew I would never survive this visit. Finally stepping onto the weathered porch we'd never gotten around to repairing, I held up my shaking fist and knocked, and then I waited. Sam's barking grew louder as he made a mad dash for the door.

God, I was even going to miss the dog.

In a matter of months, my life had become completely immersed in hers. It was to the point where I didn't even know how to exist without her. Everything reminded me of her. I couldn't eat without thinking of the meals we'd shared together. I couldn't sleep because I'd remember the nights she'd spent safe in my arms. All the while, she had belonged to another man.

I heard her a split second before she opened the door. She was yelling at Sam to be quiet. She pulled the door open, and I saw her instantly freeze. My heart lurched at the sight of her standing before me. Even in my anger, I still wanted her, and even as she stood there in stunned silence, I couldn't help but notice how beautiful she was.

Without a bit of makeup on and wearing nothing but a pair of cutoff shorts and a faded tank top, she was perfection, my natural beauty.

No, not mine, I reminded myself. *She belongs to someone else.*

"Garrett," she finally breathed out.

"We need to talk," I said quickly. My eyes darted around her in search of *him.*

She nodded in agreement. "Yes, there's so much I need to explain."

I ignored her comment. There wasn't much I really wanted her to explain. I didn't want details.

I stepped into the foyer, and my eyes continued their erratic dance around the house, searching for any clue of the bastard's presence. I didn't think I could handle seeing them together.

"He's not here," Mia said softly.

"What?"

"Aiden. He left the morning after you left."

My fists tightened at my sides, and I felt the blood heat in my veins. Visions of the two of them entangled in Mia's sheets flashed through my head. "The morning after, huh? Did you have a nice reunion with your future husband, Mia?"

"Stop. Please stop, Garrett," she begged, tears staining her cheek.

I stalked forward, taking several steps, until I could feel her ragged breath on my neck. "Why? Does it bother you that I finally found out?" I bit out.

"We were never engaged."

Taken aback, I tilted her chin upward, meeting her watery gaze. "He seemed to think you were."

"He was angry," she said. "There's so much I didn't tell you, so much I've kept hidden from both of you."

Taking my hand, she led me to the living room. Sitting next to me on the couch, she spent the next hour telling me about the life she'd had after she left me—the real life without any gaps.

She'd met someone. When I had been drinking myself to oblivion just to be able to stand human contact, she had been happy and living with someone.

It fucking hurt, but at the same time, I felt a smidgen of relief, knowing she hadn't been living in the same hell I had for the past eight years. I wouldn't wish that upon anyone.

"He really was a wonderful man, Garrett," she said.

"So, if he was so wonderful, why didn't you stay in Atlanta?" I asked with a twinge of bitterness in my voice.

I'd said, it was a smidgen of relief, a very small

smidgen. The rest of what I was feeling was just raw hostility.

"When I met Aiden, I was all alone in a new city. He was nice and charming and uncomplicated. He was focused on himself, which afforded me the only type of relationship I was able to give. He didn't want kids or a ring. He just wanted someone to share dinners with and take to work functions."

And share his bed. That part wasn't lost on me, and seeds of jealousy took root in my mind, sprouting with vengeance as I once again pictured the two of them together. I hadn't believed that Mia was celibate in the eight years we were apart, but now, I had a face to go with my worst nightmare. It was like someone describing Freddy Krueger compared to actually seeing him firsthand.

"But then, he wanted more?" I assumed.

"Yes." She nodded. "I should have seen it coming, but I did my best to ignore it. When I met him for dinner one night, I walked into a completely deserted restaurant covered in flowers and candles, and I panicked. He gave this beautiful speech about how much he loved me and how he wanted me to be the mother of his children, and all I could do was stare at the exit, trying to figure out how quickly I could make a run for it."

"Why?" I pressed, needing to know.

She took a deep breath and turned her eyes up toward mine. "At the time, I told myself it was because I was hiding so much from him. He didn't know anything about me. And most importantly," she said quietly, her eyes squeezing shut as her voice faltered, "he didn't know I couldn't have those children he wanted so desperately."

The air in my lungs suddenly halted at her confession. "What do you mean?"

Tears leaked out of the corners of her eyes, and she took a choked breath. "I should have told you earlier. I shouldn't have kept it from you for so long," she babbled through her tears.

"Mia, please, help me understand," I said gently.

"The night I miscarried...when I went into the ER, they did the procedure to...remove the baby." She paused, her tears turning into strangled sobs.

I pulled her hand into mine, stroking it with the pad of my thumb.

"It happened all so quickly, and I found out later that there was quite a bit of scarring...so much so that I can't carry another baby—ever."

Pain lanced through my heart, worse than I'd ever known. It was worse than when I had turned and seen the look of pure horror on Mia's face when she found Aiden standing in her living room. It was worse than when her mother had handed me the note that I thought would end my life forever.

The woman I loved couldn't have children. My heart was breaking for her. Ever since I'd known Mia, she'd loved children. It was how I'd known we would be okay having a child so young—because I had Mia to guide me. Giving, kind, and selfless, she would have made the best mother.

"This is what you've been hiding from me?" I asked, sweeping away a tear from her cheek.

"Yes, I was so afraid to tell you. I was afraid if I told you about Aiden, you would ask why I left, and I didn't have the courage to tell you."

I couldn't handle the separation between us any

longer. I'd come here to put as much distance between us as possible, but now, watching her grieve and crumble before me, the mere inches between us felt like miles. Wrapping my hands around her waist, I effortlessly pulled her onto my lap, cradling her in my arms, as I savored the feel of her warm body against mine.

"Why? Did you think I wouldn't love you? That I would blame you?"

"I don't know. I don't know…I'm broken," she cried.

I smoothed the hair away from her face and bent down to kiss the tears away from her soft cheek.

"Baby, I would never, ever blame you for that. You're not broken, and I could never love you less. It's not possible. If anything, it only makes me love you more."

Her frantic eyes stilled and met mine. They were red and puffy from the constant stream of tears, but she was still beautiful.

As much as I wanted to kiss her and take her for my own without looking back, I had to know that she was all mine beyond a shadow of a doubt.

"I don't want to ask, but I have to. If that is the only reason you walked away from Aiden, don't you think he deserves to know?"

"He knows. I told him the night he showed up here."

My heart picked up, and I squeezed her tighter, fearing her answer. "And?"

"And he went back to Atlanta—for good."

My eyes darted up to hers, searching her face for something, anything. "Why?"

"I said I thought, at the time, that was the reason I left. But I realized I ran from that proposal because he wasn't you."

It was all I needed to hear. My fingers dived into her

hair, pulling her closer, as my mouth found hers. It had been too long since my lips tasted hers, and I instantly devoured her, feasting on her softness like I was starved.

Needing to erase the visions of Mia and Aiden that my mind had been creating all week, I lifted her off the couch. Never breaking our kiss, I carried her up the stairs. As I rounded the corner into her bedroom, I gently nipped her lip. She moaned against my mouth, and I felt it all the way down to my cock. Finally reaching her bed, I gently laid her down and took my time removing her shorts and tank top until she was in nothing but a pair of panties and a thin lace bra.

My hands roamed over every inch of her skin, feeling the curve of her hips, the swell of her breasts, and the deep juncture of her thighs. Each brush of my hand sent shivers through her body, making her moan and arch her back in need.

"Please, Garrett," she begged.

"I'll take care of you, Mia. I'll always take care of you," I vowed.

She watched with hooded eyes as I made quick work of my clothes, lifting my shirt over my head with one hand and unbuttoning and dropping my shorts and boxers in seconds. Starting at her toes, my fingers traced her ankles, spread over the backs of her calves, and made their way up to her trembling thighs. My lips followed the same path, tracing a wet passage up her leg and continuing beyond. I kissed her flat stomach, the valley between her breasts, and finally returned to her lips. Bracing myself so I wouldn't hurt her under my weight, I lowered my body onto hers and sighed in pleasure as skin met skin. I felt like I'd finally found home again.

"This is what I want, Mia, forever. I don't care about

what you can or cannot give me. You'll never be broken in my eyes. I just want you—forever. Only you."

A single tear trailed down her cheek, and I caught it with my thumb, brushing it away. I kissed the spot where it had fallen.

"No tears. Just give yourself to me, exactly as you are. Can you do that?"

She didn't answer. Her fingers dug into my hair, and she kissed me hard. I instantly responded, returning her fiery passion with my own. Her legs wrapped around my middle, pushing my hard length against her wet heat. I growled, gripping her round ass with my hands, as I pulled her closer. I'd almost lost her. Any amount of distance seemed too much at that moment.

"Give me this for the rest of my life, Mia. It's all I need," I breathed in her hair before scattering kisses across her chin and cheek.

Lifting up on my elbows, I gently eased into her welcoming body, inch by inch, allowing both of us time to enjoy every blissful moment. Our eye contact never broke, even as I bent down and placed a tender kiss on her lips. Savoring the feel of our bodies once again connected, I went slow, taking my time to make sure every thrust hit just right. Her hips arched up to meet mine, as sweet sounds of passion escaped her lips.

I wasn't just making love to her. I was giving everything to her. I was handing over my heart despite the difficulties we'd had and the road blocks we might face in the future. She was what I wanted in this world, and I felt this overwhelming need to show her with every kiss and lingering touch I gave.

My lips found her taut nipple, and I swirled my tongue on the pink tip as I continued to love her. I picked up my pace and tilted her hips forward, hitting that sweet spot that made her cry out in pleasure. Her nails dug into my back, and I released her nipple, letting it go with a pop.

I moved up to meet her lips. "I love you, Mia Emerson. I will always love you," I vowed.

She tightened around me and cried out her release, shuddering and moaning into my mouth, as the orgasm racked through her body. As her body milked mine, I felt my balls tighten a split second before I came hard, and I shouted her name as I released into her.

I kissed her dewy wet skin and tucked her naked body into mine. I felt at peace. I didn't remember falling asleep, but sometime later, I awoke to Mia pointer finger moving up and down my chest, making tiny hearts up and down my abdomen. I smiled and placed a single kiss on her lips and jumped off the bed. She laughed at my sudden exuberance as I picked her up and carried her into the bathroom.

"Garrett!" she shouted, as I took the last few steps and set her down on the counter. She yelped as her ass hit the cold countertop. I gave a quick chuckle as I reached into the shower and turned on the water. It quickly warmed up, and I pulled us both under the warm spray. I washed her hair and took my time moving the soap, covering her body in suds. I rubbed my hands up and down her skin and watched in fascination as her nipples pebbled and hardened from my touch.

"I want to wash your hair, too," she said, squirting some of the shampoo she'd bought for me when I'd started using all of hers.

I smiled, realizing she hadn't removed it from the shower. She had been hoping I'd come back.

"How do you plan on doing that?" I asked, looking down at her to emphasize our obvious height difference.

She gave me a quick smirk and planted her arms on my shoulders, hoisting herself up, as she wound her legs around my waist. Laughing, I wrapped my arms around her hips to stabilize her. She started right away, working the shampoo into my short hair until it foamed and lathered. I enjoyed my new view as her breasts pushed against my face, and I carefully ran one of my hands down her slippery body, pushing her against the wall for support.

"You better not drop me," she said, trying her best to sound intimidating.

"Never."

We once again drained her hot water heater. Mia yelped and screamed as the temperature switched from hot to cold in seconds. We rushed out of the shower, and I wrapped her in a towel before running into her room to grab her robe. Once she was snuggled inside, I carried her to the room and laid her on the bed. I covered her with blankets for added warmth.

I quickly dressed and ran a hand down my wiry face. I needed to shave. I headed into the bathroom and gave Mia a bit of time to relax. It had been days since I'd shaved, and I was looking a bit haggard. A bit of scruff was sexy, but this was ridiculous. I was starting to look like a hobo. I grabbed the shave gel off the shelf and pulled my razor out of its spot in the cabinet.

I grinned like a damned fool. I liked seeing my stuff intermingled with hers. It gave me a sense of peace I thought I'd never find again.

I finished shaving quickly and dabbed my wet face with a towel before exiting the bathroom. I was intent on enjoying some additional quality time with Mia. Instead, I found her curled up on the bed in tears. The bottle of lotion laid next to her, covered in old photos. Her hand was clutching the ultrasound picture I'd found several weeks ago. I rushed to her side and knelt at the edge of the bed, bringing our eyes level.

"Mia," I said, pulling the ultrasound picture from her clutched fingers. "Please tell me what's wrong, so I can fix it."

"I went to grab the lotion for you, and I just had to look at it again. I look at it all the time, Garrett. I don't think you can fix it. You can't fix any of it because it's me who can't be fixed." She sat up and tugged at her robe, pulling it tightly against her body. She drew her knees up to her chest. "Today…us together like this…it's exactly what I want for the rest of my life. You're all I've ever wanted, Garrett."

I joined her on the bed, placing a tentative hand on her knee. "I'm right here. You already have me."

"I know, but what happens when you want more? I can't give it to you, Garrett. I ruined that for us a long time ago. I can't give you children. A life with me is nothing but a dead end."

The absolute joy I'd felt moments before as I'd carried her from the shower drifted away like dust in the wind as she spoke. This was not a woman who was ready to move forward with her life. This was a woman who, much like I had been for the past eight years, was still very much stuck in the past. I had done the impossible. When everyone had told me to stop looking at everything I'd lost, I'd taken their advice and made the leap. I started looking ahead and focused on all the joy I could have with Mia if I was just willing to try.

But what I hadn't realized was that she hadn't leaped

with me. She was still stuck in our memories, grieving a child we'd lost and a future we'd never have, rather than looking at the one we could have right now. That day, when she told me about the ultrasound and she spoke about bottled feelings—I'd hoped that by telling me about the miscarriage it would cure everything, but I hadn't known the whole truth, and seeing the woman in front of me now, I realized she still had so far to go.

"Mia, life with you would never be a dead end. I don't care if you could give me a hundred children or none. I didn't fall in love with you with any expectations. I fell in love with you, only you. If life had presented us with a dozen different choices for our future, I would gladly choose any of them as long as you are by my side."

I took a strangled breath. I hated myself for what I was about to say, but I knew that it needed to be said if we were ever going to move forward with our lives together.

"Mia, I'm willing to make a life with you, regardless of what kind of life that is. The future is unwritten, and I want to spend my life discovering ours together, but I can't do that while you're still grieving the past. You've been punishing yourself for far too long, and it's time to let it go."

Letting go of her hand, I kissed her softly on the forehead and stood. I felt her eyes on me as I walked to the door of the bedroom, and as I turned around, they were still watching me.

"When you're able to do that, I'll be waiting. I'll always be waiting for you."

I forced myself down the steps and out of the door, hoping the next time I returned that it would be for good.

MIA

It had been two weeks since I watched Garrett walk away as I lay helpless and unable to move forward with him. It had been fourteen days since I cried myself to sleep, clutching that sonogram in my hand, like I'd done so many nights since I'd returned home.

The next morning, I'd woken up alone with nothing but a worn black-and-white photo to comfort me, and I'd realized he was right. I had been stuck in the past. No matter how much I'd wanted to move forward, I had been bricked in behind a solid wall, separating myself from everything I wanted because I was drowning in my own regrets.

Unfortunately, my realization hadn't come with a solution or an instant cure. Eight years of blaming myself for something that, deep down, I knew I had no control over hadn't been an easy hurdle to overcome. Eight years of buried emotions take time to unearth and as much as I wanted to run back to Garrett and tell him I was miraculously cured, I knew I had to find a way through this by myself.

I'd spent the first few days going through the motions of my life, putting on a happy smile even though I felt like I was crumbling. Leah had blessedly been off work, so my happy-go-lucky routine had been, for the most part, overlooked. I'd managed to skate by without much notice. My nights had mostly been spent in silence as I had gone through every old photo I had, remembering the life we had and the life we were going to have.

I'd smiled and laughed at the goofy photos, remembering the sunny summers we'd spent at our spot by the river. My mother had never allowed me to wear a bikini, and I'd hated every suit she'd ever bought me. Much like the great shoe rebellion when I was sixteen, I'd snuck out and bought a bright pink two-piece. I'd never seen Garrett's eyes flare so feverishly. He'd dragged me into the water and pushed me against a smooth boulder, and he'd shown just how appreciative he was of my new purchase.

Not every photo had brought back happy feelings. There was one that had instantly made my lips tremble and my womb ache with emptiness. We'd taken it the day I confirmed what I'd secretly been expecting for over a month.

After many tears and a few panicked moments, Garrett had jumped off his childhood bed and reached into a drawer in his dresser, pulling out a camera. As I'd wiped tears from my eyes, I had asked him what he was doing, and he'd said he wanted our son or daughter to know how happy we were when we found out about them. So, we'd cuddled close, nudging our heads together, and snapped a photo. My eyes were rimmed with red, and my lips were puffy, but both of us were grinning from ear to ear. We had been ready for it all, but it was never meant to be.

I'd spent days doing this, dwelling in old photos, while my future was wasting away—and Garrett was waiting for me to take the leap and leave it all behind. Guilt and regrets were a funny thing. I had wanted nothing more than to run out my front door, jump in my car, drive in the direction of Garrett's apartment, and tell him I wanted him and only him for the rest of my life. But every time I'd looked at the front door or coaxed myself into putting on my shoes, I would remember the day I'd lost our child. Fear would settle back in, and I'd sink back further into my hole.

He'd said he didn't care. He'd said he wanted me. But what would happen in a few years when everyone our age was pushing around a stroller or complaining about daycare costs? How would he feel about his decision then? Would he resent me?

On one of my many nights of photo-bingeing while lying on my bed, letting my self-deprecation sink in deeper, my eyes had settled on the photo of Garrett and me standing with his parents. A twinge of pain had hit sharply at the sight of Garrett's father standing next to Garrett with an identical grin on his aged face. Garrett looked so much like him, but his eyes were all his mother's. She'd passed that trait on to both of her children, and those signature green eyes were hard to miss.

The next morning, on my day off, I had driven to a sleepy neighborhood in search of something only a mother could provide—comfort. Since my mother had never been more than a disciplinarian, I'd gone to the one woman I'd always looked up to and loved since the first minute I met her so many years ago.

"Mia," Mrs. Finnegan greeted me at her front door with an inviting smile.

"Hi, Mrs. Finnegan."

She gave me a pointed look, and I laughed, remembering her previous request that I call her Mom.

"Sorry. Hi, Mom."

Her smile broadened. "Better. Now, come on in. It's hotter than blue blazes out there. I don't think summer is going to give up quite so easily this year."

We made small talk as I followed her into the kitchen. She pulled out a pitcher of sweet tea from the fridge, and I helped by grabbing two tall glasses from the shelf, remembering where they were from my earlier visit.

"How are you doing? I feel terrible about not visiting sooner," I said as she poured our glasses and handed one to me.

"I'm doing a little better every day. There are times when I come into the living room and expect him to be sitting in that favorite chair, yelling at the TV over some stupid football game, but for the most part, my life has adjusted as best as it can."

I sat at the kitchen table, and she brought over some freshly made cookies.

"Clare made these and brought them over. She keeps bringing over sweets. I believe it's her way of coping, but I think I'm going to bust out of my clothes soon!" She laughed.

"I guess we all mourn differently."

"Yes, we do. Each of us handles loss in our own way."

She paused, and I looked up and found her comforting green eyes.

"How did you mourn, my dear?"

I took a cleansing deep breath, knowing now why I'd come this morning. It wasn't just for comfort. It was for healing.

"I don't think I have," I whispered quietly.

She nodded as if she understood or recognized the pain.

"I think it's time you let yourself do that, sweetheart," she said gently.

"But I don't know how. How do you mourn the idea of something? How do you let go of a life that never happened? There are no memories, no stories. She didn't even have a name."

"You give your lost child a name and let me do the rest."

That conversation had been a turning point for me. It had given me the strength and courage to do everything I'd accomplished in the last two weeks, and it had brought me to where I was now—standing at Garrett's front door. I was ready to say good-bye to my regrets.

With a steady hand, I took a deep breath and knocked.

I heard the radio kick off, and a set of footsteps grew louder as they made their way to the door. My heart rate accelerated with every step he took, knowing what I was going to say.

The door swung open, and there he was, standing before me in dark jeans and a green T-shirt that brought out the color of his eyes. His breath caught the moment he saw me, and what looked like relief danced across his features.

"Mia." He said my name and it sounded like a prayer as it left his lips.. "Thank God. I didn't know how much longer I could stay away."

He pulled me close, breathing me in, as my body was engulfed in his. His lips found my forehead, and he placed a soft kiss against my skin, silently telling me he loved me.

I was home.

No building or structure would ever feel as inviting and safe as Garrett's warm body wrapped around mine. Homes were not built of wood or brick. They were built by the memories and love we created in them. As long as I had Garrett, I could go anywhere, do everything, and conquer any obstacle life threw at us.

"I'm so sorry it took me so long," I said softly.

"I told you I would wait. I meant it. But that didn't mean I didn't want to see you," he confessed.

He pulled me inside and shut the door behind us before ushering us to his room.

"I just need to hold you," he admitted when I raised my eyebrow at his location selection.

Hearing no complaints from me, he lay down on the plush mattress, and I settled in next to him, breathing in a sigh of contentment.

"I missed this," I said, running my hands under the hem of his shirt to feel the tight skin of his abdomen.

He sucked in a breath as my fingers skimmed his stomach, and I smiled, knowing I could still affect him so with just a single touch.

"There's so much I want to tell you, Garrett, so much I want to explain. When you left me that day, I thought I'd never be able to pull myself out of the ocean of guilt I'd created. How could I move forward when I was the one to blame for all our failures?"

He opened his mouth to speak, but I stopped him.

"No, it's okay. I've come to terms with it now. I've realized that there are things in life that cannot be controlled. Grief is a part of life, but it can't become our life. I'd allowed grief to take over and rule my entire existence because I'd never allowed myself to say good-bye to our daughter. I'd held on to her, the grief and the life I'd never know. But it wasn't really grief I was experiencing. It was regret and shame. I was blaming myself for snuffing out her existence, and by doing so, I wasn't allowing myself to let go."

His eyes were glassy. "And did you finally say good-bye?"

"No," I answered honestly.

A bit of disappointment flashed across his face, so I continued quickly, "But I'm going to…today. We both are."

His brows furrowed together in confusion as he sat up on his elbows. "I don't understand."

"Will you go somewhere with me?" I asked.

"I'd go anywhere with you."

<hr>

We held hands as we made our way down the familiar path, the sounds of our footsteps adding to the natural rhythm of the swaying trees and chirping birds. I hadn't told him why we were here, and he hadn't asked. He just patiently waited for me to explain.

When we turned the corner and found ourselves at his family's plot, standing in front of his father's newly installed headstone, he turned to me in confusion.

"Why are we here?" he asked.

"So, we can say good-bye," I explained, pointing to the new granite marker that had been installed next to his father's.

Garrett took a step closer, his eyes scrunching together, as he read the words. "Her name was Hope?" he whispered as he fell to his knees. His fingers lightly touched the raised lettering as if he was memorizing it by feel.

I stepped forward and knelt beside him.

"Your mother told me to give her a name. She said it would help me heal and grieve. I know you always loved the name Hope."

"It's beautiful," he choked out.

We silently looked down at the memorial that marked the memory of our child.

Hope Elizabeth Finnegan

Our darling Hope. Too beautiful for Earth, but we will hold you in Heaven.

Until then...

"Why Elizabeth?" he asked, never taking his eyes off that tiny plaque.

"I wanted her to have a family name. You mother told me Elizabeth was a name that had been passed down from generation to generation."

He nodded, swallowing hard, as he fought back heavy emotions. "It's my sister's middle name as well."

"I know."

He finally looked up at me, his eyes wet from unshed tears.

"You gave her my last name," he whispered.

"She's our child, Garrett. What other name would I have given her?"

Like so many times before, he bent his head toward mine and kissed my forehead as he pulled me into his arms. "Thank you for this," he said.

"Your mother helped immensely. Without her, I think I'd still be curled up in bed, covered in old photographs, unable to forgive myself. She helped me in so many ways. She's an amazing woman."

Cupping my chin, he placed a brief, tender kiss on my lips, and I felt every emotion he was pouring into me— love, sadness, grief, but most of all, hope. We had hope for our future, our family, and our ever-growing strength. I'd named our daughter well.

He turned his head back to the bronze marker. His

vivid green eyes wandered over each word, drinking them in, savoring them.

"She would have had your smile and that cute button nose," he said with a half smile. "She would have had my eyes and my stubbornness."

"She would have been tall like you, towering above the boys in her class, with skinny long legs meant for running while being chased by her daddy."

His smile grew, and he looked down at the ground as if he was picturing her. I knew I was. I could see her image solidifying before me.

Our Hope.

"She'd have a voice just like yours and sing like an angel. I would have spent my evenings in quiet contentment just listening to the two of you making music together," he said, bringing me to tears.

"There wouldn't have been a moment of her life we wouldn't have loved her, watching her grow, seeing her rise and fall, win and lose, as she battled her way through life. We would have loved her unconditionally and without end." The sobs tore as each word stumbled out of my mouth.

"Someday, we will have our chance to love her," Garrett said, wrapping his arm around my shoulder to comfort me.

I didn't know how long we sat there, but in that time, I silently poured my soul out to that little marker in the grass. As I sobbed, Garrett held me, never letting go, as I made peace with my demons. I forgave myself for the mistakes I'd made and the regrets I'd refused to let go of. I felt my heart purge, letting go of the darkness that had settled there. I felt lighter and blessedly free.

Finally, through my grieving, I said good-bye to the

child I would never know and the life I would never have. I would never know the joy of giving birth to my own child. I'd never experience the exhilaration of finding out I was carrying Garrett's child again. This was my new reality, but one thing hadn't changed—the man by my side.

He was still next to me—holding me, loving me, and supporting me no matter what life might hold—and that made all the difference in the world.

With one final glance at Hope's marker, I kissed my fingers and placed them next to her name.

"I love you," I whispered. "Until then..."

Turning to Garrett, I smiled and said, "Let's go home."

Chapter Twenty-Six

GARRETT

I managed to turn the doorknob and push the front door open with my foot, balancing the bags of groceries in my arms, as I tried not to be mauled over by a very exuberant Sam. He jumped and danced at my arrival, and I bent down, jostling the bags, and gave him a quick pat on the head. The smell of something burning hit my nose, and I quickly rose to follow the smell.

"Mia? Are you burning something?" I called as I rounded the corner into our newly remodeled kitchen.

Long gone were the dated appliances and lackluster cabinets. Now, the kitchen was larger, bright, and functional. We'd spent months picking out new tiles for the backsplash, installing upgraded appliances, and laying down new flooring. It had been many days and nights of hard work, but it was our dream, and it was exactly what we had needed in our journey of healing.

Smoke billowed out of the oven as Mia halfheartedly tried to wave it away with a towel.

"No, it's already burned. It's dead. I killed it," she answered in defeat.

Chuckling softly, I placed the bags down on the counter and turned toward her, pulling her apron-clad body into my arms. She looked adorable in her frilly pink apron, especially since I knew she couldn't cook worth shit.

"Why didn't you wait until I got home?" I asked, feeling her huff in frustration.

"Because I wanted to help with the cooking. It's our housewarming party—which I still don't quite understand by the way. You've been living here for three months. Why are we all of a sudden having everyone over for a party?"

I couldn't help but grin. It was down right adorable that the thought of having my entire family over still definitely made her palms sweat. They'd all welcomed her into the family with open arms, but she would still get nervous every time Clare or my mother came over, worrying that she'd mess up and look bad. I didn't know how to explain to her that they were in love with her just as much as I was.

Mia sighed, looking at her baking catastrophe on top of the oven, as she bit into her top lip with worry. I wished I had spared her the pain and just explained why it was necessary to have a housewarming party three months after she'd made me the happiest man alive when she asked me to move in with her. She'd handed me a key the day we visited Hope's memorial for the first time, but I couldn't tell her the reason, not yet.

"What's this?" I asked.

I took the shiny keychain with a single key dangling on it from her outstretched hand as we wandered back down the winding pathway to the car. I stopped, turning it over it my hand, as my fingers ran over its satiny finish. On one side, our initials were engraved, intertwining together like long-lost lovers, and on the other side were two single words that stole the very air from my lungs—Welcome Home.

I'd cleared out my apartment the following day, not wanting to waste another minute of my life in the cramped, lifeless hellhole. Mia was my life, and the first time I'd walked into the front door of our house, knowing I was truly coming home, I'd finally found happiness.

We'd spent the last three months living in this house and making it our home—together. Remodeling the kitchen had just been the beginning. We'd finished painting, picked out every piece of furniture together, and spent hours hanging old and new photos on the walls. The ultrasound Mia couldn't seem to let go of was now hanging on our wall in its own frame as a reminder of the little girl who would be waiting for us when our time on this earth was done. We might be moving forward, but it didn't mean we had to forget our past.

In the last three months, we'd healed old wounds and made new memories. With the renovations almost completed, we'd managed to host Thanksgiving, and everything had gone off without a hitch, mostly because I'd kept Mia as far away from the food preparation as possible. When Christmas morning came, I'd surprised her with breakfast in bed, and we'd opened presents under our own tree, celebrating our very first holiday together in our new life.

Holding her in my arms now, I couldn't help but grin like an idiot as I remembered her absolute joy that morning. We'd already come so far. I reached down and patted the pocket of my jeans for the hundredth time that day.

Yep, still there.

I looked up, and Mia was staring at me as if waiting for an answer.

Did she ask me a question? Oh right, the party.

"What? Oh, well, we just finished remodeling the kitchen, and all of the furniture is in here finally. It's time to invite everyone over and have a housewarming party. You know, formally," I answered quickly, hoping she'd let it go and not ask any more questions.

She gave me a longer than normal stare, her eyes searching my face, and I tried to play innocent. It must have worked because she turned toward the counter and began pulling out some of the things she'd sent me to the store to retrieve.

"Okay, but when they all die because of food poisoning, I'm telling the cops it was your fault."

"Deal." I laughed. "I'll gladly go to the slammer for you, baby."

"You better."

I tossed the charred black mounds that resembled rolls from the cookie sheet into the trash and set the sheet in the sink to soak. Pulling out fresh ingredients, I popped open another can of rolls and placed them on a clean cookie sheet.

How someone could royally screw up something as simple as rolls was beyond me, but she'd managed to succeed every time she attempted. It was a good thing I didn't mind being in the kitchen. I had a feeling I'd be the head chef in our little family for the foreseeable future.

"Why don't you head upstairs and get ready?" I suggested, placing the new batch of rolls in the oven.

I saw her out of the corner of my eye as she gave herself an appraising look. She already looked presentable in nice jeans and a warm fuzzy sweater, but I knew she'd kill me if I let her stay in that outfit for what I had planned.

"I'll take care of the rest of this," I said encouragingly. "Just go upstairs and relax for a while. Why don't you put on that pretty purple dress you bought the other day?"

Her eyes perked up, and she grinned. She'd been waiting for an excuse to wear that dress ever since she brought it home. She had even contemplated returning it. As soon as I had seen it, I knew it was perfect for tonight.

She raced upstairs, and seconds later, I heard the familiar sound of singing as she moved around upstairs. I loved the sound of her singing. She sang all the time now. I hadn't really noticed it, but when she had first come back into town, I'd never heard her hum or sing at all. It was something she used to do as if it were second nature. I thought, along with so many other things, it had been swallowed up in her grief and misery.

She'd told me late one night, about a month after I'd moved in, that singing in that club had been the first time she'd heard her own voice in years. I wished I could say that our grief and pain were gone and sealed up in that grave marker my mother had installed for Hope, but wounds couldn't heal that easily, and it'd taken months of counseling and time together to get to this point.

Deep scars couldn't be healed instantaneously. They took time to heal properly, and this time around, we knew we couldn't risk doing anything half-assed. Mia had eight years of post-traumatic stress and depression to sort through, and even though I'd forgiven her for everything, I still had years of emptiness to work through.

People say counseling is for the weak.

It's not.

Liv had found an amazing therapist who had experience working with couples who had suffered the loss of a child. Mia actually began seeing her before she showed up at my doorstep that fateful autumn day and we thought it would be good to continue the process with both of us. Counseling had taken courage. Walking into an office and baring our hearts and souls to a complete stranger with the expectation that somehow the doctor had the means to help guide us through the pain and suffering we couldn't do on our own had taken immense courage. She'd helped us in ways no one else could have.

Three months later, we were stronger than ever.

Just as I was putting the finishing touches on the chicken salad, the doorbell rang, signaling our first guest.

Not wanting to appear as a rude host, Mia came flying down the stairs, pinning her hair up as she came. Her makeup had been redone, but it was understated as usual. The amethyst dress had replaced the jeans. She looked breathtaking. The plunging neckline made my brain go haywire, and her high-heeled boots gave me second thoughts about our houseguests.

Too late now.

My sister's voice was the first I heard as her and Logan entered, followed by Maddie and little Ollie. They immediately took off for Sam. Being the gentle dog he was, Sam just rolled over and took the brunt of the children's affection with grace, allowing them to climb all over him as he waited patiently.

"The place looks fantastic, guys!" Clare exclaimed. "But, um...not that different from the last time we were here. You didn't have to host anything fancy to have us over!"

Mia threw me an evil look and mouthed the words, *I told you so.*

No one else knew my ulterior motives but me. So, now, as my family was starting to arrive, I could agree that using the excuse of a housewarming party to get them all over here months after I'd moved in was pretty lame.

It would have made more sense to wait until Super Bowl Sunday or just told them I wanted to have a cook-out...in the middle of January. Yeah, that didn't make sense either.

Stealth was not my thing. I would make a terrible spy.

"Oh, you know...any excuse to have you guys over," I threw out awkwardly.

This routine continued as the rest of my family arrived.

As Declan took his wife's coat, he joked, "You know, Garrett, if you wanted to see me so badly, you didn't have to throw a party!"

I was going to kill them all.

In addition to my family, we'd also invited Logan's best friend, Colin, and his family, who my mother had basically adopted as another extension of the Finnegan family. Liv was also joining us. Everyone who was important to the two of us was here.

It was just like I'd planned. Everything was perfect.

After everyone arrived and we all had been properly greeted and hugged, we headed into the kitchen where I'd set up everything for dinner. Since it really wasn't a housewarming party, I'd gone light and casual on every-thing. Chicken salad, fresh rolls, seasonal fruit, and several other sides that had been brought by my family. Clare had gone all out and brought a huge platter of baked goods that would no doubt feed the entire block. Leah, being the minimalist, had picked up a casserole at her favorite cafe down the street.

Every time we gathered, we would still feel the stinging absence of my father. I thought we'd all come to the conclusion we'd never fully get used to the idea of life without him, but we were adjusting. We were a family with or without him, and he would hate the idea of us crumbling because he wasn't here to hold us together. So, we'd continued on as best as we could. Life moved on, and so had we. The holidays had been the hardest, but we'd found new ways to adapt, and having the young ones around always brought meaning and purpose to the season, even for those who were grieving.

We all made plates of food and scattered throughout the house. We kept the kids at the kitchen table to avoid a food catastrophe, but the adults fanned out into the living room, sitting on the couch and floor, as we enjoyed talking about work and family life.

I sat on the floor in between Mia and my mother, who was sitting above me on the sofa. I felt my mom's warm hand touch my shoulder, and I turned toward her and saw her clutching Mia's hand as she smiled.

"I'm so happy for you two. This house is beautiful. What you've done and accomplished together is beautiful."

I knew she was speaking about more than the house. We'd managed the impossible, and this house was just the physical representation of the future. Part of our healing had been coming clean with everyone we loved. There were no longer any secrets with my family. They all knew the hardships Mia and I had faced so long ago and the recent ones we'd overcome. Mia had been so nervous about telling everyone, but I knew my family. It had only made them love her more.

"Thank you, Mom," I said, sliding my hand up to grab hers.

We finished dinner, and I got kicked out of the kitchen as my family cleaned for us. As dessert was brought out, my palms started to sweat. It was just about showtime. I snuck a peek at Mia. She was leaning over the counter, checking out the goodies Clare had brought over, and talking about school. Since Clare was a high school teacher, she was always interested in Mia's recent return to college.

"It's good! I'm still a bit rusty. I feel ancient, but it's only a few classes and two semesters, so I think I'll survive."

"You are not ancient!" I reminded her.

She'd finally stopped punishing herself and enrolled back in school to get her teaching credential. It had been a decision that was all hers, and I couldn't be prouder. Of course, now that she was one step closer to her dream, she was starting to look to me to start pursuing my own.

I only had one at the moment, and I thought it was time to start living it.

Just as I was opening my mouth to make an announcement, asking everyone to gather in the living room, Clare yelped and then cursed.

"Oh, shit!" she cried.

"Mommy said a bad word!" Ollie said, which caused an uproar of laughter.

Clare turned, and I caught what all the commotion was about. She'd managed to spill her entire glass of wine down the front of her ivory-colored blouse, and it was now running down her pants onto the floor. I turned around immediately.

"My top!" she whined, shaking her arm in an attempt to whisk away some of the moisture.

Logan immediately stepped in front of her, blocking her view from the rest of the room. The men in the room immediately began chuckling.

"What are you doing?" she barked.

"Your blouse is now see-through, babe," he said with a touch of amusement.

"Oh my God," she muttered in horror.

Picking up a towel off the counter, I took several steps backward until I was in arm's reach of Logan and handed it to him. The other women in the room helped clean up around her, and Mia took her upstairs to find something else to wear.

I looked around and huffed.

Okay, so that didn't go exactly as planned, but there is still time.

After about twenty minutes, the women finally descended. Looking less stressed, Clare was now dressed in a pair of Mia's jeans and a dark brown sweater without a speck of wine anywhere.

"I need chocolate!" Clare announced as soon as she hit the bottom step, which got an encouraging agreement from everyone else in the house.

Soon, everyone was grabbing dessert plates and digging into the platter of cookies and brownies and cutting slices of Mom's homemade banana cream pie.

I guessed I would begin my plans after dessert. That was fine.

I helped myself to a brownie and sat down next to

Mia, who was snacking on a cookie and speaking to Declan about his latest project. My foot tapped nervously as I waited for everyone to finish.

How long did it take to eat a dessert?

Of course, after everyone finished, another round of dishes had to be done.

Can't do anything when there are dirty dishes in the sink.

That would surely end the world.

Once that was all done, I finally made my announcement. "Hey, guys, could I get everyone into the living room for a minute?"

They all gave me strange looks, and a few grabbed extra cookies as they went, but I managed to get all the adults and children seated quickly. Mia thankfully sat by herself in a chair, which made my life a bit easier.

"Thank you guys so much for coming. It really means a lot to Mia and me. This home has really become the embodiment of our new life together, and—"

"Oh, shoot," Leah said suddenly. "Lily's got a diaper situation, and wow, it's, um…awful. Can we pause this for about five minutes while I go take care of this?"

Pinching the bridge of my nose, I nodded as she got up and took off for the office, grabbing the diaper bag as she went.

This was not my day—at all.

They all stared up at me expectantly.

"Well, just talk among yourselves!" I said, waving my hands.

I walked into the kitchen for a breather. I heard Liv and Mia continue their earlier conversation about going to the farmers' market next week, and Clare joined in that she wanted to go as well.

Declan followed me into the kitchen, grabbing a

couple of more cookies. He said, "It's for the kids," and then he turned as he was about to walk back out. "Hey, man, you okay? You seem a bit tense."

I turned around, and he must have read something in my expression. Maybe it was because he'd been in my shoes before because his eyes suddenly went wide.

"Oh! You're gonna...oh! Here? Okay. Shit. And we keep interrupting. Yeah, that sucks. Okay, uh...I'll go make Leah hurry up."

He dashed out of the kitchen, and within a few moments, Leah was flying back into the living room, flashing me a huge grin as she found her seat. I took a deep breath and came back into the room.

"Okay, so what I was saying was, Mia and I really appreciate each and every one of you, which is why I wanted all of you to be here."

I hadn't even turned to her. My hand had barely made a single twitch to move to my pocket when Logan's cell phone went off.

"Motherfucker," I cursed under my breath.

And now, I was cursing in front of my widowed mother.

Awesome day.

"Sorry! I've got to take this. It's the hospital."

I waved him off, and he dashed into the office for privacy. Two minutes later, he returned. He broke the news that there was an emergency at the hospital, and he'd been called in. Clare rushed into action and offered to drive him. Within minutes, they'd kissed everyone and rushed out the door with the kids. Mostly everyone followed their leave, and soon, Mia and I were left with Declan and Leah, who are both dragging their feet.

Leah gave me an apologetic hug as I shook my head.

"It's okay," I whispered in her ear. "There's always the Super Bowl."

MIA

I bent down and picked up the pillow off the floor. I placed it back on the couch, fluffing it as I did. Next, I refolded the blanket the kids had pulled down to make a fort in the dining room, and I draped it over the arm of the chair. Stepping back, I admired our cozy little living room. Looking back, I remembered what it looked like when I'd first moved in—a couch covered in plastic and a pile of wood flooring. Now, it was warm and inviting and more than I could have ever imagined. I'd never imagined this house becoming my home in so many ways.

I'd bought it as my huge step out on my own. I'd thought I needed to be on my own to find myself. It had turned out that I wasn't searching for myself. I had been searching, reaching, and clawing my way back to Garrett. There were pieces of myself I still had yet to discover, but I hadn't done it alone. Coming back here to this house, this city, and this man had helped make all of that possible. I was whole again because he helped make it possible.

I no longer dwelled in the past, afraid of my future. I had no idea what our future would bring, but that was part of life, wasn't it? The great unknown. I knew there would be more tears, more struggles, and more heartache. But with them, there would also be tears of joy, happiness, and love. Life was a balancing act. Sometimes, there were moments that tipped the scales, and we found ourselves walking in shadows, but as long as we had those who loved us, we'd always find the light again.

"What are you thinking about?" Garrett asked against my ear as his arms wrapped around my waist.

"How wonderful you are," I said with a grin as I snuggled up against his warm body.

"Mmm...is that so? I think you should show me."

His hands tightened around my waist, and he spun me around until we were face-to-face. His eyes glimmered, and his mouth was curved into a wicked grin.

"Oh, yeah? And how exactly would I do that?" I asked, feigning innocence. I might have batted my eyelashes for effect.

His hands went to the hem of my dress, and he started to pull it up, higher and higher, until my black thigh-highs were exposed.

"Fuck, it's a really good thing I didn't know about these when my mother was here."

A giggle escaped my lips. "That would have not happened while your mother was in the house!"

He gave me a dubious look. "Do you not remember the many study sessions in my room or that time in the garage when my parents were inside making dinner?"

My cheeks instantly heated at the memory. He always had been a bit of a daredevil.

"Okay, point taken. But we're older now and responsible!" I added.

"Mmm...challenge accepted," he purred in my ear as he curled his palm around my backside.

"You're seriously deranged."

"That's why you love me," he said.

His lips met mine, and his hand slid up my thigh and over the lacy edge of my thigh-high. He pulled my leg around his waist. He lifted me and carried me over to the couch, and as my head hit the freshly fluffed pillow, the doorbell rang.

"Seriously? I just can't catch a break today!" Garrett cursed, causing me to snort out a laugh.

I stood, adjusting my dress and smoothing out the wrinkles, and I walked the short distance to the front door.

"It's probably Leah or Liv. They must have forgotten something," I suggested.

I looked around for any missing toys or Tupperware. I didn't see anything, but that didn't mean there wasn't anything lurking around. There were tons of hiding places.

As I pulled open the door, a gasp escaped my lips, and I froze. There, standing before me, was someone I hadn't seen in years, someone I hadn't expected to see again.

"Dad!" I exclaimed as Garrett's hand curled around me.

He didn't look anything like the man I remembered. Standing before me was someone I would have never recognized as my father if I happened to pass by him on the street or in a congested crowd.

He was dressed down, wearing jeans and a black button-down shirt. He still looked put together and handsome, but I couldn't get over the jeans. Never in my life had I ever seen my father in denim. My mother would have had a stroke.

"What are you doing here?" I asked. I was still completely bewildered by not only his physical appearance but by his mere presence alone. I hadn't even known he knew where I lived.

"Are you going to invite me in?" he asked with a slight

grin. Shoving his hands in his pockets, he rocked back on his heels in what appeared to be a nervous gesture.

"Oh, of course. Please, come in. Would you like some coffee? Dessert maybe?" I offered awkwardly.

Maybe you'd like to explain why you are standing in my foyer after eight years of silence?

He politely declined, and I took note that his impeccable manners hadn't diminished over the years. He'd always carried himself well even if he was on the quiet side.

"You remember Garrett, don't you, father?" I said, nearly choking on the rusty paternal word for the man standing before me.

My father nodded, and I watched him turn his attention to Garrett, who had remained noticeably quiet since my father had made his grand entrance. His body was tense at my side, and I knew it was taking great restraint not to take charge of the situation and defend me against the man who had caused me so much pain. Instead, he was pulling back and allowing me to lead. He was allowing me to make up my own mind, and it was one of many reasons I loved him.

"Yes," my father answered, sticking out his hand in a formal gesture toward Garrett.

Garrett stared at his outstretched hand for a moment before finally giving in and taking it in the quickest handshake known to man.

"Good to know you two made it back to each other," he said.

"It wasn't without difficulty," I said, firmly meeting his gaze.

He let out a deep breath and turned away, shoving his

hands back in his pockets again. He paced the small space in circles, like he was churning up the courage to speak.

"I left your mother," he finally said to my utter astonishment.

"What?" Garrett and I both said in unison.

"The divorce was finalized last week. I've been living in a separate apartment for five months, waiting for everything to be settled. I wanted to be sure before I contacted you."

His pacing was driving up my anxiety, so while I tried to process everything, I ushered us into the living room. I watched him take a seat in our flea market chair we'd recently bought. It was antique and had needed a bit of love, but after some new fabric and a bit of elbow grease, it had turned out great. Seeing my father in my living room, sitting among my things, was odd.

"Why? Why did you leave her?" I asked finally.

He cocked an eyebrow as surprise spread across his features, so I amended my question. "I mean, why now? After all this time?"

He nodded in understanding and settled back in his chair.

"It was you honestly. It should have always been you. I should have left her a long time ago, but I was too weak and afraid of what would happen to my life if I did. Everything I did completely and utterly revolved around that woman. I feared what would have happened to me. Hell, I feared what she would do to me if I left. I let her run my existence. I even let her destroy the one relationship I cherished more than anything. That was you."

I was flabbergasted. I always knew he loved me. He was never short on showing affection, even when my mother frowned upon it, but he had broken free from her for me, and I couldn't comprehend that.

"The last straw was when she told me you came to visit," he said.

My eyes widened, and I felt Garrett's fingers weave with mine in silent support.

"I knew she recognized me," I whispered.

"Yes, she did. She just wanted to hurt you, and from your reaction, I can see she did. When she told me you ran out of the building, most likely in tears, I knew I had to leave. Even if she ruined me, I couldn't stay chained to a woman who would do that to her own child."

"So, what now?" I asked hesitantly.

"I don't know. I'm moving back to Richmond. I always liked it here. I don't expect anything, if that's what you're asking. I know I wasn't innocent in all of this. I was as much to blame for all the pain and suffering you endured as your mother was. But I'd like to be here...if you want me to be."

My father was back in my life.

Did I want him to be?

Chapter Twenty-Seven

"So, your dad is back? How's that going?" Liv said.

I balanced the phone between my shoulder and ear while attempting to stir the pot of boiling pasta on the stove.

Is it supposed to be murky-looking like that?

"It's going, I guess," I answered vaguely.

After giving the water another swish, I turned down the temperature to medium, fearing it would boil over. That had happened last time, and it hadn't been pretty. *Water could boil at medium, right? Eventually, I'm sure.*

"So, how is Garrett taking it?" she asked.

"Well, he's obviously cautious. He's letting me decide which way I want to go."

"And which way is that?"

I sighed. I'd been back and forth with my decision over the last week. I had gone through several emotional stages with my father's reappearance in my life—surprise, anger, annoyance, elation, back to anger, and finally, numbness. I liked numbness the best. It lacked any highs or lows and didn't require decisions. Of course, it hadn't helped a damn bit either.

"I don't know. I want to believe he's being genuine. I mean, he did divorce the woman. That's pretty convincing to me."

"Damn, I would have loved to see her face when he dropped that bomb. That had to be priceless," she said with amusement.

I tried not to grin, but she was right. It was hard to picture my mother in a situation she couldn't control, and she had definitely been able to control my dad.

"Well, you know I'll support you no matter what," Liv said. "I'll hug him and welcome him back to the city, or I'll kick him in the balls. Whatever you tell me to do, babe."

That brought a smile to my face, and I could not help but laugh. "Thanks, Liv. I'll keep you updated, but I've got to go. I'm making dinner for Garrett, and then I'm headed out to dinner with my father."

I heard an audible snort before she said, "You're making dinner for Garrett? Are you trying to kill him?"

"No! I just wanted to be nice. He's been so nice this week with everything, and I feel bad for ditching him, so I wanted to have dinner ready for him when he gets home from work."

"Okay, babe, but you would have been better off ordering a pizza," she said before laughing and hanging up.

I looked down at the pot of water filled with half-limp pasta, and I sighed in frustration. *Does food hate me? I followed the directions, didn't I? Liv was right. I should probably just order a pizza.*

Picking up my phone again, I headed upstairs to freshen my makeup and grab my boots, so I'd be ready when my dad arrived. He'd called a few days ago and asked if I wouldn't mind going out to dinner with him, and I'd agreed. I knew he was making an effort, and even though I was still wary of falling back into a relationship with him, I wanted to allow him the opportunity to at least try.

Grabbing my boots in one hand, I dialed the pizza place down the street and ordered Garrett's favorite. I raced back downstairs and started the process of chucking the failed meal in the trash just as Garrett came through the door. Head lowered, he was engrossed in a phone call and dodged into the office.

"Do you have any other ideas? I'm totally tapped out," he said before he shut the door.

Okay…weird.

It wasn't the first odd moment of the week either. I'd caught him on the computer late at night. As soon as I'd entered the room, he'd quickly shut down the monitor. He'd had a number of mysterious phone calls as well, and he'd seemed on edge, not grumpy or moody. It had been just like he was about to explode.

With the dinner now trashed, I moved to the living room to slip on my shoes. As I was pulling up the last zipper of my left boot, I felt the familiar warmth of Garrett's hands running down my shoulders and arms.

"Sorry, I had to finish that call," he said, bending forward to pull me against him.

"No problem. Everything okay?"

"Yeah, I think so."

"You've been very vague lately," I said, turning to face him.

The corner of his mouth curved into a small grin, but he remained silent. Instead, he just placed a small kiss on my nose.

The doorbell rang before I had a chance to push him for answers. I gave him a look that said this conversation wasn't over, and he just chuckled. He released his hold on me, so I could answer the door.

My father looked much the same as the last time I'd seen him. He appeared very casual but still well-dressed in dark-washed jeans and a tailored button-down wool jacket. He had my blue eyes and dark hair. Luckily, I hadn't inherited much from my mother. For a dad, he was actually pretty good-looking.

He gave me a warm smile and moved in to hug me, but then he stopped himself, obviously unsure of boundaries. Unsure myself, I stood awkwardly and bit my lip.

"You ready?" he asked, shoving his hands in his coat pockets.

"Yep!" I said a bit too brightly.

I turned to say good-bye to Garrett and realized he was right there. I should have known. He'd offered to come with me, but I'd told him that I needed to do this myself. He'd squeezed my hand and told me he understood, and he'd said he would be there for me in a second if I needed him.

I kissed him sweetly on the cheek and said I'd be back shortly.

The drive was short, and we ended up at a little cafe down the street that Garrett and I loved to visit. I was surprised by my dad's choice, but figured he was trying to impress me by picking something more my style.

"This is a great place," I commented as the waiter seated us near the back.

"I always loved this place," he said, picking up the menu and smiling, like he'd just seen an old friend.

"You used to come here?" I scoffed, trying to picture my dad in one of my favorite restaurants. I looked around at the less than five star atmosphere, taking in the exposed pipes at the ceiling and the rustic wall paper.

It wasn't a dump, but it definitely wasn't the Ritz either, which was the only type of dining experience for my mother. This cafe was a mom-and-pop type of location with real food and great service. It was definitely not the type of place I'd expect to find my father.

"Yes, I always came here for lunch. It was my little secret," he said with a grin.

"What other secrets do you have?" I asked.

"I used to attend all your choir concerts, each and every one."

I gasped. My mother had never approved of me joining choir at school. She'd paid for vocal lessons, and I'd had vocal recitals every year. That had been an approved and accepted extracurricular activity. Singing in a high school jazz choir had been just some silly little hobby and not worth her time. She'd never gone to any of my recitals even though it was the one thing I'd been most proud of during my four years of school.

"I never saw you."

"I was always in the back. I remember every solo. You were fantastic."

Tears stung my eyes. "Why didn't you ever tell me?"

"Amelia, I'm a very weak man. I didn't start out that way. I think that's what attracted your mother to me in the first place, the power I could wield. I was the top of my class in law school, and I had my pick of jobs. I was going places, and she saw me for what she could gain out of me. The fool in me thought she loved me. By the time I realized her real intentions, it was too late. We had you, and I was deeply in love with her."

"Even after you found out she didn't love you?"

"We don't choose the ones we love," he said with sadness. "It took me a long time to realize my love for her was poison. It was poisoning everything in my life, including our own daughter. She had become the master of my universe, and the worst part was I had allowed it. I didn't care about her social ladder or money. I'd always just wanted to make her happy. But it was never enough."

"So, you finally broke free," I said.

"Yes, I finally decided to love myself...to love my daughter more than a woman who would never change and who would never love me back. I can't say it was easy. Despite everything, I still love her. Or I guess, I still love the memory of her, if that makes sense."

I smiled and nodded. "Yes, that makes sense."

We ate our meal and chatted a bit about my classes and work at the hospital. I asked him about his new job, and he said he was adjusting well at the new firm.

Later on, as we drove, he became silent until we made our way up to the front door.

"I guess the hardest thing I'm dealing with is how much I failed you. I spent years in this fog, hoping that somehow your mother would love me back. That entire time I was waiting, you were growing up without a father."

"You were there," I said softly.

"No, I wasn't, not as much as I could have been. And I haven't been here for eight years."

Taking his hand, as we stood on the porch, I met his gaze. "Dad, in the last few months, there's one thing I've learned about regret. You have to let it go. Otherwise, it will swallow you whole. Grieve your mistakes, but then put them in the past and move on. I'm here now, and so are you."

As it so happened, I wasn't the only one holding on to regrets.

His blue eyes watered, and for the first time in over eight years, I opened my arms and felt the loving embrace of a parent. I thought I had healed all my wounds from my past when I grieved our lost child. It turned out that I still hadn't grieved my own lost childhood.

As I stood in the embrace of my father's warm arms once again, I finally felt free.

GARRETT

That little black box had been burning a damn hole in my pocket for an entire week.

Ever since my perfect plan had failed miserably, thanks to my family and their catastrophes, work emergencies, and then Mia's father showing up, I'd been pacing our newly renovated floors. I'd spent hours on the Internet trying to figure out something, anything that would be original, spontaneous, and represent the depth of the love I had for her. I quickly discovered I couldn't find anything new and original on the Internet. *Go figure.*

Nothing was good enough for my Mia.

I was not copying someone else's idea, and I was definitely not plastering her name on a Jumbotron. Thanks to Aiden, all restaurants were out of the question, and I really didn't want to risk having my family over again for another failed party. Not to mention, she would get a little suspicious if they all suddenly showed up for a second week in a row.

I'd been on the phone with Leah almost every day, trying to come up with an idea, and so far, I had nothing. Even my idea to take Mia to New York and propose on the Empire State Building seemed lame and overdone.

Why is this so hard?

I knew it was right. I knew she was right. All I needed was the damn place and a plan.

While I was surfing around the Internet for the hundredth time that day, I heard the front door open followed by Mia's voice as she greeted me. I quickly shut down the computer and stepped out of the office. I met her in to the living room where I swept her up in my arms as she giggled and smiled. I showered her face and neck with kisses, which only made her laugh harder.

"You're a dork," she said cheerfully.

"Yes, but I'm your dork, and I'm hot."

"And so modest, too."

I gave her a sly grin and slapped her ass, causing her to yelp. I carried her to the couch and pulled her onto my lap as I made us comfortable.

"How was dinner?" I asked, already having a good idea.

Her eyes were bright and full of energy, and she couldn't stop grinning.

"It was wonderful, Garrett."

I smoothed out her hair and tucked it behind her ear, loving how soft and silky it felt between my fingers.

"I'm glad, baby. I'm so glad."

"He came to my choir concerts in high school," she said wistfully.

I smiled. "He couldn't stay away."

"He said he wants to get to know us both." She looked up at me with hesitation.

"I'd like that. He's your father, Mia. We're looking forward, right? Remember the past, but don't dwell in it. Isn't that our motto? We've all made mistakes, and that doesn't exclude him."

"I think he's wallowing in regret, just like I was. It's different, but I recognize the symptoms."

"Like father, like daughter?" I asked with a shadow of a smile.

"Yes, I guess."

"Well then, who better to help him than you?" I pointed out.

"You're right. He said it was hard to leave my mother. He said he still loves her after all these years."

"I guess I can see that. Love can be many things. Pure or tainted, healing or hurting—it's a fine line."

"I hope he can heal, like I did."

"He will," I said, placing a chaste kiss on her cheek. "He has you."

She turned in my arms, and I cherished the feel of her.

This is where I want her for the rest of my life.

"Come on, let's go to bed," I said.

"It's eight o'clock!"

"Well, you can never get too much sleep," I joked.

She gave me a doubtful look, which made me chuckle. I grabbed her around the waist and flipped her slightly before throwing her over my shoulder.

"Garrett!" she squealed.

"I'm telling you, we need to get to sleep. It's late. The sun will be up in fourteen hours!"

I made a mad dash for the stairs, and she screamed louder, banging her fists on my ass.

"Keep doing that, and I'll start spinning!"

"Ugh!" she cried out in amused frustration.

I took the stairs two at a time, which made her bounce up and down on my shoulder.

"Oh my God, I'm going to kill you, Garrett Finnegan!" she threatened as we rounded the corner to our bedroom.

I loved the orange we'd picked out for the walls. Since then, we'd sanded and re-stained all the furniture and bought new linens from some crazy home store in the mall that Mia made me walk around in for hours. It looked great, but right now, all I wanted to see was Mia naked against one of those sun-kissed walls.

Letting her slide off my shoulder, I tried to hold back my laughter as I took in her frazzled hair and beet-red face.

"You are so dead," she said, blowing an errant brown strand out of her face.

My attempt to contain my laughter failed, and it came roaring out of me. I doubled over, clutching my side, as I fought for breath.

"Jackass," Mia said with a giggle.

Pulling myself together, I clutched her waist and pulled her closer.

"That was the carefree boy I fell in love with, throwing me over the shoulder in the middle of the hallway in front of the entire school. The man staring at me now with the smoldering, made-for-sex eyes—that's the man I fell in love with all over again. Like past and present colliding, you are the perfect mix of the two now."

My eyes widened at her words, and like a lightbulb, everything fell into place.

Past and present colliding...

For the past few weeks, I'd been driving myself mad,

trying to think of the perfect way to ask Mia to marry me. I'd been convinced that this time, I had to do it bigger, grander, and in a way that she would be proud of. But hadn't I already done that?

Sitting by the river after I'd proposed the night before our graduation, neither one of us had felt like we'd been cheated of something greater. It hadn't mattered that her ring was small or that we weren't someplace public. We'd had each other.

Wasn't that all that mattered?

I pulled back from our embrace. "Grab your coat," I instructed.

"What? I thought we were going to bed?"

"Oh, we'll do that later. I want to go for a drive."

She looked at me like I had two heads, but rather than disagreeing, she just smiled warmly and followed me down the stairs.

"Where are we going?" she asked as she slipped on her coat and gloves.

As I palmed the ring box in my pocket, I smiled. "I know just the place."

GARRETT

 $\mathcal{M}$ y consciousness stirred as my eyes slowly lifted. Soft light filtered through a window, and my gaze shifted, taking in the warm sun-kissed color of the walls and the dark furniture.

I was home.

I'd dreamed of her again. This time though, she hadn't walked away from me in the satin sea of caps and gowns. She'd walked toward me.

I slumped back on my pillow and exhaled, feeling peaceful and relaxed.

It had been a busy week. Besides the party-planning, blueprints had to be completed for the next phase of the housing development I had been hired to design. Semester grades were due, and my sexy wife was nose deep in grading tests and parent-teacher conferences. She loved every minute though. Just as I'd thought, she was an amazing teacher, and her choral students adored her. I was fairly certain a few of those pimple-faced preteens even had a bit of a crush on my beautiful wife, not that I blamed them.

My hands searched the warm flannel sheets and came up empty. I looked to the right and found nothing.

Where was she?

Rising quickly, I tugged on a pair of pajama bottoms and a T-shirt, and then I headed down the stairs where I could already hear the sweet humming sounds of her voice as she sang "Happy Birthday." Turning into the kitchen, I found her dancing around in one of my old T-shirts, making a goofball of herself, as Asher giggled and cooed. Sneaking up behind her, I slipped my hands around her waist. She yelped in surprise and laughed, relaxing into my chest.

"You weren't in bed." I pouted.

"Someone needed to be fed," she said.

She pointed to Asher whose face still made me melt every single time I saw it.

"Someone is an attention hog. Where's my breakfast?" I asked, looking around at the mess she'd created.

Mia had learned a few things in the three years we'd been married. She could make a couple of dishes now without lighting the kitchen on fire, but she'd never learned the art of tidiness. The kitchen looked as if it had blown up flour.

"It's not your birthday, grumpy," she pointed out, flipping the slightly burned pancake on the griddle.

"Hmm…maybe I'll have cereal."

She turned to give me the evil eye and slapped my ass as I made my way to the other side of the kitchen.

Asher yelled, "Da!" He made his grabby hands, which resembled tiny pinchers on a crab.

I smiled, loving the sound of my child calling out to

me. It was a sound I'd thought I would never hear, yet here we were, celebrating his first birthday. I picked Asher up from his highchair and rocked him on my hip while Mia made subpar pancakes, and I realized how lucky I was, how fortunate I'd been.

I'd learned that our lives could be plotted out by pivotal moments in time. My life with Mia had been a journey, an endless string of moments and memories that kept moving us forward, propelling us to a future neither of us could imagine.

As I'd sat in that homeroom class so many years ago, staring at the girl who would one day be my wife, I'd had no idea how important that moment would become. She was the first girl I'd ever noticed and the only woman I'd wanted since. I'd thought she'd broken me on that deserted, rain-soaked street and that I'd never recover. When I'd found her on that crowded street at the farmers' market, I'd known I would never be able to let her go again.

Every moment of our lives had brought us to this one and the countless others that would follow.

"So, little dude," I said as he grabbed on to my nose and giggled, "are you ready to celebrate?"

MIA

Seeing Garrett hold our son never failed to make my heart stutter and swell with pride. He took Asher upstairs, and I set my sights on the kitchen, hoping I could get the breakfast mess cleaned by the time everyone arrived for Asher's birthday party.

Our little boy was turning one today.

I was a mother.

I'd known this fact for a year now, longer actually, but it still amazed me. It was something I'd never thought was possible, but I'd quickly learned that nothing in life was impossible. I'd known adoption was an avenue we could explore, but I'd also known it was difficult, expensive, and full of challenges.

After Garrett had proposed to me by the river on that cold winter evening in the exact spot he'd dropped to one knee so many years earlier, my heart was complete. I wouldn't need anything else in the world as long as I had him.

"What are we doing here?" I asked.

He stopped the car at our favorite spot by the river. The trees were now bare and statuesque in their grayish wintery state. Garrett grabbed his trusty blanket out of the back of the car, and we started down the path toward the water.

"I thought a little bit of alone time with our favorite spot might be nice," he said.

"In thirty-degree weather?" I asked, rubbing my hands together. I shoved them in my pockets.

I saw him smirk as he unfolded the blanket and spread it across the cold ground. He sat down and motioned for me to do the same.

"You want me to sit down on the frozen ground?" I added.

"Mmhmm," he said, smoothing out the blanket suggestively.

I rolled my eyes and planted my butt down on the cold earth next to him, yelping as my jean-clad ass hit the icy blanket.

"See? Not that bad, right?"

I just glared my answer back at him, but then I gasped as soon as he bent forward on his knees and propped one forward.

Holy shit. He was on one knee...and he just pulled out a ring box.

I suddenly didn't care about my ass anymore. Just like the first time, I went to my knees and mimicked his position so that our noses were touching.

He laughed. "Some things don't change."

I stared down at the ring box, and then my eyes drifted up to his. "No, they don't."

"I've been agonizing for weeks, trying to find the perfect place to ask you. That sham of a housewarming party was all for show. I was supposed to propose that night, but all my meticulous plans got botched. I've been scrambling all week, attempting to come up with something. Then, you made that comment about our past and present colliding, and I realized I already had the perfect spot."

"Here," I said.

"Here," he confirmed.

He opened the ring box and nestled inside was a perfect representation of everything we'd been through.

"When did you do this?" I asked.

He'd somehow managed to take my original engagement ring and added to it. He'd combined three stones, adding a larger stone in the middle and two smaller stones on either side —past, present and future.

"A few weeks ago. I'm surprised you didn't notice. It's been missing from your jewelry box for a while now. I've been sweating bullets ever since I stole it. The smaller stone to the left is your original stone."

"It's beautiful, Garrett," I said, tears trickling down my face.

"When I ask you this time, it's forever, Mia. No matter what life throws at us, we will go through it together."

I nodded as he took the delicate ring out of its box, and he placed it on the tip of my finger.

"Mia Emerson, will you do me the honor of becoming my wife?"

"Yes."

Six months later, on a Southern plantation over-looking the James River, Garrett and I had finally become husband and wife.

Looking down at my bridal set, I smiled, remembering my father walking me down the aisle and feeling nothing but peace, happiness, and hope.

I'd never expected anything more than that moment, and I never asked for it. A year later, Garrett had brought up adoption, and I had felt almost scared to ask for more.

We were happy. Did we deserve to ask for more?

He had explained to me that when two people had as much love as we did, it needed to be shared.

So, we had turned to adoption.

We'd found open adoption to be the right path for us, and the young girl who had chosen us was wonderful. She'd allowed us to attend every doctor's appointment and even be present at the birth. Seeing our child being born had been the most precious gift she could have given us.

She was young, so very young, and she had chosen to walk away completely. We had given her other options, but she'd said anything else would be too hard. It was an extremely grown-up decision, and we had respected her wishes. I'd been in her shoes—even though I'd had Garrett and she had been alone—but I remembered feeling over-whelmed from the grown-up decision that had been too much for my age.

When I'd held Asher Thomas Finnegan in my arms for the first time, I'd fallen instantly in love with him.

He was a little miracle.

I finished cleaning the kitchen and ran upstairs to make myself presentable. Then, the doorbell rang, signaling the arrival of our first party guest.

"We'll get it!" Garrett yelled from the hallway.

I exhaled in relief. I was nowhere near ready, and I was pretty sure I still had flour in my fingernails.

The doorbell chimed several more times as I ran around, putting on a flattering pair of jeans and a gauzy top. I finished the look off with some jewelry and wedged sandals, and then I flew down the stairs.

Everyone was gathered around Garrett and Asher. Our little boy was dressed in adorable jeans and a cute little vest. He'd grown so much since the day I held him in my arms for the first time. I remembered holding his tiny foot in my hand as he'd stared up at me.

"Our little guy needs a name," Garrett said softly.

I rocked our son back and forth and smiled up at Garrett from the chair.

"Asher," I answered, rising carefully from the rocker as I held our little bundle.

I gently handed him to Garrett and couldn't help the giggle that escaped as I watched him tense. Asher was so small. His tiny head looked like a doll in comparison to Garrett's massive frame.

"Asher," he repeated, as he took him in his arms. "I like that."

"It means "happy and blessed.""

Our birthday boy was passed around the room from laps to waiting arms. Clare cooed and made him laugh as she covered up her eyes in a game of peekaboo. I saw her look up at Logan with a knowing smile.

Perhaps Maddie and Ollie would be getting a new sibling soon?

Leah and Declan played blocks with Asher on the floor, and they laughed as he knocked down their carefully built towers each time. It was one of his favorite games.

My father rocked Asher back and forth when he got sleepy and put him down for a nap with the help of Garrett's mother.

"Where's Liv?" I asked suddenly, realizing we weren't yet complete.

"Oh, she just called. She said a new neighbor was moving in next door and blocking her driveway with the moving van. She should be here any minute."

Oh boy, a new neighbor? That could be interesting.

She showed up not more than five minutes later, carrying a tray of veggies and hummus. She told me the heroic tale of how she'd managed to get her car out of her driveway despite the rude new neighbor she had.

Lunch was ready. Everyone grabbed plates and served themselves from the kitchen. Nothing was ever fancy at our house, especially now that we were parents. I was proud of myself for managing to go to the store to pick up prepared chicken salad and for showering all in one day.

My once stark and empty house was now filled with color, warmth, and family. Every wall showed a glimpse from our past that had brought us to this moment. As we sat Asher in his high chair and watched him demolish his birthday cake, I couldn't help but feel a little overwhelmed.

"Hey, you okay?" Garrett asked, pulling me against his chest.

I snapped another picture of Asher and finally turned to Garrett. "We did this," I said.

His eyes softened, and he smiled. "Yeah, we did."

He bent down and placed a tender kiss on my eager lips, and I melted into his touch.

I'd walked away from love and felt my heart shatter. I'd spent eight years bottling up the pain and heartache from those emotional events. I thought I was in control, but when you are running from your life, you're never the one in control.

I never understood why I ended up driving back down that familiar highway, to the one place I swore I'd never return. Seeing Garrett standing on that street corner had been like a long overdue jolt to my heart. An awakening I so desperately needed. He saved me. He saved me by loving me and showing me that it was okay to once again love myself.

Love is many things. It's every raw human emotion all rolled up into one messy four letter word. There's no rule book and definitely no guarantees. But as I stood there in Garrett's arms, with our friends and family in a house we made a home, I knew that no matter what life threw at us, we'd always get by with just a little bit of love, hope and happiness.

***

Don't miss the last chapter of the Ready series. Liv and Jackson's story continues in *Ready or Not.*

READY OR NOT

PROLOGUE

Twenty Years Ago

I stood on the large stage and quietly bent forward, smoothing the tiny wrinkles out of my pretty pink taffeta dress. The fabric glittered and shimmered as I moved under the bright spotlights. A simple satin bow sat high on top of my head, and dark ringlets curled down my back, reminding me of all the princesses Daddy would tell me about at bedtime.

Looking around at the crowded room and the large audience standing before us, I couldn't help but smile.

I guessed I was kind of like a princess now.

"Stop fidgeting, Olivia," my mother whispered next to me.

Her pale pink coat matched my dress, but it wasn't nearly as pretty. It made her look old and stuffy. I liked it better when she used to dress in shorts and sandals, and she'd dance with me in the sprinklers when the weather got too hot and sticky to stay indoors.

I heard a tapping sound as a microphone came alive.

My attention turned to the front of the stage as the crowd exploded in applause.

Smiling, I watched my daddy step out from behind the curtain, grinning and waving, as he passed by a sea of red, white, and blue. Signs bearing his picture and name were bobbing up and down amid the crowd, and I soon found myself covering my tiny ears to block out the thundering noise.

Slender polished fingers wrapped around mine and tugged my hands back down to my sides. I looked up to find my mother wiping tears from her eyes. She gave me a tight hug, and then she whisked away salty trails that had made their way down her cheeks.

"He's no longer just ours anymore. Things are going to be different from this moment on," she said.

I glanced back at my father, who was now standing at the wooden podium. After thanking everyone in the room, he turned around and motioned for the two of us to come forward.

"I wouldn't be anyone without these two women standing beside me—my wonderful wife, June, and darling daughter, Olivia."

The crowd cheered, and I couldn't help but smile and blush a little.

I really did feel like a princess—or at least a senator's daughter.

Whatever that was.

My father always said that being a senator was a big deal. All I knew was, his face was everywhere, and soon, he'd start working at the Capitol building downtown. I'd once taken a field trip there. It looked like the White House, and everyone said it was very old.

"This is only the first step. We're making waves in

Virginia ladies and gentlemen! Victory tonight, change tomorrow!" he bellowed into the microphone.

The crowd erupted once again as he wrapped his arms around us. My mother's tears continued to flow as I smiled out at all the people cheering for my father.

She was wrong.

Daddy wasn't different. He felt the same, and he certainly looked like the same goofy dad who would tuck me in at night and sing me songs about dinosaurs and princesses having tea parties.

It was just a job. Kara was one of my friends at school, and her father had gotten a new job. The only thing that had changed in Kara's life was that she got a bigger house down the street.

We already had a big house.

I looked up at my daddy one more time as he squeezed me closer to his side and waved to the crowd.

Nothing would change.

He'd always be my hero.

CHAPTER ONE

LIV

Late.

I was always late.

I didn't know how others managed their lives so effortlessly, especially when they had responsibilities outside of themselves, like kids and husbands and a few plants.

I had only myself to manage, yet I was always running around like a nut at the last moment, trying to decide things like if the teal or brown sandals went better with my dress.

"Teal. Definitely teal," I muttered as I stared into the floor-length mirror hanging on the back of my bedroom door.

Shoe decision made, I shifted into hyperdrive and began throwing on bangle bracelets and a scarf before finishing everything off with a spritz of my favorite lavender perfume.

I flew down the stairs and made it to the door before I came to a screeching halt.

"Brown!" I yelled to no one in particular as I ran back upstairs to switch my shoes for the tenth time.

I ran back down to the first floor of my historic little house and managed to grab my keys and purse before rushing out the door. I had just turned the lock when I noticed a beast of a moving van occupying the entire street.

"What the hell?" I mumbled, looking around in a daze.

My little blue Prius was perfectly blocked in by a red monstrosity of a moving truck.

Mike's Movers was plastered on the side, and two big, bulky men were slowly moving down a ramp with a large blue dresser.

"Excuse me!" I yelled, marching over to the beefy quarterback-looking men.

"Yeah?"

"Are you aware your truck is blocking the entire street?" I asked, trying to ignore my high-pitched tone and the way my hand attached itself to my hip.

I looked like a bitch.

But I'm angry!

Beefy man number one's eyebrow arched in amusement. I had no doubt he found my annoyance cute and endearing.

"Sorry, sweetheart. It's a narrow road, and there aren't any alleyways big enough. We're going as fast as we can."

"Listen, sweetheart," I replied, making his lazy smile falter slightly, "I'm late for something, and I really need to get out of my driveway. So, if you could move your big-ass truck just a smidge and let me out, I'd be so very grateful."

Apparently, my attempt at politeness with a dash of southern charm hadn't worked. Not even a little.

The man looked at me blankly, before wiping his nose with the sleeve of his sweaty shirt. "Sorry, we're under a time crunch, lady."

"Ugh!" I cried out in frustration. "Is there an owner to all this crap?"

"There is, but he's not here right now. I think he got stuck in beach traffic on I-95. Moving here from down south, I think," he rambled.

"Awesome."

I took one last glance at the truck completely blocking in my car from getting on the road leading to my best friends' house—Mia and Garrett Finnegan.

I would be late once again.

———

An hour later, after whipping my car into gear and flying down the road as quickly as possible in the direction of Garrett and Mia's, I was finally on my way to the party.

Arguments with new neighbors and moving companies immediately vanished.

My little godson was turning one today.

It still amazed me to say that I had a godson.

When Mia Emerson had arrived on my doorstep four years ago, I'd found a shell of my former best friend. She'd looked much the same. Although older and perhaps a bit less naive than the last time I'd seen her, it had still been her peeking through those watery blue eyes—or at least part of her.

The other half she'd left behind eight years earlier when she walked away, broken and ashamed. When she'd found Garrett standing on a street corner in a farmer's market, it was like the entire world had righted itself that day.

It had taken time and a lot of healing on both sides, but eventually, they'd found a path back to each other.

Then, they'd found Asher, my beautiful little godson.

Due to a miscarriage gone wrong, Mia could never have children of her own. After their first couple of years of marriage, she and Garrett had decided to adopt and make a family of their own. Seeing my two best friends become parents was a joy I couldn't describe, and it'd made me believe that anything was possible.

Except the possibility of me ever being on time.

I glared at the stoplight that had been stuck in the annoying shade of red for what seemed like an eternity, and I silently willed it to turn green. Someone must have felt pity for me in that moment because the light miraculously turned, and I quickly made it down the last few blocks to the cute little renovated house where Garrett and Mia had been living since she returned to Richmond.

Since Garrett had moved in, the house had undergone several upgrades, and now, it was the showpiece on the block. Its fresh paint and beautiful landscaping made it one of the most sought after pieces of property in the area. But until little Asher needed more room or if they decided to add to the family, I believed the Finnegans were staying put.

I didn't bother knocking, and instead, I just entered through the front door, yelling, "Hello?"

Mia's golden retriever, Sam, came barreling down the hallway. Several small children followed behind, chasing his tail.

I gave him and the kids a proper welcome, and then I proceeded into the kitchen where the majority of the adults were crowded around the hors d'oeuvres.

"Hey, everyone. Sorry I'm late." I set down the veggie and hummus platter on the counter next to a large bowl of fruit.

"No problem." Mia grinned.

"What?" I asked, noticing the mischief in her eyes.

"Well, we're kind of used to it by now."

I chucked a kitchen towel at her head, and she burst out laughing.

"Shut up," I mumbled. "You have flour in your hair."

Her eyes widened as her hands flew up to her long brown hair, brushing away the white powder that had settled around her crown.

"I don't know how you manage to be on time for work every morning, yet you're late to everything else, Liv."

I shrugged. "Don't want to piss off my boss." I winked, which caused everyone to laugh. "Where's my—" I began asking just as the baby monitor went nuts.

Red lights started flashing as high-pitched wailing filled the room.

"Oh, there he is," I said with a grin.

"He took an extra-long nap," Garrett explained.

Mia motioned toward the stairs.

"Let me," I said. "I want to snuggle him."

My flowing teal skirt swished and floated behind me as I left the party and jogged up the stairs. I passed the master bedroom and walked down the hall until I reached Asher's nursery. Pushing open the door to the dimly lit room, I walked inside.

The soft light in the room washed out most of the

bright colors, leaving only muted, somber tones. The yellow on the walls was barely recognizable with the black shade pulled taut, but I could almost make out the tiny star shapes I'd painted on the walls months before he was brought home.

My little peanut was standing in his crib as little tears trickled down his chubby cheeks. As soon as he saw me enter, his little hands flew up, making little pinchers, as he lost the last bit of patience he had.

"Okay, okay." I laughed. "I'll spring you free," I cooed, lifting him from the crib and nestling him in my arms.

He smelled like baby shampoo, so clean and fresh. Whoever had invented that particular scent was a genius. I had no plans of making a baby anytime soon, but just a whiff of that stuff even made my chained-up ovaries constrict just the slightest bit.

After a quick diaper change, I brought Asher downstairs to the rest of the family. His grumpy attitude was completely forgotten as he set his sights on his birthday cake. Blue with brown and white polka dots, it had a giant number one–shaped candle on top. After setting his wiggly body in his highchair, we all sang as Mia carried in the cake. As she placed it down in front of him, his eyes widened in delight as Mia tried in vain to keep his little pincher fingers from diving into the frosting. She and Garrett helped blow out the candle, and then they cut a small piece for the birthday boy. Everyone watched in delight and horror as Asher demolished the cake, coating his face and high chair in frosting and chocolate cake.

"He made a big mess!" Lily said to her mother, Leah.

A quick snort followed, and Leah answered, "Baby, you did the same thing. I was cleaning chocolate out of your nose for days."

Leah gave me a quick grin, and I laughed. I loved Leah. We'd grown really close over the years, and I considered her one of my closest friends. She was the best friend of Garrett's sister, Clare Matthews.

Somehow, I'd been pulled into this crazy family, making me one of them.

The Finnegans didn't define family as a last name or bloodline. Family was being with loved ones, and everyone in this room—whether the last name was Finnegan, James, Matthews, or even Prescott, like me—was considered family.

It was the only kind of family I'd had in years.

JACKSON

"Good God, I forgot about the wallpaper," I muttered as I passed by the hallway bathroom. I dropped another box into the room that Noah had declared as his during our first walk-through.

"I'm kind of digging the toilet wallpaper, Dad," he said.

His young laughter filled the hallway as I found him leaning against the doorway, which led into the horrible bathroom.

"It's awful. Who does that?" My eyes roamed the floor-to-ceiling wallpaper that predated even me. It had probably once been a brilliant white, but it had faded into a dingy cream. The old antique toilets ranged from dusty blue to wrought iron and covered the entirety of the bathroom.

"Great Grandma," Noah answered. "Obviously."

"Yeah. She must have thought it was a good idea…in 1955."

He laughed again as I messed up his hair. Darting out

of my way as he rolled his eyes, he did what I could only describe as a Justin Bieber hair flip to move his sandy blond locks neatly back in place.

I'd tried everything to talk him out of that ridiculous haircut.

I'd lost. The hair was cool, and I just didn't get it.

Gotta love tweens.

Noah was in those special years of development when he would be torn between the simple life of a kid and the alluring complexity of a teen.

My son was just about to enter sixth grade. I wasn't quite sure what had happened to him in the last few months of grade school, but it was as if the thought and anticipation of going to middle school had suddenly turned him completely upside down and backward.

That, or aliens had abducted my real son, and this was just a stand-in. I was still unclear.

He was constantly moody, going from one extreme to another. One minute, I'd find him in his room, playing Legos and singing to himself, and then the next, he'd be yelling and screaming over being treated like a baby.

We used to talk, from feelings to *Sesame Street* and everything in between. Now, I would get shouting and a door in my face.

Was it me? Was I coddling him? Or were these raging hormones that had suddenly infiltrated his body, and they were too much for him to handle?

Part of me always wondered if it had something to do with the lack of maternal presence in his life.

What if I'm not enough?

I always tried to be all he needed, but as awesome as I was, I couldn't be a replacement for a mother.

Standing in the hallway, I watched him shuffle off to his new room, no doubt in search of his phone or iPod, and I just shook my head. I didn't have time to sulk or ponder over questions I didn't have the answers to.

That blond hair, blue-eyed boy was the only thing I had in this world.

One way or another, I had to be enough.

LIV

I was pleasantly surprised to find my street free and clear of moving vans when I arrived home several hours later, stuffed full of food and high on the smell of baby Asher's shampoo. He was my fix. I loved that little monster. As usual, Mia and Garrett had to pry him away from me.

I was twenty-eight and had no plans of marrying anytime soon—if ever. Holding my godson every so often kept those baby-wanting tendencies down to a minimum. You might make a certain life plan and fully intend on sticking to it, but that didn't mean your hormones had to get on board with you.

I wasn't against marriage, nor did I have a horrible back story to defend my reasoning. I just didn't think I had that specific gene that allowed a person to mate for life.

One guy—forever?

It sounded so permanent.

Choosing just one would be like picking a favorite piece of jewelry.

I had this gorgeous turquoise pendant. I'd picked it up at a farmers' market from a jeweler who only made one-of-a-kind designs. It'd immediately become my new favorite thing to wear. The intricate silver and dark color of turquoise went perfectly with almost everything in my closet. I'd wear it so much that my friends forgot what I looked like without it. The pendant and I had become one —that was, until I'd found an amethyst and rose quartz necklace that outdid the turquoise one in every way. I would still wear the turquoise, but it wasn't nearly as special anymore.

Isn't it the same with men—the one you're with is like a turquoise pendant until something better comes along?

So, I had just decided a long time ago to have a very large jewelry collection.

I used the same logic on the men I dated—fun and casual while it lasted but nothing permanent. Life was too short to settle.

As I parked my car on the curb in front of my house, I snuck a quick peek into my rearview mirror, trying to catch a glimpse of my new neighbor.

I'd lived next door to Mrs. Reid for as long as I could remember. She was a sweet, grandmotherly-type woman.

She used to bake cookies every Sunday until the nurses had started coming every day, and then the cookies had stopped. She wasn't much of a fan of my all-natural version. I'd presented my plate of organic chocolate chip cookies and proudly boasted that I'd used applesauce instead of oil. She'd taken one hesitant bite and crinkled her nose.

"Cookies need fat, honey," she'd told me.

I'd laughed, not feeling the least bit offended.

She had grown vegetables and roses in her backyard up until she couldn't walk without assistance, and I'd been tending to her gardens ever since. Mrs. Reid was in her late eighties when she'd passed away.

When I finally stepped out of my car, a gasp escaped my lungs as my eyes lowered to the flower beds separating our two houses.

"Who would do such a thing?" I whispered, looking down at the decapitated and ravaged flowers.

The once beautiful display of multicolored perennials was now a churned-up disaster of footprints and soil.

My heated gaze settled on the lights glowing within the house. A shadow passed by an open window upstairs in what used to be Mrs. Reid's master bedroom.

I took one step forward, ready to march over, meet my new neighbors, and give them a piece of my mind.

A strong gust of wind sent the curtain into a tailspin and suddenly the shadow solidified, and I saw the finest bare back I'd seen in years. It was tanned, broad, and so muscular that the defined muscles could be seen from two floors down. Hard, lean arms reached out toward a box and grabbed a T-shirt as I begged him to turn around—until my eyes found his ass.

Dear Lord.

My new neighbor was hot—or at least the back of him was.

Turn around, turn around, I silently begged.

The weather took that moment to remind me of its mighty power and sent a strong gust of wind whipping through the two houses. The curtain settled back in place, and I was once again left with shadows.

As the first raindrop fell, signaling the impending storm, I looked down at the once perfect garden that I had painstakingly kept alive as a tribute to my longtime friend and neighbor. It had been trampled on and was now ruined, and I felt the rage boiling back up to the surface.

Hot or not, my new neighbor was a plant-trampling

jerk, and when I got home from work tomorrow, I'd make sure he knew it.

I'd also take a moment to see if that face of his matched his perfect back and ass.

Shut up, Liv.

BUY NOW

ACKNOWLEDGMENTS

There isn't a single person on the planet I can thank more than my husband. He is more than a life partner—he is my soul. Babe, thank you for letting me chase my dreams even though I've probably become a little more insane in the process. I love you.

Secondly, thank you to my two adorable children. They've put up with my crazy travel schedule this year and handled having a slightly forgetful mother like a champ.

I have an amazing family. They give me endless support. I truly appreciate everything they do. A special thanks to my sister-in-law Julie for being my super assistant in New York! I love you!

To my talented beta readers—Evette Ashby, Shera Layn Bell, Michelle Kannan, Christy Townzen, Sarah Cook, Ami Brown, Jenni Barnds, Whitney Baer, Jennifer Wolfel and Carey Heywood—thank you SOOOO much for all of your hard work!

I wouldn't be where I am today if it wasn't for some truly amazing blogs. A special thanks to TotallyBooked, Tyhada Reads, Sassy Girls Books, Sinfully Sexy Book Review, Love N. Books, Reader's Candy, All Romance Review, The Rockstars of Romance, Anna's Attic, Three Chicks and their Books, Book Lover's Obsession and Wolfel's World of Books. I could go on and on forever.

To my amazing editing team - Jovana Shirley and Ami

Deason, thank you for loving Ready for You and putting your heart and souls into making it shine.

A big thanks goes out to Sarah Hansen for this cover.

Thank you Shanyn and everyone at Inkslingers PR for putting up with my 5,000 emails and helping me get the Ready Series out to the world! Another big thanks to my agent, Jill Marsal for always being there when I need a helping hand.

Lastly, (whew!) I have to thank my readers—the few who have been with me since I published, or maybe even earlier. The many who stumbled upon one of my books on Amazon…and the cherished who have emailed me late at night in tears because my words have touched their soul. Thank you for allowing me to become part of your lives and investing in the stories I write. I can't begin to tell you how much you've all changed my life and the lives of my family.

ABOUT THE AUTHOR

J.L. Berg is the USA Today bestselling author of the Ready Series, the Lost & Found series, and many more. Originally from California, she now resides in central Virginia with her high school sweetheart, two children, and three dogs. When she's not writing, she enjoys spending time with her family or indulging in her love for Doctor Who. J.L. Berg is represented by Jill Marsal of Marsal Lyon Literary Agency, LLC. For the latest book updates, audio news, and more, be sure to visit her website.